ALONE

Books by Loren D. Estleman

Kill Zone
Roses Are Dead
Any Man's Death
Motor City Blue
Angel Eyes
The Midnight Man
The Glass Highway
Sugartown
Every Brilliant Eye
Lady Yesterday
Downriver
Silent Thunder
Sweet Women Lie
Never Street
The Witchfinder
The Hours of the Virgin
A Smile on the Face of the Tiger
*City of Widows**
*The High Rocks**
*Billy Gashade**
*Stamping Ground**
*Aces & Eights**
*Journey of the Dead**
*Jitterbug**
*Thunder City**
*The Rocky Mountain Moving Picture Association**
*The Master Executioner**
*Black Powder, White Smoke**
*White Desert**
Sinister Heights
*Something Borrowed, Something Black**
*Port Hazard**
*Poison Blonde**
*Retro**
*Little Black Dress**
*Nicotine Kiss**
*The Undertaker's Wife**
*The Adventures of Johnny Vermillion**
*American Detective**
*Frames**
*Gas City**
*The Branch and the Scaffold**
*Alone**
*The Left-Handed Dollar** (forthcoming)

*A Forge Book

LOREN D.
ESTLEMAN

ALONE

A VALENTINO MYSTERY

A TOM DOHERTY ASSOCIATES BOOK
NEW YORK

This is a work of fiction. All of the characters, organizations, and events portrayed in this novel are either products of the author's imagination or are used fictitiously.

ALONE: A VALENTINO MYSTERY

Edited by James Frenkel

A Forge Book
Published by Tom Doherty Associates, LLC
175 Fifth Avenue
New York, NY 10010

www.tor-forge.com

Forge® is a registered trademark of Tom Doherty Associates, LLC.

Library of Congress Cataloging-in-Publication Data

Estleman, Loren D.
Alone : a Valentino mystery / Loren D. Estleman.—1st ed.
p. cm.
"A Tom Doherty Associates book."
ISBN 978-0-7653-1576-2 (alk. paper)
1. Motion picture film—Preservation—Fiction. 2. Archivists—Fiction. 3. Extortion—Fiction. 4. Murder—Investigation—Fiction. 5. Hollywood (Los Angeles, Calif.)—Fiction. I. Title.
PS3555.S84A76 2009
813'.54—dc22
2009034609

First Edition: December 2009

Printed in the United States of America

0 9 8 7 6 5 4 3 2 1

This book is dedicated to my wife, Deborah, who writes as Deborah Morgan, for companionship, support, expert opinion, and staying to watch the credits with me when everyone else has left the theater.

There is only one Garbo.
—Greta Garbo

News item, December 11, 2005:

GARBO'S LETTERS MISSING

Stockholm, Sweden—Two letters and two postcards written by Swedish screen legend Greta Garbo appear to have been stolen from a public archive, officials said Friday.

The documents, written by Garbo to her close friend Vera Schmiterlöw after the actress moved to Hollywood in the 1920s, were reported stolen from the military archives of Sweden last month after a researcher found they were missing, archivist Anders Degerstrom said.

Degerstrom said the documents had not been checked out since March 2004, according to archive records. The letters could have been stolen any time since then, he said.

This year's 100th anniversary of Garbo's birth was celebrated in Sweden with private screenings of her films and an exhibit at the Swedish National Portrait Gallery.

I

THAT TOUCH OF SPINK

1

WINGED PEGASUS GLIDED along the San Diego Freeway, soared down the ramp onto Sunset Boulevard, and swooped into West Hollywood, full of oats and hubris. There gridlock clipped its wings. It waited for the lights to change with a quizzical smirk and both eyebrows raised in a Victor Mature arch.

L.A. took little notice. A city accustomed to seeing Roman centurions in White Castle and RuPaul anywhere spared only the occasional curious glance for a flying horse in the bed of a rented trailer, even if it wore all the colors of the rainbow and BRUINS SUCK spray-painted on its plaster butt. Valentino got all the way to his last turn before someone seated on the passenger's side of a wired-together El Camino got his attention with a two-fingered whistle.

"Hey, buddy! Fill 'er up with regular!"

The man pulling the trailer smiled weakly, waved, and made the turn.

He pulled into the alley next to The Oracle Theater and braked behind a construction trailer piled high with demolition debris. Exhaling with relief, he switched off the ignition. He disliked attracting attention, and had chosen the one place in America to live where it was virtually impossible. The exchange at the intersection had nettled him.

He got out and hoisted himself up onto the wheel of the construction trailer to peer inside. It was filled mainly with sheets of dirty linoleum cratered with old cigarette burns and heaps of broken lath with bits of plaster the color of bad teeth clinging to the slats by strands of horsehair. This, too, was a relief; he lived in fear that without his supervision the workers would throw away something irreplaceable.

"What a hideous way to treat a noble creature that never existed. Where'd you find him, Fire Island?"

Valentino stepped down and turned to meet the owner of the voice. Kyle Broadhead stood outside the fire door propped open on the side of the theater, flanked by a pair of husky young men in UCLA sweatshirts: undergrads, beyond doubt, selected from the football team's expendable third string. Between them the rumpled film studies professor looked like a garden gnome. He was stuffing his pipe from his old pouch and getting more tobacco on his sweater than into the bowl.

"Not Fire Island, but close." Valentino followed his gaze to the multicolored sculpture hitched behind his car. "An Armenian rug dealer in the Valley stuck it in front of his shop to attract business. Some students from State have been decorating it once or twice a week for five years. It'll take ten gallons of mineral spirits just to get down to the original workmanship."

One of the burly UCLA boys snorted. "Everybody knows you can't trust a statie with a box of Crayolas."

"Spoken by the young man who when I asked him who directed *Stagecoach*, said Henry Ford." Broadhead walked around to the back and scowled at the BRUINS SUCK. "I hope you didn't drive past campus."

"I made an end run around it," Valentino said.

"What's it made of?" the other student asked. "Coach'll drop me if I pull a muscle."

"He'll drop you if you drop another pass," said his teammate.

Valentino said, "It's just hollow plaster. The rug dealer and I got it up there without help."

Drawing on his pipe, the professor reached up to pat Pegasus on the rump. "Welcome home, Old Paint. Your brother missed you."

Valentino untied the ropes that lashed the sculpture to the trailer and acted as guide as the students bent their shoulders to their task. They carried it down the ramp that came with the trailer and through the broad doorway into the building, Valentino saying, "Careful, careful," biting his lip as the horse's brittle ears passed a bare half inch under the top of the frame, and scurrying around ahead of them to kick hazardous pieces of rubble from their path, walking backward and gesturing gently with arms spread in front of him as if to calm down a beast of flesh and blood. Broadhead wandered in behind them, smoking.

After much grunting, mutual accusations of sloth on the part of labor, and two pinched fingers, the tie-dyed creature of mythology stood at last on a pedestal opposite its twin at the base of the grand staircase in the lobby. For the first time in more than a decade they bracketed the cracked marble steps and mouse-chewed carpet runner.

"There's teamwork," Broadhead said.

Valentino glared at him. "What's that make you, the coach? I missed the part where you contributed."

"I hired the muscle. A passing grade for twenty minutes' work."

The student with the pinched fingers took them out of his mouth. "The new one's bigger."

"It won't be once all those coats of paint have been stripped away," Valentino said. "They're both the same age. They were cast by the same artist who sculpted the original out of limestone."

"How do you figure it made it all the way down to the San Fernando Valley from here?" Broadhead asked. "Those wings don't really work."

"Vandals. Pranksters. People have been scavenging the place since it shut its doors. They got tired of it and sold it, or tossed it, and somehow it wound up in a junkshop in Burbank, waiting for someone to buy it and turn it into an advertising gimmick and post a picture of it on his Web site. That's where I found it, on the Internet. Thank God for those kids with their buckets of paint. They protected it from the rain and smog."

Broadhead blew smoke at the fallen-in ceiling. "Cost you a fortune to restore it."

"Not as much as it would've to duplicate it from scratch. The artist is dead and the original went down with the *Andrea Doria*."

"What's the point?" asked the young man who'd come through without injury. "It's just something to walk past on your way to the show."

Valentino smiled at him. "It *is* the show, or part of it. I can't explain it to you if all you know about movies is DVDs and the multiplex. I'll put you both down for free passes to the grand reopening, and then you can see for yourself."

"They'll be in AARP by then," Broadhead said. "And you'll be in a crappy nursing home, as penniless as the schnook who went broke on this dump the first time."

"A man needs a hobby."

"A hobby is something that has nothing to do with your work. You spend all week sniffing out and restoring old films and all weekend rebuilding a theater to show them in. That's like an undertaker who stuffs turkeys on his day off."

But the film archivist wasn't listening. Standing there admiring the reunited sculptures—really magnificent beasts tossing back their heads, opening their wings, and lifting their front hooves free of the earth—he saw them unsullied and unchipped, all gleaming gold leaf and electric light shining from their eyes. Between them had passed Hollywood's royalty: Swanson, Gable, Harlow, Chaplin, Bogie and Betty, James Dean, Brando, Groucho, Harpo, Chico, and Zeppo; flashguns flaring like sheet lightning as they filed in for the premiere of yet another vision from the Dream Factory. Outside, limousines lined the street on both sides for blocks, and sabers of light swiveled and crossed, bleaching the bellies of clouds a hundred stories above the pavement.

". . . Harriet think?" Broadhead was saying.

The hallucination faded. Plaster dust settled over leprous patches of linoleum, drop cloths blurred the outlines of the plugged fountain and shattered glass snack counter, pigeon filth frosted the reliefs on the walls. Chalky clouds swirled slowly in the sunlight slanting through holes in stained glass.

"What did you say?" Valentino asked.

"I said, 'What does Harriet think?' She's a forensic pathologist. Does she bring DNA home to spin in a dish in the kitchen?"

"I should call her. We're going to a thing tonight." He looked around. "Where is everyone? The place was crawling with workers this morning."

"This was how it was when we got here. Ask your contractor."

"I would if I could get him on his cell."

"He's probably in Athens, cribbing bits off the Parthenon. Maybe this will explain something. One of the jocks found it taped to the door." Broadhead took a small rectangle out of a sweater pocket and handed it to him.

It was a business card. Valentino read the message scribbled in blue ink on the back first: "Call me. D.S."

He turned it over to look at the printing:

DWIGHT SPINK

LOS ANGELES COUNTY BUILDING INSPECTOR

"What do you think it is?" he asked.

Broadhead puffed on his pipe, thickening the haze. "It can't be good. Government functionaries are like mice. If you don't see or hear them, you can pretend they don't exist."

Valentino could never get a cellular signal on the ground floor of The Oracle; there was either too much lead in the paint or the walls were too thick for modern microwaves to penetrate. He went into the auditorium, where more drop cloths hammocked the rows of seats and carpeting had been torn up in strips to expose dry rot in the floorboards, swung open a panel that looked like part of the wall, and climbed a set of steep narrow musty-smelling steps to the old projection booth. He'd furnished it with all the essentials of a bachelor living arrangement; his lease had run out on his apartment in Century City and all his money was tied up in the renovation. When his phone informed him he had service he sat on the sofa bed and dialed the number on the business card.

"Yes?" It sounded more like a challenge than a question.

"Dwight Spink, please."

"Speaking." This time Valentino heard a British accent. He

introduced himself. Then: "Yes, the theater. I sent the crew away. You have a serious problem, Mr. Valentino."

He waited, hearing his heart beating between his ears.

Spink cleared his throat in two notes, like a cellist dragging his bow back and forth across the strings. "Perhaps you're not aware that the State of California requires a separate hazardous material license for laborers engaged to remove asbestos."

"I was told all the necessary permits had been obtained."

"We're not discussing permits. Laborers who handle asbestos must be bonded and licensed as a matter of public safety and to minimize the risk of litigation."

"Did you ask them if they were licensed?"

"That isn't how it's done. When I asked to see a license, none of the men present was able to comply."

"Were any of them actually removing asbestos at the time?"

"The law makes no provisions for the odds of an inspector actually conducting an inspection when the removal is in process. Absent the certainty that an unregistered laborer would not attempt the job after I left, I ordered everyone to leave lest they all be exposed to a dangerous carcinogen."

"Isn't that the same as arresting someone because he might commit a crime?"

"No, sir, it isn't."

"I think you should be discussing this with my contractor."

"I attempted to reach Mr. Kalishnikov, but was told he was unavailable. Since public safety was involved, I took the initiative."

"I'll have him get in touch with you. I'm sure this can be resolved with a single conversation."

The cello rasped. It sounded like the opening to the theme from *Jaws*. "During my inspection I noted also that someone has been living on the premises. That neighborhood is zoned commercial, not residential."

"I understand it's zoned for both."

"There is some question as to precisely where one ends and the other begins. In any case I cannot allow the present situation to continue until the zoning board has voted and a certificate of residency is issued. Until then the person who has been living there must find outside accommodations."

"Is there anything else, Mr. Spink?"

"As a matter of fact there is. The staircase leading to the projection booth is not up to code. The treads are too narrow, the risers are too high, and the ventilation is inadequate. These things violate OSHA, the fire code, and the Clean Air Act. The stairs must come down."

"Then how am I—how will the workers get up to the booth?"

"Not being in the construction business, I wouldn't know. Whatever solution your contractor comes up with must comply. These regulations were drafted for our safety, Mr. Valentino. Yours and mine." Spink cleared his throat. "It's Friday afternoon. I will conduct another inspection Monday. If at that time the proper license is presented and the nonconforming passage to the booth and the unauthorized apartment there has been sealed off to my satisfaction, the construction may resume."

"How am I supposed to seal it off without any workers?"

"It's a simple job for a rough carpenter. We can assume he won't be messing around with asbestos."

"I haven't budgeted a carpenter until next month. Do you have any idea how much this has cost me so far?"

"It's a fair-market state," Spink said. "You pay for what you get."

When the line was clear, Valentino tried Leo Kalishnikov

again. The flamboyant contractor, who specialized in designing and building high-end home theaters and had taken on The Oracle as a personal challenge, was out of the office, and his cell phone went straight to voice mail. Valentino left an urgent message and went downstairs.

Kyle Broadhead was alone in the lobby. "I sent the defensive line home. I'm giving the clumsy one extra credit so he doesn't sue you over those mashed fingers." He read Valentino's expression. "That bad. I was right about mice, wasn't I?"

"I'm beginning to smell a rat."

2

"I WANT TO be alone," Harriet said.

"Vant," said Valentino.

"I *said* want."

"You did."

"I don't understand."

"It's 'I *vant* to be alone.' Your accent needs work."

She squinted. "Did we or did we not watch *Grand Hotel* just last week? You said it was research."

"I did and we did."

"She said, 'I want to be alone.' She pronounced the *w*, I heard it. I even had you go back and play it again to be sure."

"Beside the point. When Greta Garbo says 'want,' the world hears 'vant.' Garbo didn't have to prove she was Garbo. You do. Perception is everything."

"I don't have to prove I'm Garbo to win a silly contest."

"Look, if you don't want to play, don't. I thought it would be fun."

"Okay, don't get your moustache in a wad. I mean *vad*. Hang on while I go slip into something less comfortable."

She left him standing in her living room and went into the bedroom, leaving the door open a few inches. Harriet Johansen had answered her door wearing a fluffy robe and pink mules with a towel wound around her head; with her face freshly scrubbed she looked like a sloe-eyed little girl with ideas. Valentino wore an imperial Russian uniform: scarlet tunic with gold frogs, white riding breeches, and black stovepipe boots. A thin Ramon Novarro moustache clung to his upper lip, stuck there with spirit gum. He felt like an idiot who'd never had an idea in his life. What had he been thinking?

"I did some research on my own," Harriet called through the opening. "Did you know Greta Garbo checked into hotels using the name Harriet Brown?"

"I'd heard that."

"So we share a name, and that's how I attracted your interest. You want to sleep with Garbo."

"I honestly never made the connection until just now, when I saw you in that turban. I thought someone had colorized *The Painted Veil*."

"A towel isn't a turban. You didn't answer my question."

"You didn't ask one."

She sighed. "Do you want to sleep with Garbo?"

He touched his moustache to make sure it hadn't slipped off plumb. "Rita Hayworth once said the problem with her love life was men went to bed with Gilda and woke up with Rita Hayworth."

"Remind me who Gilda was."

"Her sexiest role. Her point was she couldn't possibly hope to fulfill their expectations."

"So I'm a letdown."

"I didn't say that. Are you trying to pick a fight?"

"I was teasing. Why are you such a grouch? I thought the idea tonight was to have fun."

"Forgive me." He meant it. "That damn theater is eating my lunch."

"Don't be so quick to condemn it. We met there, don't forget."

Which was true. It might not have been the first romance that began in a theater, but the circumstances were unusual. He'd plunged into the purchase on a whim, then discovered he'd bought the scene of a forty-year-old murder. That had brought him to the attention of the Los Angeles Police Department and its crew of criminalists, including Harriet.

He said, "I'll try to keep that in mind. It may spare you the unpleasantness of lifting my fingerprints off the throat of a bureaucrat."

"What on earth happened today?"

"Let's not spoil the night with construction talk, all right?"

"Deal. Anyway, it's out of character for John Gilbert."

"Ramon Novarro."

"Sorry. I thought it was Gilbert with the uniform and the funny moustache."

"It was. Also Conrad Nagel and Melvyn Douglas and Fredric March."

"No wonder she *vant*ed to be alone."

He looked at his watch. They were getting a late start, but such things seemed less important since he'd met Harriet. He sat on the sofa, turned on the TV, and found *The Scarlet Empress* on TCM. Marlene Dietrich, the poor man's Garbo—until she'd blossomed—spent half the movie as wide-eyed as Shirley Temple, then assassinated her demented husband, Czar of all the Russias, and became Catherine the Great overnight. She put on a dazzling uniform and was galloping a white stallion up the wooden steps of the Kremlin when Harriet coughed to get Valentino's attention. He switched off the set, turned his head—and dropped the remote on the floor.

"What's the matter? Did I overpluck?"

She stood outside the bedroom door in a daring filigreed gown glittering with crystals that left bare her shoulders and all of her midriff but her navel, concealed by a V-shaped sling connecting the brassiere to the clinging, low-slung skirt. A fantastic bejeweled headdress covered her hair and framed her oval face, the high cheekbones accentuated with highlights and shadow. Her lips made a delicate bow, and with her brows plucked ruthlessly into pencil-thin arches and extensions on her lashes, she was a full-color reproduction of Garbo in *Mata Hari*. The heels of her open-toed silver pumps added three inches to her height.

"Say something," she said. "You look like Jimmy Stewart in that Hitchcock thing."

"*Vertigo.* Except you look more like Greta than Kim Novak looked like Kim Novak." He rose. "If they don't hand you first prize the minute you step inside the door, the fix had better be in."

She stuck out her tongue, cracking the facade. "I have an unfair advantage. Not all the contestants date a guy who knows a guy who knows the wardrobe mistress at Universal."

It was a reproduction of the original costume, made for a Garbo biopic that had been shelved on the advice of the studio's lawyers. She'd still been alive then, and determined to block any production that would bring more reporters to her doorstep with camping equipment.

"I wouldn't feel too guilty," he said. "Most of the contestants can afford personal designers. But they wasted their money."

"Seriously?"

"Uh-huh."

She pointed a finger. "Just remember you're going to bed with Harriet Johansen. If you're lucky."

He offered his arm. "Ms. Brown?"

"Mr. Novarro." She took it.

He helped her on with her wrap at the door and opened it.

She stepped through. "He was gay, you know."

"You *did* do research." He drew the door shut behind them.

The smooth stone front of the Beverly Hills mansion was bathed in colored lights. Guests were still drifting in, and despite the presence of an army of parking attendants dressed in special comic-opera livery for the occasion, Valentino and Harriet waited several moments before one of them arrived to open their doors and take the wheel. The sinuous strains and brawny thump of an old-fashioned tango spilled out from inside.

A maid took Harriet's wrap in the foyer. They went into the ballroom, where a number of dancers, some with skill, danced to the music of the string quartet. Others mingled and chatted in line at the open bar.

Harriet turned to Valentino. "Now that we've made our entrance, I have to leave you alone for a while."

"Not too long, I hope."

"There's engineering involved. Next time, *I* wear the pants."

She stranded him among two or three dozen women dressed as Garbo in her various movie incarnations: disguised as a not-very-convincing young man in boots and jerkin from *Queen Christina*; hauntingly amnesiac in platinum-blonde hair and elegant evening wear from *As You Desire Me*; gung-ho Stalinist in severe suit and cloche hat from *Ninotchka*. A number of Camilles wisped about, perishing beautifully, and he counted no fewer than five Anna Christies and as many Mata Haris, although none as startling as Harriet Johansen wearing that outfit. He couldn't believe he'd never noted the resemblance. Maybe he had, on some level, and that was what had compelled him to find out more about her.

But he was satisfied that he hadn't fallen for a phantom. Funny and outgoing, dedicated to her career but never letting it interfere with her social life, Harriet was as unlike that living sphinx as could be.

When a waiter whose uniform was uncomfortably similar to his own offered him a tray loaded with stemware, Valentino thanked him and relieved him of two glasses of champagne, then retreated to a corner to observe his fellow guests from safe ground.

There were fat Garbos, old Garbos, black Garbos, an Asian Garbo, and one or two Garbos wearing heavy powder over distinct five o'clock shadows. Their escorts looked only slightly less exotic. There was one very good Erich von Stroheim, several John Gilberts, and three Charles Boyers attempting to look Napoleonic in *Conquest*. Valentino didn't spot any other Ramon Novarros, but the night was young and guests were still arriving. He'd have preferred to come as John Barrymore, but that would have been the wrong movie.

The fancy-dress couples fluttered about, sipping from flutes and spilling champagne on the glittering parquet floor. The walls and columns were ornamented in a relentless Art Deco motif, with original and reproduced posters from Garbo's most famous films and glossy black-and-white stills of that iconic face blown up ten times life size among the clamshells and stylized swans. The party had been planned to celebrate the 100th anniversary of the star's birth.

"Pardon me, old sport, but I think your britches are ringing."

A man bearing small resemblance to Clark Gable, but whose gravel-voiced impression was spot on, grinned and winked as he danced past in the arms of Garbo as Susan Lenox. Valentino realized then it was his cell he was hearing and not one of the instruments playing on the bandstand. He set the champagne glasses on a cloth-covered table and took the phone from his pocket.

"I have received your message," Leo Kalishnikov said, in the broad Balkan accent he affected for customers. "What disaster has befallen?"

Valentino turned away from the music and chatter and gave the contractor a quick summary of his conversation with the building inspector.

"Ludicrous. We aren't removing asbestos for two more weeks. What is this fellow's name?"

"Dwight Spink."

Kalishnikov said something in harsh Russian. "I know this man. He is a cossack. I'll see that a man with the proper credentials is on the site Monday."

"What about sealing off the stairs to the projection booth?"

"Nail a four-by-eight sheet of plywood over the entrance. You can manage this, yes?"

"With help. I'm not exactly handy."

"I will apply to the zoning board for a variance so you can live on the premises. That takes time. You will have to make other arrangements meanwhile."

Valentino thanked him and flipped the phone shut. When he turned back to the dance floor, his host was approaching with a hand out.

"Let me guess," Matthew Rankin said. "Lieutenant Alexis Rosanoff."

Valentino grasped the hand. "On the nose. A dozen of these people might have identified the actor, but I doubt more than one or two could have named the character in the movie."

"I have Andrea to thank for that. She was a fan of Greta's—G.G., she called her, all her friends did—for years before they connected, and continued to be one throughout her life. She dragged me to every revival theater showing her pictures on the West Coast. I sat through *Flesh and the Devil* nine times." His throat worked. "They died the same day, you know."

Fifteen years had planed only a little of the pain from the widower's tone. He was a trim, erect eighty in a beautifully cut tuxedo with flared 1930s lapels, white shirt, tie, and hair all of a piece and interrupted only by his aristocratic face with its carefully topped-off tan. He might have been an older version of the Melvyn Douglas who had played opposite Garbo three times.

"Did you know Garbo well?"

"I never met her. The friendship predated our marriage. They'd visit whenever Andrea made a buying trip to New York, and after Andrea retired they kept contact by mail. She burned the letters at Greta's request, near the end. Some of her other so-called friends had begun to sell her letters at auction."

"Mrs. Rankin was a real friend. A single Garbo letter would bring a fortune on today's market. I couldn't begin to guess at the value of an entire correspondence."

Rankin's brows carved a deep scowl line between them. "Ghouls. People will try to make a buck off anything these days. They aren't content just to hound living celebrities into self-imposed house arrest to protect their privacy; now they've begun to prey on the dead ones as well."

Valentino, taken aback by the direction the conversation had taken, complimented him on the decor.

Calming, Rankin replied that the photos and posters had come from his late wife's collection. But his guest knew the reason for the tirade. A former chemist with a hefty interest in technology, Rankin had computerized the department-store chain he'd inherited from his father-in-law and expanded into Europe. His strong executive presence, in company with his aristocratic wife, had made them public figures, with all the unwelcome attention that entailed. Since Andrea's death, Rankin had retreated into virtual seclusion, emerging only for such events as this, in respect for her memory and his own interest in film.

Enter Valentino. On behalf of the UCLA Film Preservation Department, he'd been privileged to accept generous donations from Rankin to update equipment and acquire rare prints of motion pictures long considered lost. He'd responded with alacrity to the invitation to attend the Garbo party with a guest.

His motives weren't entirely social. He picked up one of the glasses and sipped champagne, considering his approach. "How did Mrs. Rankin and Garbo become friends? She withdrew from society a long time ago."

The millionaire recovered his good humor. "They met in one of Andrea's father's stores. My dear girl was working there to prepare herself for an executive position. Greta was a salesgirl, you know, in Sweden; made her debut, in fact, in a promotional film for the store, *How Not to Dress*."

"That footage has been missing for many years."

"Your avarice is showing, young man. Everyone in your line of work knows that Greta made her a present of her own print: one former department-store clerk to another. Why didn't you just come out and ask me if I still have it?"

Valentino shrank from the directness of the old man's gaze. "I'm sorry. My cards say *Film Detective*; 'Archivist' makes people's eyes glaze over and they don't hear my pitch. Sometimes I get to believing my own publicity and try to be slick. I won't bother you about it again."

Rankin was silent for a moment. Then he laughed boomingly, drawing curious glances from some of his milling guests. "I was paraphrasing Andrea's father. If I'd asked him straight out for her hand, he'd have had me evicted from his house as a gold digger. I've waited fifty years to turn someone on the spit the way he did me that day, just before he agreed. UCLA's in my will. You'll have those reels by and by."

"Thank you, Mr. Rankin. You don't know what that means."

"A second disc on the DVD rerelease of *The Temptress*, no doubt, and a lot of hyperventilating on the part of a select group of cinema geeks. Apathy apart from that. Adam Sandler fans have done in old movies as surely as mall rats did in the department store. Call Roger. He'll arrange a screening."

"I'd like that very much."

"It's been stored under ideal conditions. I think you'll be pleased. I—Good Lord!"

Valentino put out a hand to steady his host, whose face had gone dead white beneath the tan. He appeared to be having a seizure. Then he realized that Rankin was staring at something behind him.

He turned. Harriet was approaching. The legendary head shot of Greta Garbo, full face, in the identical Mata Hari headdress, hung on the wall behind her; she seemed to be coming straight out of the frame. When Valentino turned back smiling, Rankin was no longer standing before him. He lay on the floor, pale and unconscious, with a crowd beginning to gather around him.

3

VALENTINO ENVIED THE doctor.

The man was dressed as John Barrymore, in a double-breasted *Grand Hotel*–style blazer with a coat of arms embroidered on the handkerchief pocket. His silver temples and pencil moustache were genuine, but someone who knew a good bit about prosthetics had altered his nose to resemble the straight prominent beak of the Great Profile. Beside him, the archivist in his fussy uniform felt like a sophomore in a high school play.

He was alone in Rankin's private study with Rankin, the doctor, and another male volunteer who had helped him carry the tycoon in from the ballroom and stretch him out on the leather sofa. By the time the doctor had his dress shirt open the patient had come around, but the doctor insisted on listening to his heart.

He smiled, removing the stethoscope from his ears. "Just a faint, I'd say. You might try a looser collar next time you play dress-up."

Valentino was comforted, both by the diagnosis and by the way the lamp next to the sofa showed traces of Just for Men in the doctor's moustache. His wife, who'd been with him in the ballroom, had looked big-boned and awkward in a ballerina's frilly tutu—although no less so than Garbo in that costume. Fortunately, she'd worn more becoming outfits in most of her scenes.

"It wasn't the collar." Rankin's eyes sought Valentino's. He looked every year of his age, and still a little disoriented. "Who on earth was that woman? I thought it was the guest of honor back from the grave."

"Harriet Johansen, my date. She doesn't look that way most of the time. She's a criminal expert with the LAPD. I'm very sorry she gave you a start."

"Make sure she's still here when we give out the prize for Best Look-Alike. Phyllis won't mind, will she, Ned? I'd hate to lose my personal physician over a social gaffe."

"She has a sense of humor. I told her she looked like one of the dancing hippos in *Fantasia*. I'm still standing, as you see." The doctor latched his bag and rose from the sofa. "Just to be sure, why not schedule an appointment? We won't have nearly as much fun dressing for your funeral."

Rankin assured him he would. The doctor left, followed by the man who'd helped Valentino carry in Rankin. He wore a tight morning coat over a waistcoat and checked trousers and had wound a silk stock around his neck in a fair approximation of Robert Taylor's costume in *Camille*. Valentino had considered the man's tall, wistful escort Harriet's only serious competitor for the prize.

Roger Akers, Rankin's personal assistant, entered moments later. He was a lean, high-shouldered, narrow-faced man of forty, a tightly wrapped, nervous type whom the archivist had dealt with occasionally in his exchanges with his employer. The man went straight to the sofa without a glance toward the archivist.

"I came as soon as I heard," Akers said.

"I'm sure you did. Did you finish those letters?" The old man sat up and buttoned his shirt. He hadn't completely recovered from his shock; his fingers slipped on the gold studs.

"Of course not. They said you'd collapsed."

"Well, I didn't die, so you're still employed. Help yourself to a drink, since you're here, but I expect those letters here on my desk in the morning."

"You know I don't drink. Have I ever failed to finish an assignment?"

"You've never been one to overlook a detail—or an opportunity. Now, please leave. I've something to discuss with this gentleman."

Spots of color the size of quarters glowed high on Akers' otherwise sallow cheeks, but he turned and left without comment. Thirties dance music drifted in from the ballroom, sealed off by the closing of the door.

"That was fairly unpleasant," Valentino said.

Rankin stood and refastened his tie before an antique mirror. Heavy vintage furniture anchored the room, lightened slightly by a computer with a plasma screen glowing on the massive carved desk. "His concern for my health was real. If I die, that man will have to live on an assistant's salary."

Although his curiosity was aroused, Valentino conquered the urge to pry into his host's affairs. He himself had formed an instant antipathy toward Akers. There was something of Uriah Heep in his demeanor; he only acknowledged Valentino's presence when there was business to conduct, and his attitude toward Rankin veered between toadying and contempt. Why he kept the man on was a mystery.

Rankin made no effort to dispel it. "Your stunning date," he said, fussing with the bow. "Did you say she's a police officer?"

"Not technically. She's a forensics technician. She collects and analyzes evidence, but she doesn't arrest or interrogate people, like on TV. Those things are someone else's specialty. She doesn't have a badge and isn't allowed to carry a gun."

"Nevertheless I assume she's required to report unlawful activity."

"Well, we all are, strictly speaking. But her career depends on it." Now he was keen. The atmosphere in the room had changed drastically since the assistant had come and gone.

The tycoon adjusted his cuffs, tugged at his lapels, and smoothed the snowy hair at his temples with the heels of his hands. There were now no signs of earlier disturbance. "Are you free tomorrow morning?"

A memory flashed through his mind of his contractor's advice to erect a sheet of plywood across the entrance to the nonconforming stairs in The Oracle.

"Yes. I'm off Saturdays."

"Can you come back here at ten, without Miss Johansen, and without telling her of the appointment? I don't want to place you in the position of having to duck awkward questions."

Valentino hesitated. "Something tells me this has nothing to do with my job description."

"It can, if you agree to my terms. You pose as a detective, which suggests to me you have a talent for investigation. I know you've been instrumental in bringing many lost films to light. How would you like to exercise your gift and incidentally add Greta Garbo's first appearance on screen to that list? Immediately, I mean. Not after I expire and my will finishes crawling through probate."

"I like the part about getting *How Not to Dress* for UCLA. The other part sounds illegal."

"I want to dig up something on Roger Akers. Something embarrassing, preferably criminal, but certainly of an intimidating nature."

"That *is* illegal."

"Only if you break the law to obtain it. What use I make of it isn't your concern."

"It is if there's blackmail involved. That makes me an accessory."

Rankin's smile was chilly; he was now Melvyn Douglas to the life. "There was only one blackmailer in this room, and he's left. I intend to use the information to stop him before he cleans me out and leaves nothing for my heirs."

"You're awfully quiet," Harriet said. "Are you upset that that fella in the Lord Fauntleroy getup beat you out for Best Leading Man Look-Alike?"

"Robert Taylor," Valentino corrected. "Armand Duval, to be precise, and the answer is no. His Camille had me worried for a while, but obviously I had nothing to fret about."

They were at her door. She lifted her prize—a nearly priceless period majollica vase fashioned into a full-length likeness of the actress—admired it, then lowered it to fix him with her Mata Hari–like gaze, fully primed to wring secrets from the unwary masculine gender.

"If he wants to adopt you, don't let him. What would you do with a string of department stores in this day and age?"

"He's kept his going a decade longer than most. Anyway, my birth parents might object."

He had, of course, told her of their planned meeting, but had said nothing of the sinister terms. There was no sense in upsetting her, since he had no intention of conducting what amounted to an illicit private investigation into a stranger's sordid past. But he had a movie buff's desire to see what happened next. Matthew Rankin, the wily old CEO, had anticipated that.

"Why the cloak-and-dagger? I thought our relationship was past the point where we kept secrets from each other."

"It's university business, and a long way from a sure thing. I don't want to jinx it."

"Banana oil. Is that something G.G. might say?"

"By all accounts it would be saltier than that." But he weakened before the silence of the sphinx. "You know I've been obsessed with that earliest Garbo footage for years. He's invited me to a screening." Which wasn't a lie.

"Has this something to do with what happened tonight?"

"I think so. He's eighty, after all. It may have come home to him that he doesn't have much time to arrange his affairs. Where are you going to put your vase?"

"You'll find out the next time you try to change the subject." Her eyes matched the pair in cold ceramic.

"I'm sworn to secrecy."

"About a screening? What is it, a skin flick?"

"A porno film starring Greta Garbo would be the find of the century, but I'd never show it in public for the same reasons I'm not going to betray Mr. Rankin's confidence. Some things should be kept private."

"Starting now." She went inside and pushed the door in his face.

He spent what would be his last night in The Oracle for a while, listening to the nearly human moans and sighs of an old building settling on its timbers. Exhaustion got the better of his thoughts sometime before sunrise. He awoke with the room full of dusty light. He wanted to call Harriet, but there was barely time to shower and shave at the YMCA, put on the California uniform of sport coat, T-shirt, jeans, and running shoes, and still make his meeting in Beverly Hills.

The mansion wore a grim aspect under a heavy slice of late-morning smog. The housekeeper left him in a front parlor while she went to see if her master would receive him. It was a pleasant room, done in shades of cream and yellow, with a portrait above the fireplace of Garbo in late life, expertly rendered in pastels; a gift, most likely, from G.G. to her friend, Andrea Rankin. The hair was gray, the face lined, but the expression was more peaceful than in any other likeness Valentino had seen.

It cheered him, as did the setting, and he could scarcely bring himself to believe that he had come there on a mission he could only regard as immoral. True, Roger Akers wore an air of malignancy that wasn't out of place for an extortionist, but if that was the case, what could he possibly have on a man as eminently respectable as Matthew Rankin that would move his victim to respond in kind?

He was pacing the room, following this train of thought, when a chandelier-rattling scream stopped him in mid-step.

He opened the door to the hallway just as the housekeeper came running down it, waving her arms as if to clear her path of obstacles. He stepped in front of her; they almost collided, but she stopped and stared up at him with her mouth working.

She was an Asian of about fifty and her hands were coarse, but her features were fine and of a noble caste; he suspected she was one of the many who had come West in their youth bent on stardom, only to settle in the end for a steady job and a living wage.

"What's wrong?"

"He dead." Her voice was strained. The scream had cracked it.

"Mr. Rankin? Are you sure? Did you call nine-one-one?"

"No Mr. Rankin. Mr. Akers."

4

"IS HE DEAD?"

Valentino looked at the speaker. Matthew Rankin stood on the other side of the great carved desk in the study. The squat revolver smoking in his right hand clashed with his conservative gray suit.

It was, perhaps, the first foolish question the department-store mogul had ever asked. His assistant, Roger Akers, lay on his back in front of the desk, spread-eagled, as if he'd been flattened by a sudden gale. The front of his suit coat was stained dark and a stain of the same color was spreading around him on the Persian rug. His eyes were open and glassy.

"He was a maniac," Rankin said. "He came at me with that."

He pointed at a green marble bust lying against a leg of the desk near Akers' foot. It appeared to be a naturalistic representation of Garbo at the height of her beauty. An empty wooden pedestal stood beside the door. Valentino had not noticed either the night before, but he'd been too preoccupied with the fainting and its aftermath to inventory the contents of the room.

The door stood open. The voice of the housekeeper, lapsing in and out of her native tongue as she jabbered to an emergency operator over a telephone, was distracting. Valentino closed the door and the room was silent.

Rankin looked down at his hand, seemed to realize for the first time he was holding a gun, and dropped it on his desk with a clunk. Valentino knelt then and searched for Akers' pulse, mainly for his host's benefit. He had none, although his wrist was still warm. The stench of spent powder burned Valentino's nostrils. He stood, shaking his head.

Fortunately, Rankin's big swivel chair was behind him, because his knees gave out then and he dropped into it. His face was ashen beneath the tan. "He wanted more money to keep quiet. I refused. He threatened to go public with what he knew. I told him to go ahead. You see, I was confident you'd come through for me and we'd stalemate him.

"He went into a rage. I tell you, I've seen men ruined, but I've never seen one react with such violence. I've kept this gun in the drawer for years, for my protection. I don't even remember picking it up. He scooped up that bust and raised it above his head and I knew he meant to split open my skull with it."

Valentino studied the dead man's face. It was twisted with anger or surprise.

"Whatever he was using to blackmail you, it will have to come out now. It might work in your defense. What was it?"

The desk's top drawer was open; presumably, it was the one that had contained the revolver. Rankin nodded—a purely mechanical operation, disengaged from rational thought—and rummaged through its contents with shaking hands. At last he drew in a deep breath, let it out raggedly, and laid a sheet of paper on the desk.

Valentino had to step over the corpse to retrieve it. A shudder racked him as he did so.

It was a handwritten letter reproduced on ordinary copy paper. There was no date or signature and the text was written in a foreign language. He'd never seen Swedish, but he knew in a flash that was what it was. "*Liebe* Andrea," read the salutation.

"Someone I knew dropped a bundle at Christie's on a rare Garbo inscription," he said. "It looks like the same writing. Is this a letter to your wife?"

"Can you read it?"

"A word here and there, from my high school German, which is related, but I've forgotten most of what I learned. There appear to be some tender sentiments here."

"Andrea's mother was Swedish. They spoke in that language when they didn't want anyone eavesdropping; it was another bond between Andrea and Greta. I picked up a little over the years, by osmosis." He drew another rattling breath. "It's a love letter."

Valentino chose his words carefully, but there was no way to ask the question without intruding. It was a grotesque enough conversation without the presence of a corpse. "Did they have a sexual relationship?"

"Not that I ever suspected, but the letter's explicit. Aren't you shocked?"

"Hardly, this late in the day. And lesbian rumors hounded Garbo her whole life. She didn't conform to the demure image most people associated with femininity when she was young, and sometimes she was seen wearing slacks in public. Even her most conscientious biographers haven't been able to track down any hard evidence. This would be—persuasive." He'd almost said *a smoking gun.* "How did Akers get hold of it?"

"Snooping, how else? He must have found it somewhere in the house. It had to have meant a lot to Andrea or she'd have burned it with the others. She wasn't the type to overlook things. He gave me this copy: a souvenir, he said. I never saw the original. I assume he kept it in a safe place."

"We're enlightened now. It wouldn't be that big a scandal."

"It would be insufferable. My wife was a very private woman, much like Greta. If this had gotten out when she was alive, it would have killed her. I'm betraying her memory just by showing you the letter." He sat up straight, the executive in charge for the first time since Valentino had come into the room. "Give it back. I'm going to destroy it."

Valentino drew the letter out of his reach. "If you did, you would stand trial for murder. It's hard to make a case for self-defense without establishing a motive for mayhem on the part of the deceased."

"I don't care about myself." Rankin laid a hand on the revolver. "Give it back, I said."

"You won't shoot me."

"I shot Roger."

"He was threatening you with a blunt instrument. All I have is a piece of paper. Anyway, it wouldn't do any good. The police are bound to find the original when they go through Akers' personal effects."

The stony facade cracked. The old man sat back, his face drained of color and life. As the first siren came within earshot, Valentino reached out and nudged the revolver to the far corner of the desk from Rankin.

Valentino's only personal contact with the Beverly Hills Police Department had been to ask directions of an officer seated behind the wheel of a squad car. That encounter, and some movies he'd seen, had not prepared him for the detective lieutenant who arrived at Matthew Rankin's house behind the uniformed police.

Beverly Hills cops were polite. Ray Padilla had the manners of a derelict working Hollywood and Vine.

Beverly Hills cops went by the book. Ray Padilla had never read a book in his life.

Beverly Hills cops knew how to wear Armani and which gold clip went with which hundred-dollar tie. Ray Padilla wore pumpkin-colored polyester and a green bowling shirt.

The man was cast against type.

"Valentino, huh?" He made marks in a spiral pad with a ballpoint pen with advertising on it.

The archivist braced himself, but Padilla didn't comment on the name. He needed a haircut, and the dead cigarette clamped between his teeth managed to observe the department's on-duty smoking ban while violating its spirit. When he removed it, which was only to replace it with a fresh one from a pack of Kools, the filter tip looked as if a hamster had been at it.

They were standing in the front parlor, which had lost much of its charm in the presence of a detective from Homicide. Others in his team were interviewing Rankin in a spare bedroom and the housekeeper in the kitchen, and technicians were at work in the study lifting prints and measuring blood patterns. The morgue crew waited in the foyer for the medical examiner to finish inspecting the body before they could remove it.

"You touched the gun?" Padilla had an irritating habit of clicking his pen repeatedly while waiting for an answer.

"Only with the back of my hand. Mr. Rankin was agitated. I was afraid of what he might do with it in his state."

"Suicidal?"

"I'm not qualified to judge. Given the circumstances I just thought it was a good idea."

He'd said nothing of the old man's attempt to take the letter from him at gunpoint. He felt as protective of him as Rankin had of his late wife's reputation. Anyway it had seemed a half-hearted threat at best.

"What is it you do again?"

"I look for movies."

"That shouldn't take long in this town."

"Beverly Hills?"

Padilla masticated his cigarette. "Hollywood. The Monster That Ate Southern California. You can't sit on the john without seeing Natalie Wood in a monitor in the stall. My kid brother got a ticket for yanking out the air bag in the middle of his steering wheel and installing a DVD player. He asked me to fix it. As if."

Valentino tried not to sigh. Of all the cops in Los Angeles County, he had to draw one who hated movies.

"The films I'm paid to look for haven't been seen in decades. I'm a preservationist."

"Sounds like you put up pickles in jars."

"I leave that part to others. I'm a hunter and gatherer, and in some small way a detective."

The lieutenant turned his bleak eyes on him. "Some detective. You didn't even hear the shot."

"The study is soundproof. I noticed that last night, when

you could only hear the music of a live orchestra when the door was open."

"Yeah, the party. You say Rankin and Akers had words?"

"I said that twice. I told you what they were."

"You'll tell it all again before we're through. I'm a detective, in a large way. That's how I do things." Click, click. "Any drugs at this party? You see Rankin take anything?"

"Definitely not. It wasn't that kind of party."

"Good. I stood in a courtroom once and watched a rich man's son walk on a manslaughter rap because he was on Ecstasy at the time."

"It was a perfectly respectable affair."

"Yeah. Grownups in crazy costumes."

"Lieutenant, do you have any reason to believe Mr. Rankin wasn't defending himself when he shot his assistant?"

Padilla looked as if he was considering answering when someone knocked. He barked, and a female officer in uniform came in holding up a transparent Ziploc bag by one corner. Sealed inside was the copy of the Garbo letter. "Print team scanned it, Lieutenant."

"You'll find mine on it," Valentino said. "They're on file at UCLA."

The lieutenant didn't appear to be listening. He was holding the Swedish letter in front of him as if he were reading it. Valentino was pretty sure he was posing.

The officer was still standing there when Padilla lowered the sheet. "Did I forget to tip you?"

"The chief of detectives is here."

"What'd he use, a helicopter?"

"I heard him say it's a high-profile case."

"We don't get any other kind. Tell him I'm on my way." When

she left, he pointed his pen at Valentino. "We've got your contact info. Any trips planned?"

"No, but I'm in the middle of changing addresses. You can reach me on my cell or through the university."

"Sure you didn't hear a shot? Maybe you thought it was a door slamming."

"Positive."

"What I don't like about it is not being able to fix the time. It could have happened ten minutes before the housekeeper looked in on Rankin. Plenty of time for him to dress the set to fit his story."

"You can test the soundproofing for yourself."

"Gee, I didn't think of that. I guess you *are* a detective." He flipped shut the pad. "Okay, Valentino. Hop on your camel and hump it out of here."

He knew something like that had been coming.

The foyer now was jammed with people, nearly as many as had filled the ballroom the night before. Uniforms and plainclothesmen and -women stood about in klatches, and every time one of them went out or came in through the front door, officers stationed there had to push it back against reporters clamoring to enter. The bullet that had ended Roger Akers' life had shattered all the years and money that Matthew Rankin had invested in his privacy. Valentino felt the tragedy as if he were in its center.

The chief of detectives—Valentino had heard the name Conroy when a reporter had cried for his attention—conformed far more closely to his concept of a Beverly Hills cop. A tall man in his forties with a sixty-dollar haircut, he wore a midnight-blue suit cut to his solid frame and gold-rimmed glasses with tinted lenses. When Padilla approached him, Conroy asked the lieutenant if he was having a hot flash.

"No, sir."

"Plainclothes detail doesn't mean you can go about in public dressed like you're in the lineup. The next time we meet I want to see a necktie and not your Adam's apple."

"Yes, sir."

"Now, what've we got?"

Valentino made his way around the officers at the door and into the desert glare of TV lights and stuttering strobes on the front porch, microphones poking at him and questions tumbling over one another like lemmings. "Who are you?" seemed to be the theme. He shouldered his way through the crowd and trailed a number of reporters out to his car, where two of them tried to block his path but parted when he gunned the motor. The experience gave him a new appreciation of the word *press*.

5

HE LAUGHED ALOUD when he saw Kyle Broadhead.

It was the first time since leaving the Rankin house he'd felt anything but gloom. The shooting, the implications of the Garbo letter, the police interview, the assault by reporters, and his inability to raise Harriet on his cell had made him as dreary as the smog that lay on the roof of The Oracle like a ton of moldy cheese.

He'd reached the professor at home and found him eager to help out with the carpentry project. On the way to the theater, Valentino had stopped at Home Depot and bought a four-by-eight sheet of plywood and a bungee cord, intending to slide as much of the sheet as he could into his trunk and tie down the lid, only to find that it was too wide for the trunk. He'd gone back inside, exchanged the bungee for thirty feet of rope, and tied the sheet to the roof of the car, making sure to leave the door handle free on the driver's side for him to climb in behind the wheel. For the second time in as many days, he felt like a clown transporting flotsam across the City of Angels.

Broadhead greeted him in the lobby, wearing a brand new pair of bib-front overalls, painfully blue and as stiff as aluminum, over a checked flannel shirt with its factory creases showing. His shaggy hair boiled out from under a Dodgers cap and his feet were shod in his favorite pair of worn Italian loafers. Their low heels allowed the cuffs of the overalls to touch the floor in back.

He scowled at Valentino's reaction. "What's the matter? Haven't you ever seen a man dressed for honest work?"

"You look like you're in the Witness Protection Program."

"At least I don't look like an unemployed actor. You got a place for nails in that sport coat?"

He stopped laughing. "I forgot nails."

"Now, *that's* funny." Broadhead bent suddenly and lifted a handmade wooden toolbox loaded with hammers and squares and Mason jars filled with nails of various lengths and girth. "I could rebuild New Orleans with just what's in here."

"Where'd you get that?"

"From my grandfather, on his deathbed. He was a master cabinetmaker. I've waited all these years for his genes to kick in." He scooped a short-handled hammer out of the box. "This is older than I am. It came with him from Sheffield. Someone made a mistake and left the head too long in the flames. It's triple tempered, harder than an industrial diamond. He called it Thor's Knob. You know what 'knob' means in England?"

"Stop waving it around. I'm developing a case of hammer envy. Kyle, we're just nailing up a board."

"There are no small projects, only small workers." He set the toolbox down on a stack of lumber, drew out a pair of heavy leather work gloves, tugged them on, and hoisted the box. "Let's do this thing."

"I have to go up and pack a bag first. Unless you have clothes in your house that fit me." Broadhead had agreed to put him up until he found other living arrangements.

"I don't even have any that fit me."

They went into the auditorium and up the stairs to the projection booth, leaving the toolbox behind. As Valentino opened drawers and transferred shirts, underwear, trousers, and socks to the suitcase on the sofa bed, Broadhead looked around. "I'll miss this room. Every time I'm in it I expect to make another exciting discovery."

"It gave us a complete print of *Greed*. It doesn't owe us anything."

"Putting in new stairs is going to cost you some floor space."

"I won't need it if I can get a good deal on a digital projector. You can fit a dozen of them in one of those old Bell and Howells."

"Aren't you planning to screen anything from the university library?"

"Sure. It's going digital."

"That just started. It'll take ten years just to transfer the inventory from safety stock to discs. Some of it's still on silver nitrate. Oh, wait." Broadhead chuckled. "I forgot. By the time you get this pile of bricks ready for show, they'll be implanting movies in our brains."

"I don't know how I'd get along without your encouragement."

"I think I liked you better when you were making sport of my apparel. Did you and Harriet have a fight?"

"Sort of, but that's not the worst of it." Valentino stopped packing and told him what had happened at Matthew Rankin's house.

Broadhead listened without comment, then dug his pipe and tobacco pouch out of his bib pockets and began stuffing the bowl. "So you think Garbo was a dyke?"

"I know you enjoy being a curmudgeon, but irony doesn't make an ugly word any less ugly," Valentino said. "If what Rankin says is true, she was at least bisexual, or entertained fantasies in that direction, and Andrea Rankin shared them; or at the very least did nothing to discourage them. But that's ancient history. I'm more concerned about Rankin. Lieutenant Padilla seemed hell-bent on charging him with murder."

"Well, motives don't get much stronger." Broadhead got the pipe going and crushed out the match on the floor.

"But if he was planning to kill Akers, why offer me a deal to dig something up on him?"

"Maybe he needed a witness."

"He had his housekeeper."

"Servants are like spouses. Prosecutors don't assign them much weight in court. All he had to do was pop Akers and dump the bust off the pedestal so it would look like he dropped it when he fell. It's not hard to put a dead man's fingerprints on a chunk of marble."

Valentino said, "I'm glad he picked me for a witness, if that's what it was about, instead of you. You've already got him measured for the gas chamber."

"Lethal injection, in this state. I'm not saying anything this Padilla isn't already thinking."

"There's just one hole in that theory. If Rankin plotted to kill Akers to keep that letter a secret, why'd he give me the copy when I asked him what Akers had on him?"

"You said yourself the original has to be somewhere. But it's a good point. If he planned the murder, he'd have worked out some way to get his hands on the original and destroy them both."

"Which suggests his innocence."

"Of premeditation, possibly," Broadhead said, puffing. "It doesn't mean he didn't lose his cool, maybe because Akers was taunting him, and shoot him without stopping to consider the consequences."

"At least it wouldn't make him a cold-blooded killer."

"Manslaughter is still a jailable offense, and at his age, a year could be a life sentence." He studied Valentino's face. "I didn't know you had any close friends among the plutocracy."

"I don't. But he's been a good friend to the Film Preservation Department, and I don't like to see anyone railroaded."

"Of course, this has nothing to do with the promise he made."

The archivist unfolded a shirt and refolded it the same way. "I suppose that's part of it."

"I'm as interested as you are in rescuing the history of cinema from the ravages of time. Helping a murderer to escape the consequences of his crime is a steep price to pay to recover a couple of reels of celluloid."

"I agree. By the same token I'd let them go to the devil if they got in the way of clearing an innocent man."

Broadhead let his pipe go out. "We set a bad precedent by interfering in an official police investigation to prevent *Greed* from rotting away in a non-climate-controlled evidence room. I've never seen *How Not to Dress*, nor has anyone else who's still breathing his own oxygen, but I doubt a promotional documentary conceived and executed to bring customers into a department store that closed its doors under Gustav the Fifth is worth a felony record for obstruction of justice."

"I never said a word about interfering with the police."

"You didn't. That's what has me worried."

"I've got my hands full with this pile of bricks, not to

mention Dwight Spink. The sleuths' union hasn't a thing to fear from me."

Broadhead smiled. "That's all I needed to hear. I wouldn't want to be accused of harboring a wanted man." He pointed at Valentino's coffeemaker. "You might want to take that with you. I haven't had a taste of caffeine since Elaine died. I can't sleep more than an hour at a time even without it."

"Without it I can't wake up. Thanks again for letting me crash at your place. At the rate I'm going I couldn't swing a week at the Bates Motel."

"I still think you ought to bunk at Harriet's. I have it on the authority of my dear departed wife that I'd drive Gandhi to violence after two nights under the same roof."

"That would be problematic."

"Bring her flowers. For some reason that always worked with Elaine. You could have knocked me over with a bus the first time she fell for it. I guess there's a reason some things hang around long enough to become clichés."

"We'll work it out. It's just too early in the relationship to show up at her door with a toothbrush."

"You're the expert. Thank God I don't have to chew over that kind of thing anymore. The wind from the grave can be quite liberating."

Valentino closed and latched the suitcase. "I thought you were working up the courage to plight your troth with the fair Fanta."

"I was, until I did the simple arithmetic. Do you have any idea how many numbers have come and gone between my Social Security number and hers? I was eligible for AARP when she was learning how to finger paint."

"How does she feel?"

"I haven't asked her. She's interning with a legal firm downtown and studying law at night. She hardly has time to think about a decrepit old monomaniac."

"You're not decrepit."

Broadhead struck another match. "How much does a bachelor need to pack? I wouldn't leave a decent piece of plywood unguarded in a neighborhood like this for ten minutes. One of your neighbors is probably building a deck behind his refrigerator box as we speak."

Valentino unplugged his coffeemaker, tucked it under one arm, hoisted the suitcase, and took one last look around. Spare as it was, the projection booth had been his home for weeks, and he shared with Broadhead the sense of discovery that would always bathe that room with golden light. He turned his back on it and led the way downstairs.

He was glad Leo Kalishnikov had not been present to see the variety of mishaps a lifelong academic and a practical film scholar could bring to the simple business of boarding up the entrance to a staircase. They managed to knock a corner off the plywood sheet carrying it through the doorway, bent several nails fixing it in place, had to pull it down and start all over again when it failed to cover the doorway, mashed two thumbs (both Valentino's), and performed microsurgery removing a splinter from the heel of Valentino's right palm with a pair of pliers and an application of mineral spirits to prevent infection; the sting had shot Valentino to his feet and chipped one of Broadhead's teeth when he bit down on his pipe stem. At length the barricade was in place and the professor returned his tools to his box.

"Remind me to lay a wreath on my grandfather's grave next Memorial Day," he said. "My father always looked down on him because he didn't finish his formal education."

"You know, thousands of ordinary homeowners do this kind of thing every weekend."

"I think you and I agree this isn't an ordinary home."

Valentino thanked him for his help, even though he hadn't provided much, sitting in one of the draped theater seats smoking and making observations, and drove them from there to Broadhead's house in a cul-de-sac off Beverly Glen Boulevard, the unfashionable section north of Sunset. It was a brick box with functional shutters, a relic of the sleepy Los Angeles of retirement housing and milk wagons, just a five-minute walk from the UCLA campus. The professor seldom took his thrifty compact car out of the garage, and then only to annoy their department head, whose SUV burned gas like weeds. Broadhead directed Valentino to the guest bedroom and knocked out his pipe in a smoking stand by the dilapidated armchair in front of the TV while his guest carried in his suitcase and coffeemaker.

The first eight bars of the theme to *Gone With the Wind* bleated; it was Valentino's ring tone. He answered his cell clumsily. His thumbs were still throbbing.

"I got your messages," Harriet said. "If you'd told me what you were up to with Matthew Rankin, I might have answered them sooner."

"How'd you know about that?"

"Garbo's letter just landed on my desk. You also might want to check out today's *Times*."

He walked out of the guest room holding the phone to his ear just as Broadhead was closing the front door. He had a rolled-up copy of the *Los Angeles Times* in one hand.

Valentino took it from him and shook it open. His picture was on the front page with his name in the caption. His face looked washed out in the glare of the strobe with Rankin's house in the background.

6

"YOU'RE NOT VERY photogenic, you know. I guess it was your personality I fell for."

"I come off better when I'm not ambushed. They must have traced my license plate number. I didn't answer any of their questions or tell them my name."

They were in the break room outside the forensics laboratory at Los Angeles Police headquarters, where Harriet worked six days most weeks. The *Times* was spread on the table between them, collecting crumbs from her tuna sandwich.

"'Rankin confidant,' it says." She chewed and swallowed. "They probably connected his donations to the university to you. Beverly Hills cops put the wraps on tight or the newsies wouldn't be snatching at straws."

"Meanwhile I'm fair game. They're bound to link me to the Oracle. Having to clear out of there may turn out to be a blessing in disguise." He hesitated. "Does this meeting mean I'm forgiven?"

"Blackmail, it says here. I take it he asked you to help get him out from under. That's a legitimate reason to keep a secret."

"I had a better one than just that. He wanted me to dig up dirt on Akers so he could bargain with him on level ground."

She met his gaze. In her work clothes and regular makeup, with no headdress covering her short, ash-blonde hair, she looked less like Garbo than last night, but she still had the chilly stare.

"I wasn't going to do it," he said. "I went out of nosiness. And because he'd dangled *How Not to Dress* in front of me as incentive."

"Thank God." She picked up her sandwich. "I was afraid you were leading a double life. Turns out the one you're leading just got away from you. You told this to the police?"

"Yes, and so will Rankin, if he has the kind of attorney he can afford and takes his advice. It helps corroborate his version of what happened."

"Tag. You're it."

"What's that mean?"

She swallowed tuna and washed it down with diet Coke. "Hiding out at Kyle's place won't protect you from the press. You'll need plastic surgery and a new name. I'd suggest Kato Kaelin, but that might make things worse."

He changed the subject. "How did the Garbo letter wind up in your caseload? Beverly Hills has its own facilities."

"Not as good as ours. We've got the best in the state. It's a reciprocal thing: L.A. goes to the hills when we want to know which wine to serve with the veal at the commissioner's banquet." She took a folded sheet out of a pocket of her smock and spread it on the table. A glop of mayonnaise fell from her sandwich onto the text, smearing the ink when she brushed at it.

"What kind of way is that to treat evidence?"

"Chill out. We ran off a dozen copies from the fax they sent us. It's Swedish, all right. Would you like a translation?"

"I thought Johansen was Danish."

"It still is. My father taught Scandinavian Literature at the University of South Dakota. He believed in starting at home, and he felt about translations the way you feel about colorizing black-and-white films. I never got a handle on Finnish, but I aced the rest."

"How is it I'm just finding this out now?"

"Do you really want to get back on the subject of full disclosure?"

"No, ma'am."

She finished her meal, pushed aside the clutter, and gave the letter a pop. "This is a recap of a rendezvous between Andrea Rankin and Greta Garbo in New York City, sometime in nineteen forty-nine or fifty: They went to see *All the King's Men,* and I looked up the running dates. The rest is pretty steamy. You want it grope by grope or just a summary?"

"Neither. I can wait for the tabloids to get hold of it and spill all the salacious details. I'd sort of hoped there weren't any, and that Rankin's Swedish wasn't as good as he let on."

"Sorry, Val. She was human."

"I know that. It would be nice if just one star were left to shine untarnished in the firmament."

"Apart from sounding pompous, that's homophobic."

"That's an automatic reaction on your part. If a person's sexual preference didn't matter, the columnists and talk-show hosts wouldn't whisper and giggle so much whenever someone famous got outed. As for me, I'd be just as worked up if Garbo had a hot-and-heavy affair with Harry Truman. I prefer my *Titanics* at the bottom of the ocean, my Jack the Rippers unidentified, and my Garbos mysterious."

"But not your shootings."

"I like Matthew Rankin, but I have a professional stake in this one as well. If he goes to prison, my department won't take possession of *How Not to Dress* until he dies and his heirs finish fighting over the will. He says it's being kept under climate-controlled conditions, but that's no guarantee someone won't crank up the thermostat after he passes."

"Seems to me we had this conversation before, when *Greed* was in police lockup."

"There's also the real possibility the will may be broken and we'll never see those reels."

"That's your obsession, and it got a man killed. If you'd told the police Rankin was being blackmailed, Roger Akers would be in jail instead of the morgue, and Rankin wouldn't be in custody."

"I promised him I wouldn't."

She put down the letter. "I may be part of the law enforcement community, but I'm also your friend. Didn't you ever think you could discuss a matter of questionable legality with me and I wouldn't go running off to report it?"

"You're right. I'm sorry." He leaned his elbows on the table and spread his hands. "I never knew Andrea Rankin. She died of a sudden heart attack just when they were planning retirement together. He was as anxious to protect her privacy as I am Garbo's. Neither one of us was capable of making a wise choice under those circumstances."

"For someone who's a casual acquaintance, you make him sound like a bosom buddy."

"Kyle said the same thing. I denied it, but maybe you're both right. At the very least I admire the old man. When the bottom fell out of the department-store business, right in the middle of his bereavement, he could have bailed, but he didn't. Instead he pumped his personal fortune back into the chain to drag it into the computer age, at a time when most industries thought the technology was witchcraft. He kept thousands of people employed. Then when things turned around, he used some of the profits to help out the film preservation program, asking nothing in return. I'd have offered my help without his having to promise anything. Short of breaking the law," he added.

"I accept your apology." She picked up the letter. "The fingerprint people in Beverly Hills are pretty good. They matched the victim's prints to the letter and to the marble bust, so at least part of Rankin's story checks out."

"Lieutenant Padilla says he could have pressed Akers' fingers to the bust after he was dead. I guess the same goes for the letter. He might have had the time, since we can't pinpoint the exact moment of death because nobody heard the shot."

"For that matter, getting Akers to handle the letter when he was alive wouldn't have been much of a challenge. He was Rankin's assistant, after all. Which leaves just the letter. The contents, I mean."

"I wouldn't say 'just.' If your graphologist confirms it was written by Greta Garbo, it would go a long way toward exonerating Rankin. An extortionist couldn't hope for better material."

"We ran into a snag there," she said. "He needs authenticated samples of her writing for comparison. We tried MGM, but all they have is her signature on old contracts on file. That's not enough. None of the movie museums we tried could help us. What was she, illiterate?"

"No, just very, very private. For years, MGM kept one of her friends on the payroll because they couldn't make contact with Garbo except through her."

"Her own studio? Why'd they put up with it?"

He stroked his thumb with a forefinger. There was a bruise under the nail where he'd smacked it with the hammer. "Money in the bank. She saved the studio twice: when she signed with it, and when talkies came along and she was the only player under contract who didn't sound like Mickey Mouse."

"There's a name for that kind of behavior. Sociopathic."

"Or maybe she was just ahead of her time. With all the paparazzi running around these days, celebrities have to live in armed compounds and never go outside without a platoon of bodyguards. But she did go to extraordinary lengths to avoid autograph hunters. I had one glimpse years ago of a brief inscription on an early photo. George Washington's easier. Did you try the Swedish military archives?"

"Why military?"

"She never gave up her native citizenship, visited home often, and my guess is she was impressed by army security, so she donated her personal documents there."

"Okay, we'll get them on the horn and have them fax samples."

"Law enforcement's certainly come a long way since *The Asphalt Jungle*."

"I wouldn't get my hopes up," she said. "Our guy has doubts."

"Your graphologist? How can he, without the samples in hand?"

She swiveled the paper on the table and slid it toward him. "Anything about this strike you as odd?"

He studied the hand, which was simple but delicate. Finally he sat back shaking his head. "I'm an expert in one thing, and this isn't it. And the only Swedish I know is *Smörgasbord*."

"*Smörgasbord*," she corrected; but he couldn't hear any difference in her pronunciation. "Remember, I said Garbo was human. We're imperfect creatures. No one writes a character in cursive exactly the same way twice in succession. The shape and slant vary, so does the thickness of the line. But look at this."

She drew the plastic straw from her drink cup and used it as a pointer, leaving droplets of diluted cola wherever it touched the paper. "All these *s*'s are identical. Same goes for the *t*'s and *y*'s and the rest of the alphabet. Even the commas are the same. And don't get me started on the umlauts."

"By all means, let's forget the umlauts." He bent closer to the letter. "It's obvious, when you point it out. I'm impressed."

"Stop trying to butter me up. I'm not over my mad. It was the graphologist who spotted it. One of the supernerds in Cyber Crime came up with the explanation. Did you know it's possible to create your own font, even from something as personal as handwriting? You know what a font is?"

"The shape of a letter. I'm not a complete Luddite."

"All you have to do is scan it in, and if you're handy with a mouse you can sculpt the alphabet in upper and lower case and all the punctuation, type it up on the keyboard, and print it out."

"Akers handled all of Rankin's correspondence. He must have spent a lot of time at the computer. Experience is a great teacher."

"My eight-year-old cousin designed the logo for her mother's home business. She flunked recess."

"But assuming the forgery fooled Rankin, he must have known it was printed out on a computer. A pen makes an uneven texture you can feel with your fingers."

"All he ever saw was a photocopy. There never was an original."

"Rankin may not have invented the microchip, but he was

one of the first to recognize its importance. You'd think he'd have noticed the suspicious consistency of the characters."

"*I* didn't," she said, "until it was pointed out to me. Neither did you, and we're both trained to spot fakes. He was predisposed to accept it as genuine, based on his wife's close ties with Garbo and his own fears for her good name. Maybe he suspected there was more to their friendship than met the eye."

"Maybe he knew there was." He was glum.

She snapped her fingers, startling him. "Do us all a favor and get a grip on the twenty-first century, okay? She's dead, Andrea's dead, and Roger Akers is dead as hell. Matthew Rankin is alive and looking at prison or worse. If you're serious about helping him, you need to stay out of soft focus."

"If Akers faked the letter, maybe the program's still in his computer."

"Now you're cooking. Padilla confiscated and tagged every modem in the house for evidence. That's standard procedure. Beverly Hills has the edge on us when it comes to computer specialists. We gave them everything I've told you. If he didn't wipe out the hard drive—and I mean times ten; you'd be surprised how much those geeks can squeeze out of one that's been erased—they'll turn it. But it'll take time if he made a decent job of it."

"How much time?"

Her smile was sour. "Time enough for you to get a good dose of what your idol spent most of her life running away from. Rankin, too."

"It's too late to help him with that," he said. "How'd you like to quit this job and come to work for me as my reverse press agent? Keep me out of the spotlight instead of put me in it?"

"Hang on to that good humor. You'll need it when you find yourself wading neck deep in media just to get to a public toilet. Now." She scrutinized the cola spots on the photocopy, then crumpled it and used it to wipe her hands. "In order to forge this letter, Akers had to have had access to something fairly lengthy written by Garbo in her own hand, providing him with a complete alphabet and punctuation. You can write a lot of letters without using everything. Which brings us back around to the problem of securing samples. Where'd he get them? Padilla's crew tossed the house and found nothing."

"Rankin told me his wife destroyed Garbo's letters to her as a favor to her friend. But he also said this one might have escaped to fall into Akers' hands."

"Too convenient. Just the one he needed? That should have been a red flag."

"How important is it to clear up all the loose ends?"

She sat back and crossed her arms. "How do you like it when you're deep into a screening and all of a sudden a card pops up saying 'scene missing'?"

"I hate it. It takes me right out of the story."

"That's just how a jury feels."

7

ANARCHY WAS TOO conservative a term to apply to life in the Broadhead household. The situation teetered somewhere between eternal revolution and a full rout.

To show his appreciation for putting him up, Valentino stopped at Safeway after his talk with Harriet, bought a precooked rotisserie chicken, potato salad, and tossed greens from the deli section and a fresh apple pie from the bakery, and finding the house unoccupied dressed the table and set out the spread in the dining room, which he suspected hadn't been used since the death of Broadhead's wife four years before; Swanson and Mrs. Paul reigned in the freezer and a folding tray table exercised squatter's rights in the living room. He chilled a bottle of Chardonnay and was drawing the cork when the front door opened and shut.

"Hi, honey, I'm home. Whoa! Someone's been channeling Martha Stewart."

Valentino left the kitchen carrying two full wineglasses to find his housemate standing in the entrance to the dining room, a half-eaten taco in one hand and a jumbo milk shake in the other. He'd traded his overalls for an old tweed coat and unpressed slacks and plunked on his favorite cloth cap.

"It's ten to six," Valentino said. "I'd hoped by serving dinner early to avoid this very thing."

"I eat when I'm hungry, sleep when I'm tired. I let my watch wind down and threw it away. The stove's been broken for two years. Don't tell me you fixed it. You practically had to call Bob Vila to slap up a piece of plywood."

"I bought everything prepared. My fault; I should have checked with you." Valentino set down the glasses. "Why don't you drink some wine and watch me eat?"

Broadhead parked the remains of his meal on a plate, picked up one of the glasses, and drained it standing up. "Thanks." He put it down. "Can't stay. Fanta's picking me up in a few minutes." He strode toward his bedroom, peeling out of his coat.

He came back out as Valentino was finishing his salad. Now he had on pleated khakis and a sport shirt that clashed with his cap. "How do I look?"

"That depends. Are you playing golf with Porky Pig?"

"We're going to the rec center. She's taking me rollerblading."

"You rollerblade?"

"I don't know. I never tried."

"I hope your hospitalization plan is better than mine. Want to catch the Lakers game later? We can sit in front of the tube and eat cold chicken sandwiches."

"Sorry. *Battleship Potemkin*'s playing tonight at the art museum. She's never seen it."

"Don't talk during the Odessa Steps sequence." Valentino helped himself to chicken and potato salad.

"Since when do you watch basketball?"

"I decided to take your advice and broaden my interests."

"I hate to leave you alone your first evening. Why don't you—"

Valentino held up his fork, stopping him. "If you finish that sentence, you'll never make it out of the rec center alive. Fanta will see to that. I'll be fine. I'm just grateful to have a roof over my head."

"You're not by any chance a morning person, are you?"

"Aren't you? You're always in your office when I get to work."

"Yes, but I don't sleep more than two hours a night since Elaine died, and they're not always back to back. If you're the kind that goes to bed early, I'm going to disturb you with my nocturnal habits."

"What do you do, clog dance?"

"Let's just say the things that go bump in the night are terrified of me."

Valentino wanted to pursue this line of conversation, but the doorbell rang. He had a clear view from his place at the table when Broadhead answered it and Fanta came in. She had the professor in both arms and a leglock before she saw they weren't alone. She unwound herself and flashed Valentino a broad, unabashed grin. She was a willowy twenty with long straight glossy black hair and a tan that promised to go well beyond her halter top and shorts. Her feet were stuck in clunky black combat boots.

"Hey," she greeted. She took in the table setting. "Radical. Very Oprah."

"I said Martha Stewart," Broadhead said.

"Right. I get them mixed up."

"It's easy to mistake a short fat black woman for a tall blonde ex-convict."

Valentino stood. "Hello, Fanta. How are you getting along with the law?"

"Why, has my parole officer been looking for me?"

"She's in the top one percent of her class." Broadhead tucked in his shirt, which had come out when she'd mauled him. "She just started her internship and the firm she works for wants her to report to them first thing she clears the bar."

"I said no," she said. "I'm going to work directly for the studios, trying cases of copyright infringement."

Valentino said, "I hope you talk them into spending part of your first big settlement on film preservation."

"I will. I'm still jazzed from our excellent *Greed* adventure. Any big finds lately? That lost reel of *Metropolis*? The alternate ending to *Casablanca*, Bergman ditches Paul Henreid and flies off with Bogie?"

"At the moment I'm shooting for an eighty-year-old promo for a department store."

The grin faded. She shrugged. "I guess they can't all be special. I hear you're bunking with Kyle. Spooks run you out of the Oracle?"

"No, just the L.A. County Building Inspection Department."

"Ooh, scary." She turned to Broadhead. "You ready to bust some moves?"

He nodded. "I just hope that's where the busting stops."

She got to the door first and opened it for him. As he passed through, she swept the cap off his head, sent it sailing toward the sofa, waved to Valentino, and followed Broadhead out, pulling the door shut behind her.

Alone in the quiet house, Valentino finished his meal, decided against the apple pie, put the leftovers in the refrigerator, and washed dishes. Later, sunk among the tired springs in Broadhead's old armchair, he watched the Lakers play for three minutes, then flipped around until he found *The Postman Always Rings Twice* on TCM, but he got restless after a half hour and surfed through the rest of the channels; he'd always considered the film a pale shadow of *Double Indemnity*, and in any case Lana Turner was no distraction when one's mind was racing with Greta Garbo. But there was no sign of the Swedish Sphinx on any of the movie channels and he switched off the TV and cable box. He drank a second glass of wine and went to bed.

A high-pitched whine sat him straight up in dead blackness. He turned on the bedside lamp and peered at the alarm clock; 3:16 A.M. He got up, groped with his feet for his slippers, climbed into his robe, and stepped through the door to find every room in the house ablaze with light. He followed the noise into the kitchen.

Broadhead stood at the counter with his back to the door, holding the top on an old green blender with one hand. He wore his cap and a shabby blue caftan streaked with purple that covered him to his feet. The blender was gyrating maniacally and sounded like a jet plane taking off.

Valentino shouted twice, but got no reaction. He crossed the room and touched Broadhead's shoulder. The professor jumped, saw him, and turned off the blender. The noise took nearly a minute to wind down.

"Did I wake you? I warned you about my nocturnal habits."

"What are you making?"

"I'm not sure. It started out to be a margarita, but I left that behind when I threw in the eggplant. Nightcap?" He took off the top.

"It's more like breakfast. No, thanks. Do you do this every morning?"

"Sometimes I make chili fries."

"With a margarita?"

"I don't recommend it. Last time it took me forty minutes to clean out the microwave. Of course, I drank the margarita before I made the fries."

"How was rollerblading?"

"Turns out she was kidding about that. We had a nice dinner and went to the movie. Fanta thought the Odessa Steps sequence was better than when DiPalma swiped it for *The Untouchables*." He took a frosted stemmed glass out of the freezer and poured the mixture into it. It was beige, with aubergine bits floating on top.

"You went straight to dinner? You had a taco just before you left the house."

"I told you, I eat when I'm hungry. Some days I gorge all day long, then fast for a week. I sleep the same way. You would too, if you ever spent time in a Yugoslavian prison."

"Someday maybe you'll tell me that whole story."

"Someday's today. Grab a glass from the cupboard, will you? You can have this one." He held it out.

"Rain check. I'm going back to bed."

"Suit yourself. I only get the urge to tell the story once every five years."

Sleep was slow to return. At one point a whirring noise forced him to turn over onto his stomach and bury his head under his pillow. It sounded like the ventilation fan of a microwave oven.

Monday morning he made a detour to The Oracle before work. He was gratified to find the door open and pickups and cars belonging to construction workers parked in the alley. The sight of another vehicle caused his chest to tighten: a green sedan with the county seal on the door in gold.

A red Vespa scooter he didn't recognize leaned on its kickstand near the door. He had to walk around it to enter. Inside the lobby, relief washed through him. Leo Kalishnikov was there in person.

The theater designer was dressed conservatively by his standards, in a fawn-colored western-style suit with embroidery and black snakeskin cowboy boots. Their three-inch heels and the tall crown of his white ten-gallon hat brought him up to about five and a half feet. He was in conversation with a man in coveralls and a yellow hard hat who had to stoop to look him in the eye; Kalishnikov seldom raised his head to speak with anyone, no matter how tall. All around them, men and one woman stood on ladders, bent over sawhorses, and tested power tools. The sounds they made, so similar to the ones that had disturbed his sleep, were music now.

"Mr. Valentino! Come, come!" The designer beckoned with a hand in a deerskin glove.

Valentino went over and shook it. "I didn't see your limo outside."

"I placed it in storage and sent Rupert on holiday. This energy crisis is everyone's responsibility, no? My scooter, it is still outside? Not stolen? Vroom-vroom!" Laughing, he made a twisting motion with his hand.

Valentino assured him it was still there, and Kalishnikov introduced him to the man in the hard hat. "Mr. Mercado is a serious man, a courageous man. He removes asbestos as a profession."

Mercado extricated his hand from Valentino's with some difficulty. "All this way from San Berdoo just to show my license to an inspector. What's that do to your energy crisis?"

"*Cuidado*! Spink has not left the building." The designer spoke in low tones. To Valentino, he said, "We have averted disaster, as you see. Wherever did you find this magnificent beast?" He reached up to pat the knee of the particolored Pegasus at the base of the stairs.

Valentino gave him a brief account of his discovery. It seemed a small triumph next to Kalishnikov's. "I can't thank you enough for attending to this personally. I was sure it would take a week to untangle the red tape."

"No sweat." All but a tiny vestige of the Russian's accent dropped away. "The lower you go on the government food chain, the more bullies you run into. Creatures like Spink get a boot out of beating up on home owners, but when it comes to dealing with an experienced contractor they shrivel up like—Ah, Mr. Spink! How did you find the auditorium? Magical, is it not?" The Eastern Bloc was back with a vengeance.

"It's a wreck. The real magic trick is how this building managed to escape condemnation."

The man who'd answered had entered through one of the leather-cushioned doors that separated the lobby from the theater proper. He was as small as Kalishnikov without the hat and heels, pear-shaped in a black polyester suit that puckered in all the worst places and pouched above the back of his neck, but it was his head that claimed first notice. It was all out of proportion to his body: large, long, and bald to the crown, with watery blue eyes, a Kilroy nose, and a crooked row of bottom teeth that showed when he opened his mouth to speak.

The designer performed introductions. Dwight Spink laid a hand in Valentino's palm and slid it free, leaving a clammy trail. "Are you socially conscious, Mr. Valentino?"

Valentino hesitated, then replied that he liked to think he was.

"In that case, I strongly recommend you knock down this grotesquerie and donate the lot to the city for a homeless shelter. As it stands—and it barely does—it's a useless relic of a hedonistic time that thankfully has passed, and a firetrap besides. Are you aware there is only one emergency exit from that public room, and that it's chained and padlocked?"

"Um, it was that way when I bought the building. I assume the former owners did it for security purposes. It had been broken into several times."

"By the poor disenfranchised, no doubt, looking for sanctuary. Another argument in favor of replacing it with a shelter."

"They ripped out all the copper pipe to sell for scrap. I thought you were here to inspect credentials and the entrance to the projection booth."

"Yes, yes, the licensing seems to be in order and the treacherous stairwell and nonconforming residential accommodations addressed, after a fashion. That board looks as if a monkey put it up."

"You didn't give me much time." His face felt hot.

"Just an observation. Mr. Kalishnikov has received my written approval for the corrections. This exit situation must be addressed before any construction begins in the public room."

"I don't have a key for the padlock."

Kalishnikov called to a man cutting a piece of tin for the hacksaw in his tool chest.

Spink squinted at a Timex strapped to the underside of his wrist. "I haven't time for that. I'm due at a housing project in Watts in twenty minutes. I'm going to have to issue a stop-work order and come back for a follow-up inspection tomorrow. No, Friday. I'm booked up the next three days."

Kalishnikov said, "The carpenters are coming in this afternoon. They only have blueprints for the auditorium." Once again his accent had slipped.

"Then you should have corrected the violation before this. You know the code as well as I."

"I doubt that." Suddenly the designer smiled brilliantly. "Can you spare one minute, Mr. Spink?"

"Just that. The traffic situation in Los Angeles will continue to be a disgrace until we ban automobiles from the city limits."

Kalishnikov unbuttoned his western jacket and spread it open, exposing a hand-tooled leather holster under his left arm with the initials *L.K.* carved into it in loops, as if they had been spelled out with a lariat. He jerked out a big stag-handled revolver with a shiny nickel finish. Valentino recoiled. Spink squeaked and turned gray. The Russian smiled tightly. "If you will follow."

Spink seemed poised for flight, but all the workers in the room had stopped to watch, blocking his path to the street. He turned, and he and Valentino trailed Kalishnikov into the auditorium.

At the fire exit he waved them back, then planted his feet, pointed the revolver at the padlock slung from the chain, closed one eye, and fired. The report made Valentino's ears ring; Spink clasped his hands to both of his.

Things always worked more smoothly on film. It took a second shot to shatter the lock. Kalishnikov holstered the gun, fastened his jacket, and jerked loose the chain. He threw it to the floor.

"'Throw down the box.'" He grinned at Valentino. "This is a line, yes? From which western movie?"

"Pretty much all of them."

They looked at Spink. The inspector produced a pad and

pen, scribbled on the top sheet with a quaking hand, and gave it to Kalishnikov. "The fire code requires a second exit before the building can be opened to the public."

"But of course."

"Your methods are reprehensible."

"Whereas yours are open to interpretation."

Spink left. The designer watched him go, fanning himself with the sheet from the pad. "I won't charge you for that."

Valentino thanked him. His ears were still ringing.

"No need. Bullets are cheap. Spink's the one who's going to cost you."

II

EAST OF SWEDEN

8

VALENTINO CONDUCTED HIS efforts on behalf of the Film Preservation Department—and drew upon Kyle Broadhead's extensive experience for advice—from a window-challenged beige brick facility that had at one time provided heat and electricity to all the buildings on campus. Just enough remodeling had been done to make the chance visitor wonder whether it was a power plant on its way to becoming an office complex or an office complex on its way to becoming a power plant. Only the two cineastes had kept quarters there continuously since it was renovated; for everyone else it was a stopping place on the way up or out. Broadhead called it the UCLA Cartoon Studio.

The first time he'd said it, Valentino had asked him why.

"When Jack Warner found out the Warner Brothers cartoon studio wasn't responsible for Mickey Mouse, he shut it down. We're always one recession away from a Walgreen's on this spot."

Today, Valentino paused on his way from the parking garage

to observe a jumble of cars and satellite trucks perched around the plant building, some of them on the grass. Someone in the crowd that was gathered there spotted him as he was turning to retreat. Feet pounded the sidewalk. He took a deep breath, let it out, and turned back into the stampede.

"Mr. Valentino, how long have you known Matthew Rankin?"

"Did you see the shooting?"

"Was Roger Akers blackmailing Rankin?"

"What was he using for blackmail?"

"Will you testify if there's a trial?"

"Do the police think you're an accomplice?"

"Are you an accomplice?"

"Who are you wearing?"

A microphone stuck him in the eye, "Hey!"

"Oh, sorry."

He blinked. He could feel the eye starting to swell. "The answer to all your questions is 'I don't know.' If you'll excuse me, I have work to do." He took advantage of a shift in the crowd to plunge through an opening. He sprinted the rest of the way to the entrance, tears streaming from his bruised eye. Shoe leather slapped concrete just behind his own heels. Annoyance turned to panic.

The door didn't budge when he tugged on the handle. He'd never known it to be locked during business hours.

Caught in the tsunami of reporters and their questions, he smacked the door with his palms and shouted to a uniformed guard inside. The man shook his gray head. Valentino scooped out his wallet and pressed his university ID against the glass.

The lock clicked. The guard pulled the door open just wide enough for him to slide in sideways, then shouldered it shut against the horde. Valentino recognized him then.

"I thought you worked in the parking garage."

"Campus police reassigned me here today." His eyes narrowed behind heavy bifocals. "You're the one always forgets his pass. Chaplin."

"Valentino. You just saw my ID."

"I only look at faces. You sure are a lot of trouble. We got to pull officers off important details just to flush out all these unauthorized personnel. Where'd you get the shiner?"

"Power of the press." He got into the elevator and pushed the button.

Ruth was at her desk in the common area. She never was not at her desk except when she slept, if she slept. Valentino held the opinion that she did all her resting in a coffin in one of the abandoned heating tunnels beneath the building.

At a distance of twenty feet, she was a well-groomed brunette of thirty-five, fashionable in her dress but not accustomed to smile unless something amused her. At half that distance she was a gargoyle of sixty or older, weatherproofed by a dozen coats of brittle lacquer that would shatter the second her lips moved more than a centimeter above or below a straight line. No one ever got closer than that. Until quitting time, when she hoisted herself onto her muscular calves, shouldered her enormous Gucci bag, and clickety-clicked out on stiletto heels, she directed all of Valentino's and Broadhead's telephone calls and processed all their letters and e-mails in a blur of fingers that no camera, film or digital, could fix in space. "Half hummingbird, half grizzly, that's our Ruth," Broadhead had said, the first time Valentino came to him with a complaint about her attitude. "I understand her maiden name was Less."

"Where'd you get that?"

"Billy Wilder. She did some temp work for him after Harry Cohn died and before she came to work here. He also said, 'I fled Hitler for *this*?' "

Now Valentino found her waiting to pounce when he got off the elevator.

"A cop was here for you." *With handcuffs*, her tone seemed to imply. "He left this."

He took the card she'd thrust at him. It bore the etching of a police shield and the name *Lieutenant Ray Z. Padilla.*

"I wonder what the Z stands for?" he asked.

"Maybe he wrote it on the other side."

He intercepted her granite gaze. "Is it really necessary I turn it over to find out?"

"Don't flatter yourself. I stopped reading your personal correspondence two years ago. I got a bigger thrill out of Rin-Tin-Tin's."

"Rin-Tin-Tin got fan mail?"

"Bitches, all of them."

He turned the card over and read:

EITHER CALL ME OR TURN ON YOUR FUCKING CELL.

P.

Padilla's hand was as jagged as his personality. Valentino checked his phone, saw it was indeed turned off, and made the correction. It rang.

"Where are you?" Padilla said.

"At the office."

"Stick. I'm on my way."

"Lieutenant?"

"Yeah?"

"What's the Z stand for?"

"Xylophone."

The cell went dead. He turned it off and touched his right

eye. It was tender. He asked Ruth if he could trouble her for some ice.

"The nearest machine is in the student center. I can't leave my post. Been brawling?"

"I got punched out by a reporter."

"What are you, dyslexic? That's supposed to be the other way around."

He went into the bathroom he shared with Broadhead and Ruth—if she ever used it—and assessed the damage in the mirror above the sink. A crescent of white showed between the swollen lids; the skin around the socket was turning the color of the eggplant in Broadhead's margaritas. He folded his handkerchief, wet it with cold water, and held it to the bruise. He could feel the heat drying the fabric. He let the tap run longer and wetted the handkerchief again, but it was already warm when he got to his office.

He cleared a pile of musty movie magazines off his chair and dropped into it, leaning back and propping the damp cloth in place. It was the Monday of Mondays in a week that promised nothing but.

At least the throbbing kept him from dozing off. He'd gotten a little more sleep Sunday night, but not enough to catch up with what he'd lost Saturday. He'd awakened at 4:40 to see a blade of light under his door and gone out to find Broadhead asleep in his armchair with a Japanese quiz show playing on TV with the sound off. Broadhead, the world's foremost authority on the history and theory of film, showed little interest in the subject in private, preferring reality television to the timeless gems of world cinema. Valentino suspected that connecting with nonfictitious characters in credible situations helped the professor put in perspective the time he'd spent in a foreign prison charged with espionage. Broadhead maintained he'd been innocently engaged on a search for the 1912 version of *Quo Vadis?*; but his reluctance to discuss details caused his friend some doubt.

Valentino had made the mistake of turning off the set. This had stirred Broadhead, who had insisted upon making espresso for them both. He'd drunk three cups to his guest's one, regaling him with off-color anecdotes of the personal lives of the great European directors, told to him in confidence by the directors themselves. His guest had been too enthralled to interrupt him; when he'd finally packed it in, shortly after six, the caffeine in his system had stood all his cells on edge. The beeping of his alarm clock had come as a relief.

Broadhead, of course, had left the house by then. Valentino had made a note to ask him if he ever got to work early enough to catch Ruth combing her native Transylvanian soil out of her hair.

His intercom razzed. His instincts told him it had been going on for some time. He took away the handkerchief, which was dry as parchment, and looked at the toggle, working up the courage to press it. Padilla had undoubtedly returned to grill him further about Rankin, and he'd be more difficult to put off than the media.

He pressed the toggle. "Yes, Ruth."

"I was about to come banging on your door. What do you do in there all alone?"

"Movie stuff. You wouldn't understand." He was just frazzled enough not to care if she was offended. Whatever she lacked in motion picture scholarship she more than made up for in industry gossip. She'd known Rock Hudson's secret before Rock Hudson had, and possessed all the dope on Mel Gibson's DUIL bust before the sheriff in Malibu read the report.

She didn't rise to the bait, shaming him with her uncharacteristic restraint. "Someone to see you."

"Lieutenant Padilla?"

"A salesman."

He frowned. "Send him away. Don't you screen visitors anymore?"

"He has an administration pass."

That stalled him. Before he could respond, his door was opening.

"Mr. Valentino? Red Ollinger, Midnite Magic Theater Systems." The visitor stuck out his card.

Valentino glanced at the silhouette of an old-time crank-action movie camera on the pasteboard and put it down to shake the man's insistent hand. Ollinger was built like a former fullback going to seed, with a spare tire spoiling the lines of his electric blue blazer and flecks of gray in his curly red hair. He was carrying a fine leather briefcase with gold latches and his initials stamped on the flap in the same precious metal.

"How'd you get past the guard in the lobby?" Valentino asked.

"Our parent firm does a lot of business with your department. I went to the administration building and they gave me a pass. I know you're a busy man, so I won't take more than a few minutes of your time. Have you made any decisions on the equipment you want installed in the Oracle?" He unlatched his case as he spoke.

"I'm not at that stage of—"

"Yes, I took the liberty of dropping by this morning. It's a war zone now, but you'll want to think about a power source and wiring before the walls go back up. Video and audio technology were still in the Stone Age the last time a first-run feature played there." He spread open a brochure on the desk. "I can put you behind this baby for forty-five thousand dollars."

Valentino stared at a full-color photo of a digital motion picture projector. It resembled the cockpit of an airliner: dials, stabilizers, touch-screen panels, and rows of chrome-plated and color-coded portals for plugging jacks into. It seemed naked and indecent without the oversize mouse-ear film magazines that had identified projectors since before the dawn of Hollywood.

He looked up. "What can you put me behind for forty-five hundred?"

Ollinger seemed unfazed. "For that, I can set you up with a sixty-inch plasma screen, a DVR, and a pretty good surround-sound system for a basement in the suburbs. You don't want that."

"I don't?"

"You do not. I can let you have this projector and state-of-the-art audio that plays *and* records for sixty thousand flat. You can monitor the audience reaction while the feature's playing and eliminate the need for preview cards. I'm talking audial *and* visual; the system works on the wire-cam principle, with multiple units, exclusive to the manufacturer. No one else has it."

"The Oracle isn't a first-run theater, Mr. Ollinger. The—"

"Red."

"Red. The audience reaction is pretty much history."

"This feature also discourages pirates from smuggling camcorders in by photographing them during the commission of the crime."

"Taking pictures of people taking pictures of pictures." Valentino thought of the girl on the Morton's salt box, carrying a Morton's salt box with a picture of a girl on it carrying a Morton's salt box, ad infinitum. "Again, that's not a concern for a revival house. Everything on the bill is already available on tape and disc and on the Internet."

Ollinger's glad-hand expression slipped. "That's nuts. Why would they pay to see the same picture they can watch in the comfort of their own homes?"

"I'm banking they will, to help offset expenses on what started out as a glorified screening room to aid in my work. The Oracle will offer its patrons the experience of viewing time-honored classics remastered to provide the same effect they had when they premiered, in the shared environment in which they were intended to be seen. UCLA will do the remastering. Can your technology do the rest?"

"Why bother? Any old theater can do that."

"That's the idea." Valentino folded the business card inside the brochure and put it in a drawer. "I'm very busy today. I'll look this over first chance I get. If I'm interested I'll call you."

The salesman wound himself back up. "I wouldn't wait too long. The manufacturer's introducing a new model next month, with three-D imaging. That's why I can offer you this price. It's going to fly out of the warehouse."

"So what you're flogging is the state of *this* month's art. What's the difference between it and the expiration date on bananas?" As soon as he said it, he wished he hadn't; challenging a huckster's pitch was not the way to get rid of him.

Ollinger's face became earnest. "Every item in our catalogue is backed by a lifetime warranty. Replacement components will always be available. Now, when can I arrange a demonstration?"

Ruth called on the intercom then. Valentino was never so happy to learn the police were at the door.

9

PADILLA WAS WEARING the same orange sport coat (at least, Valentino hoped there were no others) atop a windowpane-plaid shirt of similar man-made material, but in deference to his chief of detectives had closed the collar with a bolo made of braided horsehair with a turquoise slide. He passed Red Ollinger on his way out, glanced around at the movie-related clutter, and shifted his unlit cigarette to the other side of his mouth.

"Looks like Ted Turner threw up in here."

"What can I do for you, Lieutenant?"

"For starters you can tell me why you left Matthew Rankin's little fainting spell out of our interview Saturday."

"I forgot about it."

"None of the people I interviewed who were at the party forgot."

"His doctor was present. He examined Rankin and said it was nothing serious, so I didn't think it was significant. You asked me about the shooting the next morning."

"I also asked you if you'd noticed anything unusual about Rankin's behavior recently. Falling on your face in the middle of a ballroom full of people qualifies in my book."

"Well, it slipped my mind. I just don't see what the incident had to do with what happened afterwards."

"Why'd he faint?"

Valentino felt a pang of embarrassment. "When I tell you, I'm sure you'll agree it was insignificant. He'd planned the party to observe the hundredth anniversary of Greta Garbo's birth. As you know, Garbo and the late Mrs. Rankin were close friends."

"They don't get much closer. I read the letter."

"I know, but—" He stopped himself; rallying his thoughts to defend the star's reputation, he'd been about to point out the flaw that cast doubt on the letter, then realized he might get Harriet into trouble for sharing details of a criminal investigation with a civilian. "All the women at the party came in costume as Garbo in her various movie roles. The lady I was escorting happened to bear a closer resemblance to her than any of the others. When Rankin saw her, it jarred him. It must have been almost as much of a shock as if his wife had returned from the grave."

"Harriet Johansen." Padilla had his notebook out. "She took first place in the look-alike contest. She's a forensics tech with LAPD. Next time you feel like withholding information, bear in mind I'm a cop who does his homework."

"I wasn't withholding anything."

"You and Johansen discuss the case?"

Here it came. "Only casually. We're friends."

"She told you the blackmail letter shapes up to be a fake. You call that casual?"

"You talked to her, didn't you?"

"You're damn right I did, and I put in a complaint with her

team captain. If it was up to me she'd be on suspension. You're a suspect in an official homicide investigation. Or you were." He snapped shut the notebook and jammed it into his hip pocket.

"Why past tense?"

"Rankin was arraigned this morning. The judge released him on his own recognizance. We pulled Roger Akers' bank statements and matched regular deposits of between five and ten thousand dollars going back six months; they matched withdrawals from Rankin's accounts according to statements provided by Rankin's lawyer. That supports his claim his assistant was extorting money from him. Even the fact the letter's probably a fake works out in his favor. The more effort Akers put into it, the more likely he was to lose his temper when Rankin put the brakes on the gravy train and try to brain him with bric-a-brac. My chief of detectives is considering recommending the prosecutor drop charges. Meanwhile I've been reassigned."

Valentino's relief shaded into curiosity. "If you're off the case, what are you doing here?"

Padilla dropped his mangled cigarette into an ashtray that hadn't held one since it left Schwab's Drug Store and stuck a fresh one between his lips. It bobbed up and down as he spoke. "Don't blame me, blame Robert Blake and O.J. I have a hard time working up the enthusiasm to tank a nineteen-year-old gangbanger for life for shanking another gangbanger when people who have all the advantages walk away for the same crime. This guy Rankin has a mansion in Beverly Hills, a penthouse in Manhattan, a villa in France, and a private jet. I've seen his passport; during the six months Akers was bleeding him, he'd been to London, Amsterdam, Tokyo, Stockholm, Tuscany, and the Galapagos, which I don't even know what that is. He spent more in the souvenir shops than he was paying Akers to keep that letter under lock and key, and he still wanted to bribe you to get him off his back. It's that sense of entitlement that grinds my gut. I got two weeks' personal time coming. I'm making this one my hobby."

"So this isn't an official visit."

"It's official as hell. No police officer is ever off duty. If I turn something that can be used in evidence, the department will be right behind me. Individual initiative's hot since the Terminator went to Sacramento." His teeth ground on his filter tip when he referred to Arnold Schwarzenegger; the man seemed to harbor a pathological hatred for movies and movie stars.

"How does your department feel about personal vendettas?"

"Nothing of the kind. I was ready to wrap this one up as justifiable homicide, then I found out what happened at the party. Rankin's a heavyweight, an alpha male in a dog-eat-dog business. No history of illness according to his doctor, who's been seeing him for twenty years. He did a tour in Korea, got a medal of valor. He didn't faint when the bullets were buzzing around his ears, didn't faint when the medal was being pinned to his chest, didn't faint when his wife became terminal or when department stores went down the toilet or when he got all those shots to hop all over the globe. Suddenly a pretty girl rigged out like a dead actress shows up at his blowout and he drops like a bucket of mush. Twelve hours later his assistant is dead by his hand. That's why I asked about any change in Rankin's behavior. There's always a connection, always."

"Coincidences bother me, too," Valentino said, "in films. Screenplays are supposed to make sense. That's one of the many places where movies differ from life."

"You know a lot more about that than I do. I haven't been to one since Clint Eastwood started playing with monkeys."

"You haven't gone to the movies in twenty-five years?"

"Why? They changed?"

The archivist waved his hands, dismissing a subject that would take twenty minutes to explain. "So do you get a lot of gangbangers in Beverly Hills?"

"They got cars now." He laid a second mutilated cigarette next to the first. "You know what Rankin wore to his arraignment? No? It was on TV."

"The only thing I've seen recently on TV is a Japanese quiz show."

"A thousand-dollar suit. I guess his best one was at the cleaner's. He was in lockup over the weekend and they let his lawyer bring him a complete change of clothes every day. Everyone else goes to court in the county jumpsuit. I guess you think I'm hammering on the rich."

"It crossed my mind."

"Well, I'm not. I hope to be rich someday myself. This is America; you never know when that four-oh-one-K I got will climb out of the grave and up to the top of the Hollywood Bowl. I'm not mad at Rankin. I got a bone to pick with the system for treating him like a weekend guest instead of a possible offender who might be around for a while. Who needs a defense lawyer when the prosecutor's in on the joke?"

"If you're hounding an innocent eighty-year-old man, your department will turn on you faster than you can say 'vascular stroke.'"

"If shooting a man down at point-blank range didn't bust a vessel, he's as indestructible as they come. As for the brass back at headquarters, I'm already hanging on by one little toe. I'd've been a precinct captain by now if I spent as much on a necktie as I do on my suits. They could find a hundred reasons to can me if I didn't have the best arrest record in Homicide. Don't worry about me."

"I'm not. I'm worried about Matthew Rankin. If he's getting special privileges, he's earned them."

"I expected you to feel that way. He's the moneybags keeps your racket afloat. I saw his bank statements, remember."

"Do you have any other questions, Lieutenant?"

"Just one. Who pasted you in the eye?"

"Did you see the press party downstairs?"

"Ah. Got up close and personal with the equipment. So how's it feel getting star treatment?"

"I vant to be alone."

Padilla grinned and let himself out.

Ruth came on the intercom as Valentino was dumping the lieutenant's masticated Kools into his wastebasket. He couldn't remember the last time he'd been so popular. Usually the office was just a place to put up his feet between making inquiries about something rare and unobtainable and waiting for someone to call back to confirm it.

"Who is it now, the FBI?" he asked.

"A lawyer." The curious fact about her voice coming through an outmoded speaker that made everyone else sound as if he were speaking through a comb and tissue paper was that it was the same in person. "He says he represents Matthew Rankin."

"What does he want?"

Silence ticked. After thirty seconds she came back on. "Turns out he wants to discuss Rankin's case. I guessed that, but it took a while to wade through the Latin."

The man she was talking about had to have heard her. He

wondered if she'd simply been born lacking the gene for discretion, the way some people were born without legs or with the heart on the wrong side. "Send him in."

The door opened almost immediately. "Mr. Valentino? Clifford Adams: Klein, Benito, Lohengrin, Adams, and Adams. I'm the first Adams. No relation to the second. He traces his ancestry to Greenland."

Valentino rose to shake his visitor's hand. Adams was tall and trim, encased in gray Armani with a thin violet stripe, with a tie to match, and as black as unexposed silver nitrate; his skin glistened with the same liquid sheen. His well-shaped shaven head threw back light in flat sheets. Valentino suspected he ran waxed paper over it twice daily. His extravagantly orthodonted smile made Valentino's pupils shrink.

He carried no briefcase. Both hands were empty. The archivist thought that a nice touch. He always sat straighter in his seat whenever an actor went the extra mile to explode the stereotype.

"Lohengrin," Valentino said.

Adams uncased his teeth again, throwing the room into dazzling negative. It was like a desert shot coming hard on a nighttime campfire scene in a western. "A fictional member of the cast, as it were. The late Messrs. Klein and Benito were very aware of the cultural nature of Los Angeles, and felt their names alone sounded too much like a burlesque act. Wagner's epic happened to be playing at the Music Center the week they hung out their shingle—quite literally, I might add. L.A. was an oil boomtown then and sign painters were doing land-office business." He shut off the grin, leaving behind little chain haloes of light. "Unfortunately, the laws of corporation make it difficult to correct the caprices of a more innocent time.

I can't tell you how many billable hours we lose explaining the derivation of that one name."

"Something tells me you could to the penny, if you felt so inclined."

A spark of mutual understanding flashed between the two, and they sat. The lawyer took in the posters and stills framed in rows, shelves of bobble-head Charlie Chaplins and W.C. Fieldses, stacks of shooting scripts bound with brads, jumbles of VHS tapes, DVDs, and laser discs, and books on motion picture history leaning drunkenly against one another and spilling to the floor, bloated with colored slips of paper marking pages and passages for further study. "I like this space," he said. "I'm junior to the other Adams, who has a policy of office uniformity. All chrome and glass and black leather and nothing on the walls that doesn't meet his approval. It's like sitting in an airport waiting room."

"Why does a junior partner represent Matthew Rankin?"

"I brought him into the firm. That's how I made partner." Nothing in Adams' demeanor showed that the conversation had shifted gears. He was obviously trained for the courtroom, where a flicker of reaction from the defense could sway a jury the wrong way. "As you may know, Mr. Rankin was released from custody this morning. He's at home, recuperating from his ordeal."

"I hope he's well. I'm sure he wouldn't have spent more than two hours in custody if he'd been arrested on a weekday."

"Thank you for that compliment. I did manage to interrupt one judge's softball game to obtain a writ of habeas corpus, but the police in Beverly Hills were determined to charge my client with manslaughter. A lot of people who learned our legal system from gangster movies think habeas is a get-out-of-jail-free card, but that's only when the authorities have no evidence to detain the suspect. In this case they had Roger Akers and the weapon that killed him."

"This is the second time this morning I've been obliged to defend the movies, Mr. Adams. If people want to know how the courts work, they should read a book on the subject. Thomas Edison, one of the inventors of the motion-picture process, considered it a toy. Movies are supposed to be fun, not educational."

Adams waited politely through this address, then resumed as if there had been no interruption. "By this morning, of course, the prosecutor knew the absurdity of his case and made no objection to Mr. Rankins' release. Of course, the firm will file a suit against the city for false arrest, unlawful incarceration, defamation of character, and emotional stress as soon as the charges are dropped."

"You're certain they will be?" Valentino wondered if the firm had a spy in the police department. But the lawyer was discreet.

"It's prima facie, and a foregone conclusion. There is no evidence against my client's statement, because he's innocent. An individual who believes his life is in danger in his own home is entitled to employ deadly force in the defense of his person, even in California."

"I'm sure you didn't come here, braving the ladies and gentlemen of the Fourth Estate swarming downstairs, to deliver a lecture on elementary law. What's your mission?"

Again, the attorney appeared intractable. "Mr. Rankin asked me to invite you to his home this evening at seven, for cocktails and dinner. He wants to thank you for your defense of his character throughout this heinous episode."

"That's not necessary. I merely told the police the truth as I saw it."

"You say 'merely,' as if it's a minor thing. You'd be surprised how rare truth becomes when justice thunders. I'm the messenger in this situation because the prosecution may interpret even so humble an invitation as evidence of payment for collusion. Attorney-client privilege entitles me to proffer it without submitting to interrogation should the police catch wind of it."

Valentino said, "I must look more pathetic than I am, if they think I'd perjure myself for a lamb chop and a glass of merlot."

The lawyer let his pearlies blaze. "Poached salmon, I'm informed, and a riesling reputed to be irreproachable. He also asked me to employ all my powers of persuasion to ensure that you bring Ms. Johansen with you. Apparently he found her quite charming. Will you accept?"

"It's short notice. I'll have to check with her, and then there's the problem of shaking the press, unless he wants to set places for them at the table. I don't have any experience at that. Wouldn't he rather do it another night, after they lose interest?"

"Mr. Rankin has all the experience required—and the security—to keep the jackals at bay. He's been a private man a very long time." Before the other could respond he added, "There is in addition a matter of unfinished business he wishes to discuss with you, regarding—" He paused to flick through his mental BlackBerry. "—*How Not to Dress*. Did I get that right? I know nothing of the significance of the allusion."

Valentino's pulse rate spiked. His life had become so crowded over the space of a few days that he'd almost forgotten Rankin's offer of the film in return for his cooperation in the counter-blackmail scheme. He'd assumed it had expired with Roger Akers. Including Harriet in the invitation suggested that this time there were no extralegal strings attached; however,

Rankin had clearly intended him to reach that conclusion. He'd hardly had time to be charmed by Harriet between laying eyes on her for the first time and fainting dead away.

He proceeded with caution. "Will you be at the dinner?"

"No. I know less about the retail business than I do about movies, so I'm afraid I'm a boring companion for him socially."

"Seven o'clock," Valentino said, encouraged by this information. "Thank you, Mr. Adams."

The lawyer rose. "I'd try a piece of steak on that eye."

"I'm in the middle of a construction project. Tofu, maybe?"

After Adams left, chuckling politely, Valentino tried to reach Harriet at police headquarters, but the person he got said she was at a crime scene and would be answering her cell only for official business. He left a message for her to call back.

His day resumed at its normal pace. He set up his Moviola and cranked through footage of turn-of-the-twentieth-century L.A. for the public library, a contract job, noting and numbering frames needing restoration by the technicians in the lab. The work was time-consuming, but intensely interesting, and he pursued it straight through lunch. He was rewinding the reel, preparing to leave, when Ruth put through a call from Harriet.

"Domestic murder," she said when he asked how her day went. "Those amateurs sure make a mess. Hey, I got a dressing-down from my team captain. Apparently I treated with the enemy when I told you what we'd learned from the Garbo letter."

"I'm sorry."

"Don't be. I ignored him. Want to hear the latest?"

He paused. He'd been about to mention the invitation from Matthew Rankin. "Not if it gets you fired."

"This place would fall apart without me. I'm the only one on the detail who can operate a spectograph and brew a decent pot of decaffeinated."

"In that case, go ahead."

"We took your advice and put in a request with the Swedish Military Archives for copies of samples of Greta Garbo's handwriting to compare with the fake love letter. If you remember, we had to confirm similarity before we tackled the problem of where Akers obtained a specimen extensive enough to scan into his computer and make it plausible."

"I remember." He sat up straighter. He sensed something coming his way.

"The curator got back to us an hour later. He was so uptight he kept forgetting his English. The last time anyone looked at the documents was a year ago last March, when an independent researcher checked them out and then checked them back in. Sometime between then and this morning, two long letters and two postcards were removed. No one knows what happened to them."

10

"VAL, ARE YOU there?"

He'd been silent a second longer than needed to take in the information she'd given him. In a flash, he'd remembered something Lieutenant Padilla had said, and had almost blurted it out, but vetoed the urge because it looked as bad for Matthew Rankin as it did for Roger Akers—possibly worse—and in any case if the police didn't want Harriet talking to Valentino about the investigation he wasn't disposed to tell them anything they could find out for themselves. He didn't like Ray Padilla; the man could wage his personal crusade against the upper class by himself.

"Sorry," he said. "I was in deep shock. Garbo accepted their security, and she didn't place her faith lightly. Do they have any idea what happened?"

"Not yet. They're rattled, too. But for us it opens up a whole new line of speculation. Akers needed to gain access to that material, and it goes missing just about the time he started making substantial monthly deposits in his savings account. If we can establish how it got from a locked file in Sweden to a mansion in Beverly Hills, we can drop the lid on the case. Any ideas?"

"None whatsoever," he lied.

"And you call yourself a film detective."

He decided to derail that train of thought. "Are the archives going public with this discovery?"

"Not yet. They've asked us to keep it from the press until they can come up with some kind of strategy. My opinion? They'll offer a fat reward for the documents' return, to steer attention away from a colossal blunder. If I were the curator I'd just wait for them to show up on eBay."

"Whoever was smart enough to sneak them out from under armed guard is probably smart enough not to try to peddle them publicly."

She spoke to someone on her end. "Tom, who broke that Picasso case?"

Valentino heard a murmuring in the background. It sounded like "Danielle."

"Right. Thanks." She spoke into the receiver. "Danielle Cox works Wire Fraud. Last year four men broke into a house in Bel-Air, walked around a high-tech security system with five backups, and left with one-point-two million in Picasso drawings from a private collection. They posted them on eBay. Danielle traced them to the robbers in forty-five minutes. No one's smart all the way around third base."

"How much of this is confidential?"

"The Picasso perps are public record, and guests of the state for the next fifteen to twenty. And the whole department knows about the other thing. Stockholm must know it's going to be a race between its media team and whoever leaks it to the press on this end."

"You're leaking it to me."

"You're not the press. How are you two getting along, by the way?"

"So far it's First Amendment, one, Valentino, zero. Don't be alarmed next time you see me. You've heard about someone getting a black eye in the newspapers?" He told her about his encounter with the microphone.

Her tone softened. "Why don't you come to my place tonight and I'll put a compress on it? Ancient Danish recipe, guaranteed to reduce swelling, cure the grippe, and repel vampires."

"Actually, I was just about to ask you if you're free tonight. We're invited to dinner at Rankin's."

"That might be a conflict of interest on my part," she said after a moment. "He's still under suspicion."

"The invitation came from his attorney. He seemed confident the prosecution will drop charges. So does Lieutenant Padilla, your nemesis." He decided not to mention Padilla's personal interest in the case. He was sorry he'd mentioned him at all. He didn't want to spend quality time with Harriet discussing the man. He hoped she wouldn't pursue the subject.

"Are you there?" he asked after a moment.

"I was just wondering what I should wear. He's seen the Garbo outfit."

He said he was sure she'd think of something and arranged to call for her at six-fifteen.

When he locked his office Ruth was at her desk, lacquering her nails a stoplight red, to match her lips. As a rule, not many demands were made upon their department, so she kept her own personal cosmetics counter in the drawers of her desk with which to while away the hours. Her nails were fully an inch and a half long, apparently homegrown, and filed to bayonet points. How she managed to type with them as fast as she did and without making errors was too deep a mystery for a mere film detective to solve.

"I'm glad things slowed down finally," she said without looking up from the operation. "If things kept up the way they did this morning I would've had to put in for a raise. I don't know what to do with the money I make now."

"I didn't realize the university was so generous to its clerical staff."

"It pays less than Taco Bell. When you've been around this burg as long as I have, you've bought everything worth having and seen everything worth looking at. After that you're just treading water till death."

"How would you like to invest in a theater restoration project that will bring glory to our fair city for decades to come?"

She blew on her nails. He swore he saw a wisp of flame. "I said I didn't know what to do with it. I didn't say I was looking for a furnace to shovel it into. Go shake your cup on Sunset. Sell maps to the movie stars' homes. There are still some people who think they live in the United States."

"There's always travel. When was the last time you took a vacation?"

"Whenever it was, I found someone sitting at my desk when I got back. That weirdo son of a bitch Howard Hughes never wasted a minute replacing a female employee who wouldn't put out. And not only female. But you can pay to read my autobiography when it hits the stores, just like everyone else."

He hoped for the sake of his adopted hometown she never published it. The city might survive the Big One, but not that.

Harriet Johansen's otherworldly resemblance to Greta Garbo had vanished with the costume, replaced by a beauty that was hers entirely. Her short, smoky blonde hair clung to a head that seemed to have been shaped specifically not to be concealed beneath heavy tresses, and the slightly Far Eastern tilt of her eyes, which suggested a bloodline other than Scandinavian, compelled Valentino as he drove to make remarks that required her to turn her head his way to respond.

"Are you admiring me again?" she said.

"Guilty."

"Well, stop it. I'm self-conscious enough. I know I'm dressed all wrong." She was wearing a blue cocktail dress that brought out the color in her eyes.

"You look elegant. I, on the other hand, look like the guest of honor at a lynching. I can't remember the last time I wore a necktie."

"You should more often. You're too old to pass for the drummer in a grunge band."

"Says you. I've still got one of my baby teeth. You lose the habit of duding up when you spend as much time as I do rummaging through the dusty back rooms of junk shops looking for *Charlie Chan Carries On*."

"You're better equipped for that than you are to interrogate suspects in homicides."

"That again. There's no law against being curious." He'd confided his idea to her, and had regretted it almost immediately. It was easy to forget, once she'd hung up her green work smock, that she was basically a cop.

"There is when it involves obstruction of justice. This beef with Padilla's going to land you in the pokey."

"Do they still call it that?"

"Don't try going off topic with me. My powers of concentration are my livelihood."

"I'm responding to a social invitation. I didn't even know

about the missing letters when I accepted. If the subject comes up—"

"It will. You'll make sure of that."

"If it does," he pressed on, "I have the right to ask a question or two. But I'm looking forward to a pleasant evening. I admire our host. After the weekend he's had, the fact that he'd rather entertain you and me than turn in early and try to forget it is flattering."

"The last time he invited you to his home it was to bribe you to commit a felony."

"He had an agenda then, I admit. But he's as good as free and clear now. His secret is out, or soon will be; you said yourself the police can't plug all the leaks, and anyway it's a lie. And his claim of self-defense is holding. All he wants us to do for him is enjoy the poached salmon."

"I hope he doesn't serve it with the head still on."

"You're funny. You dissect dead people all day but you can't eat a fish when it's staring at you."

"I don't eat the people either."

Recluse though he was, and notwithstanding the experience of the past few days, Matthew Rankin proved a charming host. He greeted them in a large quiet living room with a full-length portrait of his late wife hanging above a massive fireplace of marble and brushed steel, served cocktails from an elaborate bar, and told Harriet she must never again impersonate anyone else and let others aspire instead to her loveliness.

"I said almost the same thing," Valentino said. "Maybe she'll believe it coming from you."

"Maybe if you expressed yourself as well." She sipped at her martini.

Rankin wore a midnight blue suit that fit him like a sheath, with a liquid-silk necktie that made Valentino feel as underdressed as Ray Padilla. Apart from a slight puffiness beneath his eyes, the department-store magnate looked as rested as if he'd spent the weekend in the country. He'd steered aside words of sympathy, showing more concern for Valentino's embattled face. His brow darkened when he heard the explanation.

"Did the pests follow you here? I pay a private security company to throw people like that into the street."

"That won't be necessary tonight. Campus police escorted me to my car and I was able to leave the stragglers behind in city traffic. One of the advantages of earning an archivist's salary is I drive a car that doesn't stick out."

"A gang of them was camped on the curb when I got home," Rankin said. "The police sent a squad-car team to break them up as a traffic obstruction. Clifford Adams says the department is trying to get on my good side before I take it to court."

Harriet asked if Beverly Hills had dropped the charges against him.

Rankin gulped single-malt Scotch and shook his head. "Adams says they will tomorrow. If they moved as fast to clear an innocent man as they did to besmirch his reputation in the first place"—he smiled apologetically—"but let's not talk about that. I'm going to be a self-indulgent host and inform you both you're in for a treat tonight."

"The meal sounds wonderful." Valentino drank from his glass of imported beer.

"I meant dessert. That I'm serving in my home theater."

The Asian housekeeper came to the doorway to announce that dinner was served. She looked far more composed than she had the other morning, in the demure livery of a mature maid-servant and a slight scent of tarragon; in addition to performing as Rankin's majordoma, it appeared she ran the kitchen as well. They adjourned to the dining room.

Whatever language challenges faced the housekeeper (whose English was still better than Valentino's Chinese—or was it Korean? A platoon of European actors pretending to be Asian detectives had hindered his ability to distinguish between the nationalities), she was more than equal to that posed by the culinary art. The salmon was moist but flaky, with a most delicate flavor, and each of the several side dishes would have qualified as an entree in any restaurant in southern California. The wine their host had selected, a product of his own vineyard in the Napa Valley, accompanied them all to perfection. When the woman brought out the last course, sweetened ices topped with a dollop of cognac, the table applauded her. She flushed deeply and withdrew with a slight bow.

Throughout the meal, Rankin asked his guests questions about their work that demonstrated more than polite interest and unusual knowledge.

"Those television programs about criminal technicians are claptrap, I know," he told Harriet. "One of my companies works closely with the police departments of several major municipalities, tailoring computer equipment to their needs. If the screenwriters concentrated on pure science and left the cop-show clichés to the actors playing actual cops, they'd be more entertaining and certainly more accurate. Which search method do you prefer, spiral or grid?"

She touched her napkin to her lips. "Neither. I start at the corners of the room and work my way toward the center."

"Wherever did you get that idea?"

"From my father."

"Was he a criminalist?"

"He was an academic. But that's the way he assembled jigsaw puzzles, and he never left one unfinished."

Rankin laughed. Then he turned to Valentino. "My buyers keep me supplied with films restored for DVD distribution. I've seen the comparisons with the damaged stock; the difference is night and day. Just how do you reclaim what no longer exists?"

"My specialty is finding footage, not restoring it," Valentino said. "But the technicians have been patient enough to let me watch as long as I keep my mouth shut and don't touch anything. Once they've struck off a safety print from silver nitrate, they transfer it to a high-definition master tape. They can't do anything to make up for a missing section of more than a few frames, apart from inserting a 'scene missing' card, which is an admission of failure on my part as a scrounger, but they can perform a frame-by-frame improvement process by sampling the frames surrounding one that's been compromised by dirt and blemishes. The space between is only a blip in time, too fast for the naked eye to encompass. In effect, the techies borrow elements of dark and light from the better frames and apply them to the scratched and stained ones to obtain a match."

"It sounds like Photoshop."

"Times a hundred. It's much more tedious to watch than it is to hear about. Three or four reels with moderate damage can run up two hundred hours in the lab. But when the proper pains are taken the end product is smooth and undectable. It's called the Lazarus Technique."

"Splendid! No wonder you and Ms. Johansen wound up together. Your work is almost identical."

"Not quite," she said. "Val's goes up on marquees and in millions of home theaters. Mine goes into evidence files and graveyards."

This allusion caused Rankin's smile to collapse. He leaned forward from his place at the head of the table, looking at Valentino. "I can't thank you enough for your support these past few days. My own business manager suggested I keep my picture off the cover of the quarterly report, to avoid frightening away investors with my black reputation. You're one of the few who didn't cheer my fall from grace, and you resisted pressure to blab to the media the circumstances of that ghastly letter. Giving you Andrea's print of *How Not to Dress* is a small enough gesture—"

Valentino came upright in his chair, interrupting him. Deliberately he kept his gaze from Harriet's. He knew she was sending him silent signals to lay off.

"I'm sorry," he said, "but I can't let you finish that thought without asking one question."

His host sat back slightly, drawing his brows together. But he nodded.

"Mr. Rankin, when was the last time you visited Stockholm?"

11

MATTHEW RANKIN STUDIED his wineglass as intently as if it were made of fortune tellers' crystal. "I don't remember mentioning to you I'd ever been to Stockholm."

"You didn't. Lieutenant Padilla saw it stamped in your passport. He's jealous of people who dress better than he does and can afford to travel beyond Long Beach."

"You don't know that," Harriet said. "Don't be a snob."

"The question's a non sequitur," Rankin said, "but I assume you'll explain. It would have been autumn of last year. I attended a reception there for a researcher friend who was sharing the Nobel Prize with another fellow. He used to work for me, developing software. His name—"

"That's not necessary, sir. I'm not going to check up on you, although the police probably will. They're bound to make the same connection I did. Did you by any chance visit the Swedish Military Archives while you were there?"

"No. I'd hoped to—Andrea would've insisted I pay my respects to Greta by looking at her letters—but I had to cut my trip short to put out a fire in the department-store end of my operation. It's not the sort of thing you can do from near the Arctic Circle."

"Did Roger Akers accompany you on that trip?"

"Of course. That was his function as my assistant, to see to the mundane details. I'm too old and travel has become too much of an ordeal to waste time arguing with hotel clerks over what constitutes a king-size bed in Sweden."

"Do you know if Akers went to the archives?"

"He did not. That was a personal mission. There'd have been no point in sending him in my place."

Valentino let out air. "Well, that's that."

"Was Akers with you the whole time?" Harriet asked.

Valentino looked at her. For someone who was quick to point out that forensic technicians never conducted interrogations, she seemed to be on the scent of something. Her eyes were bright and her back was straight.

Rankin looked wry. "Well, we didn't sleep together, but the archives close in the evening. The rest of the time—no, wait." He drummed his fingers on the stem of his glass. "One afternoon I sent him out to pick up a particular brand of cigars to give to my friend as a gift, his favorite label. Roger was gone two hours. He said he had to visit three smoke shops before he found one that had the brand in stock. Is that helpful?"

Valentino looked at Harriet. He was suddenly very conscious of the narrow ledge he stood on with the law. Her attention was on Rankin.

"This was last autumn?" she asked.

"The autumn before. I wish you'd tell me why it's important."

"Sometime between a year ago last spring and this morning, a number of letters disappeared from the Garbo collection in

Stockholm. Both the Beverly Hills Police and the LAPD are working on the theory that whoever stole them may have used the material to create a computer program to forge the letter Akers was using to extort money from you. Placing him within reach of the archives anytime during that period would remove reasonable doubt, not only that he'd planned the scheme from the start, but also that he went to a good deal of risk to set it up. That suggests a strong motive for violent rage when you refused to go on paying him and corroborates your claim of self-defense when he came at you with a marble bust."

Rankin was silent for a moment. Then he refilled his glass from the bottle, forgetting to offer to do the same for his guests. His hand quaked and his face blanched beneath the tan. Valentino thought the tycoon was going to faint again. Then he drank a long draft and set down the glass, a flush climbing his cheeks.

"When the police told me the letter was a forgery, I naturally assumed Roger had discovered a piece of correspondence that Andrea had neglected to destroy and used it for a model. I thought it was serendipity. What you suggest is monstrous. Squeezing money is one thing, but this is so premeditated. How could I have worked so closely with someone for so long and never suspect he was so cold-blooded?"

Valentino said, "Maybe you were too close to see it. You appreciated his machinelike efficiency without stopping to wonder how far it went."

"Airline and hotel records should confirm Akers was with you in Stockholm," Harriet said. "I may be going out on a limb here, but it seems to me you're as good as off the hook."

Valentino proposed a toast to vindication, but Rankin vetoed it. This time he topped off all their glasses and lifted his. "To friendship: Andrea's and Greta's, yours and Ms. Johansen's and mine. Wholesome, straightforward, and without agenda." They drank. "And now dessert."

Harriet said, "Didn't we already have it?"

"We had sweets. A satisfying meal ends on a more substantial note." Rankin tapped a spoon against his glass. It chimed, and the housekeeper appeared in the doorway. "Mrs. Soon, coffee in the theater, if you please."

The basement auditorium bore all the hallmarks of a Leo Kalishnikov design. They entered through an Art Deco lobby and sat in deep plush seats arranged stadium style in graduated rows facing a stage and proscenium flanked by red velvet curtains. Valentino recognized some of the same original Garbo posters that had decorated the ballroom, now encased in locked glass cabinets with sconces inspired by Frank Lloyd Wright glowing between. Although it was scaled down to accommodate a dozen or so guests, the room provided a hint of everything Valentino hoped for from the Russian's efforts with The Oracle.

Seated next to Harriet with Valentino on her other side, the host waited until the housekeeper had served their coffee in black-and-white china cups, which they placed on spacious trays between the seats, then flipped the switch on an intercom at his elbow. "Phil, you cued up?"

"Yes, sir," buzzed a reedy voice from the speaker.

"Whenever you're ready." Rankin switched off and smiled at the others. "Phil's belonged to the projectionists' union almost as long as it's existed. I acquired him from Grauman's when they pensioned him off."

Valentino scarcely heard him. He felt the old excitement coming on, as he did whenever the lights came down and the screen became luminous. He found Harriet's hand and squeezed it. She squeezed back.

The beam shot through the darkness, setting millions of dust motes afire in a shaft from the booth in the rear above the heads of the audience. It was the mother of all illusions; experts in physics insisted that light was invisible until it landed on something tangible. The countdown began, the numerals jumping off plumb, intended as they were to be seen only by those insiders who saw the raw cut—*nine* and *six* spelled out as an aid to editors to avoid splicing them in upside-down—then onto the screen crept a simple letterpress title card: *How Not to Dress,* surely the least possible dramatic introduction to the greatest star the silver screen would ever know.

A dreary period promotional feature, crafted to showcase merchandise available to post–World War I department-store shoppers weary of the drab recycled material available while the globe was in turmoil, the two reels were notable only for providing the first glimpse on record of an immortal star at sixteen, whose plump figure and awkward deportment had disqualified her from the more glamorous footage devoted to sartorial propriety. Yet Valentino saw in young Greta Lovisa Gustafson that Certain Something that separated the greats from the vast gray crowd. Muffled in unbecoming layers of sweaters, scarves, and dowdy hats, the daughter of Swedish peasant farmers looked out upon the spectators with that same sleepy, up-from-under gaze that would conquer the world before she was twenty. But he admitted to himself that her debut on film, valuable artifact that it was, would prove undiverting for general audiences. It would be relegated to the second disc of a two-disc set, undoubtedly framing *Flesh and the Devil* or *The Temptress,* and go largely unseen beyond a curious first glimpse. As history, however, it was irreplaceable.

"So that's what all the shouting's about. I don't get it."

Harriet's comment jarred him out of his reverie. The film had finished clattering through the gate and they were staring at a blank screen.

"That's the general reaction," said Rankin, before Valentino could rally himself to Garbo's defense. "People say the same thing the first time they've heard Bix Beiderbecke on the cornet, or look at Van Gogh's early sketches before they've seen *Starry Night*. You're unfamiliar with her later work?"

"I remember seeing part of *Grand Hotel* on TV when I was little, and of course Val screened *Mata Hari* for me before we planned my costume for the party. I was too young the first time, and then I was distracted the next because I was too busy studying details to appreciate the rest. I'm not sure she has much to offer to the generation that grew up since rhinoplasty and breast implants. I'm sorry, Val. I knew you wanted me to be blown away, but she may have saved her best moments for glamour photographers." She squeezed his hand tighter.

"I expected something on that order." Rankin clicked his switch. "Phil, fire up the digital."

"Yes, sir."

Rankin spoke to the others. "Nothing so exclusive this time, I'm afraid. I got this remastered disc from Ted Turner. It goes into general release next month."

The movie was *The Temptress*. A short five years had elapsed between the actress' uncertain debut and her entrance on the scene of a gala masquerade at age twenty-one, but when Antonio Moreno persuaded the mysterious guest to remove her mask, it seemed to Valentino as if the world had entered a new orbit. Ethereally slender, astonishingly beautiful, her preternaturally long eyelashes casting shadows on her high cheekbones, Garbo slunk through a breakneck four reels, gathering men's hearts like flowers and destroying their lives as easily as plucking away the petals. Had she approached the role as a scheming seductress, it might never have risen above any of the vamps standard at the time, and Garbo herself might have faded to a vague memory of a name along with Theda Bara and Louise Brooks, who lived on only as exotic faces on the screen savers of cinema geeks. Instead, her Elena drifted from European villa to Argentine wilderness to the slums of Paris, innocently unaware of the potency of her venom or its effect. With updated settings and costumes, full color, and a soundtrack, the film might have succeeded in any modern first-run house; but only with Garbo in the lead. Compared to her performance, Julia Roberts, Reese Witherspoon, and Halle Berry did little more than make faces for the camera.

The final image faded, of a dissipated temptress walking the Parisian streets looking for the price of a drink ("I meet so many men"). Harriet stared at the blank screen, her profile sharpening as the lights came back up.

She caught Valentino looking at her and wiped her eyes quickly. "Having a musical score helped."

"'Fess up," he said. "She got you, too."

Rankin came to her rescue. "Why not? She practically invented the chick flick. But men came in herds to see her as well."

He got up and excused himself to go talk to Phil. When he left she said, "Exactly what happened to her between sixteen and twenty-one, besides puberty?"

Valentino said, "Mauritz Stiller. He took her and molded her into what we just saw. He directed her in *Gösta Berlings Saga*, taught her how to sit and stand and move and dress—some say to make love, too, but there's no more evidence to support that than her so-called lesbianism—and when MGM brought him from Sweden to direct pictures for them he forced her on the studio in a package deal. By the end of the decade, he was a dead has-been, and his creature was the toast of two hemispheres. That's showbiz."

Matthew Rankin came back down the aisle, carrying two shallow black boxes stacked one atop the other and secured with straps. Each was big enough to contain a large pizza. Valentino and Harriet stepped out to meet him.

"This is the safety print," Rankin said. "I'll put someone in touch to make transportation arrangements for the nitrate print tomorrow. It's been stored at a steady thirty-five degrees Fahrenheit and is in the same condition it was when I put it down. You saw the quality of the safety."

Harriet read the label. "*Fran topp till ta*. It translates as *From Head to Toe*. I don't—"

"That was the original title in Swedish. It was changed to *How Not to Dress* for English-speaking audiences." Rankin was looking at Valentino. "This stock doesn't need much babying, but I wouldn't leave it in the trunk overnight."

Valentino took away his burden. It was heavy. Nearly two thousand feet of celluloid wound onto two steel reels and packed in polypropylene and aluminum brought physical substance to a medium usually referred to in terms of light. "I accept it on behalf of the UCLA Film Preservation Department. Should I send the receipt here?"

"I'm not giving it to the university. I'm giving it to you. Do with it what you like, but if you donate it, as I'm sure you will, by all means get a receipt. The tax deduction will defray some of the cost of your construction project. You went a roundabout way of earning it, but you freed me from a grotesque state of affairs, and cleared the reputations of two great women. I know Andrea would have wanted you to have it."

He stammered his thanks. Rankin accompanied them outside to their car, and when Valentino had secured the boxes with care in the trunk and shut the lid, the archivist and the tycoon clasped hands. Rankin stood with one hand raised until the curve of the driveway swept his image from the rearview mirror.

"Congratulations, Val," Harriet said. "I'm sure you'll watch it again as soon as you can get to a projector. It's the next best thing to a private conversation with her."

"It's better." He turned into the street. "Silence lasts longer."

12

ON TUESDAY, THE day after the prisoner was released, the Los Angeles County Prosecutor called a press conference to announce that his office had dropped all charges against Matthew Rankin except one misdemeanor count of discharging a firearm inside the Beverly Hills city limits, with a recommendation to the judge to sentence him to time served. (Later that day, this charge, too, was dropped.) Questions were directed to the commissioner of the Beverly Hills Police Department, who directed them in turn to his chief of detectives, who adjusted his tinted glasses and displayed all the symptoms of acid reflux. The unphotogenic Lieutenant Ray Padilla was not present.

On Wednesday, a van marked with the three convergent triangles of a vehicle containing hazardous material arrived at the UCLA Film Preservation Department laboratory, and a two-man crew assisted technicians in transferring two reels of silver nitrate film packed in boxes from the van to ventilated archival cabinets inside the building. (Kyle Broadhead alternately referred to the two teams dressed in hooded hazmat suits and shiny black neoprene gloves as "Morlocks" and "Oompa-loompas.") *How Not to Dress* had moved into its permanent home.

On Thursday, Dwight Spink red-tagged the grand staircase in the lobby of The Oracle for failure to meet safety regulations requiring a space of no more than three and one-half inches between the turned mahogany ballustrades in the banister railing. The inspector explained that children were inclined to get their heads stuck. Leo Kalishnikov suggested installing brass rods between the ballustrades at an additional cost of $2,500, not counting labor.

Later that same day, Spink approved the change but cited evidence of vermin activity on the premises that violated the health laws. Valentino got the inspector on the phone.

"They're mice, not rats," he said. "Rats don't hang around a place when there's no food. I learned that much growing up on a farm in Indiana."

"I suggest the construction workers have been less than thorough cleaning up after themselves at the end of their lunch breaks. Hire an exterminator, Mr. Valentino."

Valentino tracked down Kalishnikov at an excavation for a basement in Glendale, where the owner of a Mercedes dealership was planning to build his house around a home theater twice as big as Matthew Rankin's in Beverly Hills. The theater designer wore an oilcloth cape and a yellow hard hat with a plume and stood in pirate boots up to his ankles in greasy clay. He took in the latest news with a shake of his head.

"Spink smells blood in the water," he said. "The only way you're going to get him off your back is to ask him his price and pay it."

"You mean bribe him?"

"I would not use the word in his presence." Kalishnikov slipped back into his accent. "His kind is cautious. He hopes by turning the screws to cause you to bring up the subject of emolument. That way he cannot be accused of initiating the negotiations."

"What if I report him to the county?"

"For what, fulfilling his official responsibilities? Every matter he has brought up is legitimate. Most inspectors overlook minor things such as rodents, of which there is a healthy colony residing in the basement of City Hall. The building code is as long as the Bible and just as contradictory: One cannot conform to half the regulations without violating the other half. Spink has a zealot's own knowledge of county scripture."

"Well, I won't pay him off. I've had all to do with blackmail I care to."

"I applaud your integrity. I hope your pockets are deep enough to support it." He rolled up the blueprint he'd been studying. "Bite the bullet and pay the two bucks. Otherwise the Oracle will take as long to put up as the Great Pyramid, and you'll be buried in debt underneath it."

Returning to his office, Valentino had Ruth put through a call to an exterminator, who calculated square footage and gave him an estimate of eight hundred dollars for the job.

"They're mice, not escaped tigers. How much can it cost to set out a few traps?"

"It isn't a Tom and Jerry cartoon, mister. I have to get a permit from the city, and then the building has to be evacuated and tented before I can start spraying."

"How long does that take?"

"Oh, I can do it in an afternoon."

"That's not so bad. I was afraid I'd have to stop construction for a couple of days."

"Well, that's the actual spraying. The place will need three days to air out before anyone can go back in."

Valentino groaned and told him to go ahead. When he hung up, Broadhead was standing in the doorway. "Rats in the revue?"

"Just one." Valentino told him what Kalishnikov had said.

"He's right," Broadhead said. "Pay the two dollars."

"Not if it *were* two dollars. It's because people knuckle under to corruption that it flourishes. If I did, I'd never be able to look at the place again without thinking of that civil-service Uriah Heep."

"Well, it's your Chapter Eleven. I just dropped by to ask if you were thinking of serving roast pig or something like that tonight."

"Dinner's the farthest thing from my thoughts. Why?"

"Fanta and I are driving up the coast. We're staying the weekend in a bed-and-breakfast."

"Don't you have a class to teach tomorrow?"

"I'm sure I do, but if I showed up after all this time I'd just confuse my T.A. and the students." He made a gurgling noise through his unlit pipe. "I'm going to pop the question."

"What happened to your case of cold feet?"

"Fanta's are warm enough for both of us. I'm still too old for her, but I figure marriage to her will kill me off while she's still young enough to shop for a second husband closer to her age."

"Kyle, you're an incurable romantic."

"I wouldn't be doing this if I weren't. What do you think Elaine would say?"

"I think she'd be happy you found someone to look after you. You know, this is the end of eggplant margaritas at midnight."

"That's okay, I was starting to get on my own nerves. That's what happens when you live alone. On a completely unrelated subject, how are you and Harriet getting along?"

"She sat with me through *How Not to Dress*."

"It's love, then. I screened it this morning." He grasped the doorknob. "Remember what I said about living alone. It's an unnatural state."

Alone that night in Broadhead's house, Valentino called Harriet and told her about his day.

"I was going to tell you about mine," she said when he'd finished. "Suddenly, trying to trace the only tooth in a homeless man's decomposing head to the dentist who filled it doesn't seem so bad. You aren't going to pay the little jerk, are you?"

He smiled at the living room wall. "You're the first person I've spoken to who didn't try to persuade me to."

"You wouldn't be who I thought you were if you did."

"I hope you still feel that way when I finish falling from the top of the zoning tree, hitting every branch on the way down."

"There's another way," she said. "Turn him in."

"Kalishnikov says he's too slippery. It'd be my word against his."

"Not if you had evidence."

He laughed shortly. "Now *you* think I'm a detective. I'm going back to calling myself a lowly archivist."

"You can find something on him. You found *Greed*."

"I'm beginning to think they'll put that on my headstone. I'm not even sure Kalishnikov is right about Spink. Maybe he's just an overachiever."

"If that's true, he should lose interest soon. Spending all that time at one site can't be a wise investment of taxpayers' money."

"I knew talking to you would cheer me up," he said. "Listen, Mom and Dad left me in charge of the house this weekend. Why don't you come over tonight? I'll roast a pig."

"I'm not sure what that means, but I can't. I'm working a double shift. How about tomorrow night?"

"Tomorrow night I'm in Tijuana, trying to talk a retired director of Mexican movies out of his life's work."

"You and I are starting to sound like the typical professional couple."

"If you call tracing teeth and bullfighting films typical."

"Welcome to Hollywood."

Irving Thalberg shifts in his seat, unwraps a small white pill from tinfoil, and places it under his tongue. Frances Marion, veteran scenarist that she is, has never seen the slender, delicate-appearing head of production display so much agitation.

"Are you all right?" She whispers, but not low enough to prevent a woman seated in the row in front of them from turning and shushing her. Every seat in the theater is occupied; unaware of the sneak preview scheduled to follow the comedy short. San Bernadino moviegoers have nevertheless provided a capacity crowd to see the main feature, The Kiss, *Garbo's last silent—evidence of unprecedented loyalty to the star in this talkie-dominated year of 1930. An audible gasp of pleasurable anticipation has greeted the title card for* Anna Christie, *accompanied by the legendary name. But Thalberg seems unmollified.*

He ignores the interruption. "If you must know, I'm as nervous as a schoolgirl. Gilbert's fall has the entire industry on edge."

Marion's own unease is twofold. Audiences reacted with universal disapproval to John Gilbert's voice heard for the first time in Redemption. *His career is in shambles, and MGM has lost one of the most bankable stars in its stable. Everything depends on how well—or ill—a speaking Garbo goes over. This, together with rumors of Thalberg's fragile health, has Marion concerned for the studio's future should the genius behind its success expire, possibly in this very theater. The first full year of the Great Depression does not smile upon unemployed screenwriters.*

"We've been living on borrowed time for three years," Marion reminds her employer. "She couldn't go on making silents forever."

"I'm not so sure. There isn't a thing predictable about that impossible creature."

The woman shushes them again. Garbo has entered, fifteen minutes into the first reel.

She leans against the door frame in a shabby waterfront bar, demonstrably exhausted, dressed in glamorous dowd in a cloche hat and a simple dark jacket over a low-cut blouse with wilted ruffles and a skirt reaching to mid-calf, plain shoes with two-inch heels on her feet, which some iconoclasts have described as large. As she slumps to a table hauling a plain suitcase, the auditorium is eerily silent—before a talking picture. Even silent films have always been accompanied by a musical score to match the mood. Not so much as a cough or a nervous giggle breaks the tension.

Thalberg leans close to Marion. "Garbo is holding them in the palm of her hand."

"She hasn't opened her mouth yet."

Seated with her suitcase beside her on the floor, she makes eye contact with the waiter for the first time. Her lips part. The air quivers. Marion is quivering too.

"Gimme a visky," says Garbo in that queer husky voice; no coach has interceded to dilute the heavy Scandinavian accent. "Chincher ale on the side." As the waiter heads off, she turns her head his way. "And don't be stingy, ba-bee."

The stillness following this first line makes the one that preceded it seem absolutely rowdy. Thalberg reaches over and grips Marion's wrist tightly. He has never before made physical contact with her.

And then the audience is on its feet, pounding its palms together in an artillery battery. One talented individual puts two fingers in his mouth and blasts an ear-splitting whistle. Moments elapse, and several on-screen lines are drowned out, before the viewers resume their seats, thirsty as drunkards for the next beautiful foghorn note from that celebrated breast.

"By God!" Thalberg isn't whispering now. "By God, Frances! We're saved!"

The woman in front of them turns her full face on them, stiff with indignation. "Please! Garbo's talking!"

Valentino's alarm clock rang. He came to consciousness, completely disoriented. He'd brought a DVD of *Anna Christie* home to Broadhead's house from the office and watched it on the professor's television before going to bed. He had no idea where he'd gotten the details of his dream; Hollywood lore stopped when Irving Thalberg had told Frances Marion, who'd adapted the scenario from Eugene O'Neill's play about a Swedish prostitute, that Garbo had held her audience in the palm of her hand. The rest of the story was based on rave reviews and box-office totals. Encouraged by the success of her first talking feature, Garbo might have gone on making movies with her name above the title until she'd died at age 82, had she not retired in her thirty-sixth year into a life of relentless seclusion.

He roused himself sufficiently to flick the switch on the alarm and fall back onto his pillow, only to stir again when the ringing continued; it was the telephone on the nightstand. He fumbled the receiver off its cradle and muttered something into the mouthpiece.

It was Harriet. "Turn on CNN, quick."

"What?"

She repeated it. "Call me back." The connection broke.

He stumbled out into the living room, turned on the set, and surfed to the proper channel. The female anchor was talking about Iraq. He had to wait three minutes until the scroll at the bottom brought him fully awake.

He didn't call Harriet back right away. Instead he dialed Matthew Rankin's unlisted number in Beverly Hills.

13

RANKIN HIMSELF ANSWERED on the third ring. Valentino realized suddenly how late it was and that the housekeeper had probably gone to bed. "Did I wake you?"

"No, I'm just sitting here in my study, combing the Net for an estimate of how much my employees are cheating me out of. I think the experience of last week has snarled my sleeping rhythms for good."

"The Swedish Military Archives have gone public with the theft. It's on the news channel."

"I imagine that took courage on their part. I wish some of our own institutions were as forthcoming."

"I'm afraid there's more. You know how the press is when it smells two breaking stories that appear to be related. Someone leaked to them the content of Roger Akers' phony Garbo letter."

A short silence slammed. "Who?"

"A source with the Beverly Hills Police Department who asked not to be identified." It didn't have to be Ray Padilla.

Harriet had said keeping secrets wasn't law enforcement's strong suit; but it was only the one percent of uncertainty that kept Valentino from sharing his suspicions with the tycoon. "They've got just enough of the facts to reach the same conclusion you did at the beginning. They think the letter's real, and they're reporting it as if it's among the material missing from Sweden. As they see it, Garbo and Andrea were having a lesbian affair and that's what Akers was using to squeeze you."

"The hyenas! I'll sue them right off the air."

"You'd just be throwing gasoline on the fire. When they find out Akers was in Stockholm, they'll treat it as confirmation, along with any strenuous action on your part to squash the story. I'm surprised you haven't heard from them before this."

"My number's unlisted."

"If I were you I'd change it, or discontinue the service. Telephone operators aren't paid much, and the media have money to burn."

The silence this time was longer. When Rankin spoke again his tone was level. "I'll take your advice. Thank you for the warning. I'll triple my security. If you need to contact me, call Clifford Adams."

"There's one other way to handle it," Valentino said. "I doubt you'd like it, but it may be more effective."

"I'm listening."

"Call a press conference. Tell them the letter was forged and how it was done. They'll swarm around you like bees for a couple of days, but when the authorities back you up they'll find something else to boost ratings. In the meantime you'll have set the record straight about Andrea and Garbo."

"It will come out anyway, without my having to expose myself to the swarm."

"It will take longer, maybe long enough for the rumor to

grow legs of its own. Forgive me for presuming, Mr. Rankin, but I know how things work in this town, and I think you've been too busy insulating yourself from the outside world to understand. Without a host to feed on, a fifteen-second sound bite dies after a few days, but whenever a story lasts long enough to grow sidebars, travel the talk-show circuit, and get argued about at dinner parties, it can hang around as long as Paul Bunyan. The stigma may linger forever."

"I disagree. A lie cannot live, and I can't bear to wallow in the muck for even fifteen seconds." Rankin thanked him again and excused himself to wake up his lawyer.

It was as bad as Valentino had predicted.

Throughout the weekend, every time he looked at a TV screen or passed a newsstand, Greta Garbo's bewitching face gazed out at him. News libraries throughout the country were ransacked for decades-old studio glamour shots, telephoto candids, and pictures she'd posed for in the very early years before she began refusing to give interviews altogether. Oddly—or perhaps predictably—very few showed her in the fullness of her later years, despite the comparative availability of snapshots taken with her consent by her small circle of intimates; those that displayed her in gray hair and wrinkles were almost invariably blurred and grainy, showing a frumpily dressed matron in concealing hats, suffocating scarves, and the ubiquitous sunglasses adopted by generations of actresses eager to show the world they were as unapproachable as Garbo. These last never strayed beyond the width of a column, or glimmered longer than a few seconds over the shoulders of broadcast anchors. It was as Camille and Mata Hari and Ninotchka and Anna Karenina and the Swedish Sphinx of twentysomething that she filled pages and screens and the covers of magazines. It wasn't so much that the camera had fallen in love with her all over again as that it had never abandoned its infatuation.

For Valentino, the phenomenon certainly brightened the sprawling acultural scenery of Los Angeles. He abhorred only the dirty-little-boy attitude that accompanied it, as if sexual tolerance were suspended and suddenly everyone was either straight or a fag. Even the lesbian organizations that came forward to embrace the icon as one of their own seemed merely to be exploiting her for their own purposes. The world had conspired to turn her into the very object she'd gone underground to avoid becoming.

But rock bottom had not yet revealed itself; not when the right-wing owner of a cable franchise in Missouri banned the showing of any of Garbo's films on his station, and not even when a national tabloid composited Garbo's and Andrea Rankin's heads on the bodies of an entangled pair of lingerie-clad women on its front page, claiming exclusive evidence of their illicit relationship. Rock bottom came when the television program *Law & Order* ran a teaser on NBC of an episode "ripped from the headlines," about a legendary star's guilty secret exposed long after her death, with a sordid murder blended in for extra spice. Valentino had spent most of his adult life in the entertainment capital, but had never known a scandal to metastasize so rapidly.

He heard people discussing the story even in Tijuana, where the archivist sat in a steamy rented room above a laundry, nibbling at a glass of tequila and trying to pin down the tenant regarding the existence and condition of a dozen films he'd shot for pesos on the dollar during the short colorful heyday of the B movie revolution south of the border. The director, fat, seventy-five, and sweating tequila from every pore, was best known for a series about the leader of a gang of transvestite bandidos, six films produced back to back throughout the summer of 1958. Valentino suspected they might find an appreciative new audience in the postcamp world of the twenty-first century, which had embraced the best of Ed Wood and the worst of Roger Corman. However, after two hours he confirmed that the poor old fellow possessed no prints of his work after all, and had responded to his guest's query to interview him only to alleviate his loneliness. Valentino spent an additional forty-five minutes out of pity, thanked him for his time, and surreptitiously parked fifty dollars in American bills under a tobacco can on his way out.

He was grateful that his fifteen minutes of fame seemed to have departed with his black eye. No one appeared to be following him, going south or north, and when he stopped for gas he attracted no notice. The defenders of the First Amendment had lost interest in the shooting at the Rankin estate and reverted to their natural preference for sex and bringing low the mighty. That left Valentino entirely out of the loop.

When he got back to Broadhead's house, feeling wilted and drained of all ambition and energy, he found his host seated in front of his TV watching the first season of *Temptation Island* on DVD. Something about his deflated posture in the old armchair suggested the set might have been off for all the attention he was paying to the intrigue onscreen.

"I thought you weren't coming back until tomorrow," Valentino said.

"Bed-and-breakfast joints bring out my claustrophobia. A man could suffocate in one of those big poofy beds. Fanta turned down my proposal," he added.

"I'm sorry, Kyle. Is it the age difference?" Valentino sank into the sofa.

"Astonishingly, no. She said she can't be married to a man with no aspirations. Evidently I've been resting on my laurels ever since I published *The Persistence of Vision*. I barely teach, I don't research, I don't write. I'm the coot sitting in the corner criticizing everyone else's efforts without making any of my own."

"She said that?"

"She was more diplomatic, but the meaning is the same. I'm a slacker."

"Didn't you tell me you were writing a new book?"

He tapped his bulging brow. "It's all paying itself out in the echo box. I tried to make her understand that my method is an extension of John Ford's editing *Stagecoach* and *The Informer* in the camera, so that when all the footage was in the can all the editor of record had to do was piece it together."

"What did she say?"

"It was scatological in nature. There are limits to the young lady's diplomacy."

"She dumped you."

"No. Hers is not an all-or-nothing generation. We're going to the Greek Theater next week. If it's *Electra* I'm walking out." He scooped the bowl of his pipe inside an open tobacco can on the table beside his chair and tamped it with his thumb. The action reminded Valentino suddenly of the can in the old director's lonely shabby quarters in Tijuana.

"Did she say anything else?"

"Stop smoking and lose weight, but thank God she wasn't adamant about that."

"She's right."

Broadhead paused with the pipe between his teeth and a match poised to strike on the side of the box. He glared at his guest from under the tumble of dust-colored hair on his forehead. "A man who has no vices has no experience against which to measure the conduct of his acquaintances."

"I wasn't talking about your weight and your smoking. I spent the day with an old man who pretended he had something I wanted, just so I'd spend time with him. He wasn't a patch on you in his prime, but the life he's living now isn't that much different from yours. You've just got a better location. There's nothing seriously wrong with microwaving chili fries in the wee hours, but I don't think you even like them."

"They have the consistency of the stuff that collects in rain gutters."

"So why not use the time and actually write the book?"

"Here's a question for you." The professor struck the match, got his pipe going, shook out the flame, and dropped the stump in an ashtray containing a smoldering heap of slag. "When will you be able to move back into the Oracle?"

"So you moved out." Harriet shut the door on the delivery man and laid the pizza boxes side by side on the table in her dinette: medium pepperoni for Valentino, breadsticks with ranch dipping sauce for her. Valentino always knew whether she'd taken part in an autopsy recently, based on her attitude toward red sauce and meat.

"Lock, stock, and pride. He asked me where I was going and I said the Holiday Inn. We shook hands. In between there was a lot of standing around with our hands in our pockets, trying to work up the courage to apologize. Didn't happen."

"Men."

"Women. All of you generalize too much."

She made a gesture and took the napkin he offered. "I'm

surprised you lasted this long. When's the last time you saw anything by Neil Simon?"

"Wes Craven is closer to the mark. Kyle keeps vampire hours."

"Obviously he didn't throw you out because you took Fanta's side. He had to lash out at someone when she turned him down. Do you think they'll break up?"

"It looks that way, despite what he said. He's a loon in a lot of ways, but he has traditional ideas about courtship. The last time he wooed a girl they wound up married for twenty-five years. And Fanta's young and attractive and smart. She's bound to meet a good-looking young lawyer and establish something with pretensions toward permanency."

"So much for the smart part."

He peeled up a pepperoni and munched at it. "I'm not so sure he blew up at me over the sting to his vanity. I don't know just what nerve I touched, but I don't think that was it."

"Writer's block?" She plunged a breadstick into the little plastic medicine cup.

"He'd bathe me in scorn if I suggested that to his face. He's always said writer's block has the same foundation in reality as plumber's and housepainter's block."

"Denial." She took a bite. "Did you say 'wooed a girl'?"

Cinderella Man, one of a handful of recent films Valentino considered worthy of preserving for future generations, was playing on AMC. They ate in front of it, washing down the respectable fast-food fare with chianti. When the film ended, Harriet said, "It's pretty late to be checking into a motel. You won't get much back from the investment beyond a night's sleep."

"You don't know how wonderful that sounds. The only thing

that could spoil it would be the noise from a blender someone smuggled into the next room."

She regarded him over her wine, a low-key shot that put red lights in her pupils. "You're just no good at all at taking a hint, are you?"

"I'm better at avoiding them."

"What's the matter, I still smell of formaldehyde?"

"If you did, the cologne companies would hound you for the formula. Stop trying to pretend you have no sex appeal. Impersonating Greta Garbo doesn't mean you can act."

"I'm not suggesting you move in," she said. "I'm not your Mexican director. Living alone suits me fine. I've got round-the-clock bathroom privileges and when I set something down it's still there when I need it."

He sipped his wine. The residual effects of the afternoon's tequila were still present; his head was attached to his body by a thin filament, like a balloon filled with helium. "Sleeping arrangements?"

"Well, there's the sofa, but as you can see it's a futon. The Japanese have a lot more to answer for than Pearl Harbor."

"Just for tonight," he said. "I'll look for an extended stay place tomorrow. Kalishnikov is confident he'll swing a variance when the zoning board meets this week so I can move back into the theater. Maybe by next weekend I can leave the vagabond life behind."

"Your apartment's in the projection booth. How will you get to it, levitation?"

"Oddly enough, he informs me that an eighty-dollar aluminum extension ladder with a three-hundred-pound load limit is a preferable alternative to a stout set of nonconforming stairs, according to the County of Los Angeles."

She put down her glass and slid closer to him on the futon. Warmth radiated from her body. “Are we going to spend the rest of the night discussing zoning ordinances, or are we going to fool around?”

14

THERE FOLLOWED A tense period during which Valentino kept to his office and Broadhead to his. Once only, the younger man miscalculated his timing, or the professor fell behind schedule, and they arrived at the same time. The brief silent elevator ride to their floor seemed interminable. When the doors slid open they broke for cover without pausing at Ruth's desk. The intercom buzzed as soon as Valentino shut his door.

"What's the fight about?" Ruth asked. "Can't agree on the name of the fourth Stooge?"

"Shemp. And stop using office equipment for personal communications."

"I thought it was Zeppo."

"That was the fourth Marx brother."

"Right. I dated him once. Did you know he was Jewish?"

"They were all Jewish, Ruth."

"I thought Chico was Italian."

"What did I say about office equipment?"

"If I waited for business to come along all the wires would corrode." She clicked off.

When the buzzer sounded again he mashed down the toggle and said, "What is it now, the fourth Musketeer?"

"That cop's on the line."

"What cop?" He'd genuinely forgotten.

She might not have heard him. His telephone button lighted up. He hesitated, then lifted the receiver and spoke his name.

"Ray Padilla. Your pet billionaire's dug deep in his burrow. I can't get any closer to him than his lawyer. I thought maybe you could put me in contact."

"Are you back on the case?"

"There is no case, didn't you hear? Rankin's scot-free, Garbo's a dyke, and I've been suspended without pay pending a hearing to can my butt from the force. It seems I leaked sensitive information to the press."

Valentino made a pumping motion with his fist. But he kept his tone level. "In view of all that, what do you have to talk about with Rankin?"

"To begin with I want to ask him why he didn't spot the letter for a phony. The man practically invented the computer. He should've seen everything the lab rats at the LAPD saw."

"Obviously he didn't. He paid Akers blood money to keep the letter under wraps."

"He paid him for something. We've only got Rankin's word it was over the letter."

"Some people think he was inclined to believe it was real because of previous rumors and lingering doubts."

"You don't make more money than God with a history of jumping to conclusions."

"I don't understand you, Lieutenant. Your job is hanging by

a thread. Do you hate the wealthy so much you'd risk snapping it just to make one of them more miserable than he already is?"

"I've got nothing against the rich. I've never given up hope I'll be one someday, but I'm a cop, so it isn't likely. But I am a cop. A man's dead who didn't contribute anything worthwhile to society while he was alive, but the statutes on homicide don't say anything about how life's spent, just how it ended. So what about getting me in touch?"

"I can't help you. I'd like to say I'm sorry, but I'm not. I can't reach him myself without going through Clifford Adams."

"Well, thanks for nothing." Padilla's tone changed. "How's the shiner?"

"I found out they go away when people stop sticking microphones in your eye."

"I heard something like that. It's my good luck the department's in no hurry to stand me up in front of the press." The line clicked.

At lunchtime, Valentino thought, picked up the telephone to call Broadhead, put it back down, picked it up again, and called Harriet, but she told him she had a heavy caseload and was eating at her desk. "Why don't you call Kyle and mend that fence?"

"I tried, but I wound up dialing your number instead."

"You're twenty feet away from him. Get your angular hindquarters out of your chair and walk across the hall and knock on his door. Honestly, Val, sometimes you're like a high school kid who's too shy to ask a girl out."

"My hindquarters are angular?"

"You could slice cheese."

After the conversation he sat another five minutes, then got up and went out and crossed in front of Ruth's desk and rapped on Broadhead's door. When thirty seconds went by without a response, he knocked again.

Ruth said, "He left ten minutes ago."

He turned her way. She was poking at a salad in a plastic container with a fork, plastic also. He'd pegged her for a carnivore. "If you knew that, why'd you let me go on standing here like an idiot?"

"I'm on lunch."

He decided to go to the student union and see what was in the vending machines. On the sidewalk he spotted a big, redheaded man he recognized, too late to duck for cover. He couldn't believe he'd been too preoccupied to notice that neon-blue blazer in time to take defensive measures.

"Mr. Valentino! Red Ollinger, Midnite Magic Theater Systems. Remember me?"

Valentino retrieved his hand from the salesman's flipperlike palm. "You're hard to forget. You make an impression. If you'll excuse me, I'm in—"

"Sure. You're a busy man. I just wanted to tell you we made our first public test of the digivid recording system at Grauman's over the weekend."

"Digivid?"

"You know, the digital projector and webcam setup to surveil the audience while playing the feature. I gave you the brochure."

"Yes. I haven't had—"

"It caught a rotten kid flipping malted milk balls over the railing of the balcony. That's how sensitive it is."

"Congratulations. Will you be sentencing him to life at hard labor or lethal injection?"

"That's the manager's headache. The point is exhibitors will know instantly how the audience reacts—there's always some posing when they fill out those cards—and of course pirates will be caught red-handed. We're trying out a new slogan: 'Watch them watch.' What do you think?"

"I think the DVD rental business should make you man of the year. There won't be a cricket in any theater in this country when words gets out. This may come as a surprise to someone living in Hollywood, but most people don't go out to be looked at. They prefer to be let alone and unobserved."

Ollinger scratched the spare tire around his middle. "Well, good luck with your enterprise. You'll need it. You think more like the guy that buys the tickets than the guy that sells them."

"Then you understand me. I'm not looking to make a profit, just to keep from sinking in too deep."

"You don't need projection equipment. What you need is water wings."

Valentino ate a sandwich in the cafeteria—it tasted like the cellophane it had been wrapped in—and went to the graduate library to look up old Los Angeles for the historical project he was doing on commission. He walked past an occupied carrel, stopped, and reversed himself for a closer look at the occupant. Kyle Broadhead sat hunched over a heap of books, shielding an open volume like an old lion guarding its kill.

"Hiding out in the last place anybody'd think to look for you?" Valentino asked.

Broadhead started and looked up. His eyes were baleful above the tops of his reading glasses. "I warned the administration the library was turning into a shelter for the homeless. Are you down to eating from Dumpsters yet?"

"Close. I had lunch at the union." Valentino read the title

on one of the stacked spines. "*Hitchcock/Truffaut*. Are you doing research?"

"Certainly not. Can't a man read during his lunch hour without being interrogated like the Unabomber?"

"You're getting ready to write a book."

"What would be the point?" He slapped shut the one he'd been reading and sat back. "Everything's been written that can be. Nothing new has been said about the cinema since the Lumiere brothers, and they've been dead since the last ice age. Even my one leap into the mire only added to the compost." He flicked his fingers toward his own *Persistence of Vision*, sandwiched between a biography of D.W. Griffith and Shelley Winters' tell-all memoirs.

"It's seminal."

"So's masturbation, but I wouldn't go public with that either. If I read one more line of tripe about Welles' seven-minute tracking shot in *Touch of Evil*, I'll dig up the fat clown and slap the pork chop out of his hands."

"What about a straight autobiography? *My Life in the Celluloid Trenches*."

"I almost drowned once. My past flashed before my eyes. I fell asleep." Broadhead traded the book for another from the stack and spread it open. "Sorry I threw you out."

"What?" Valentino had barely heard him.

"I'm an irritable old gasbag infatuated with a girl who's younger than green wine. I should've thanked you for pointing it out instead of throwing you into the street."

"I didn't say anything like that."

"You were tactful, but that was the effect. The room's yours if you want it. I haven't even changed the sheets."

"As tempting as you make it sound, I'm okay. I expect to be home soon, among the nail guns and circular saws."

"Are you sure? I was thinking of making chili fries for supper."

Valentino laughed. Broadhead stuck out a hand without looking up from the page. Valentino shook it.

III

PALE WRITER

15

HE DETECTED NO traces of industrial-strength insecticide when he strolled among the construction debris. The exterminator had folded his tent and stolen away; *stolen* being the operative word. Valentino folded and pocketed his copy of the work completion order, for which he'd traded a check for eight hundred. It pleased him to see the carpenters and plasterers eating their sandwiches and sipping their sports drinks without apparent fear of toxic fumes (and, he noted, keeping scrupulous track of crumbs and spills), although ordinarily he'd have been impatient about the work that wasn't getting done. He assumed labor regulations forbade the practical concept of taking breaks in shifts instead of shutting down a project for sixty minutes at a stretch. The sight of a Frisbee on the floor made him scowl. No one took an hour to eat, and the bored workers filled the rest of the time flinging a projectile across a room filled with fragile and irreplaceable architectural treasures. He'd talk to Kalishnikov about that.

For the first time, however, progress was visible. Someone

who knew his way around solvents had stripped the rescued Pegasus statue of its coat of many colors without apparent damage to the frail skin, and the mythical beast bore once again its close fraternal resemblance to the creature on the other side of the grand staircase. The brass rods intended to close the unacceptable gap between the original ballustrades had been delivered and lay in a glittering stack, half attired in the brown paper and tough plastic bands that had bound them. Painters had begun the meticulous business of dissolving and scraping layers of grime, pigeon filth, and cheap varnish from the frieze of fantastic characters from legend that continued around the base of the entablature that supported the coffered ceiling, and the coffers themselves were reclaiming their reddish copper sheen from the verdigris that had dulled them for fifty years. (Valentino reveled in the new vocabulary he'd acquired from listening closely to his contractor.)

The Oracle displayed signs of emerging from the primordial muck, and its owner began to believe he might live to see the evolution through to the end.

Unfortunately, Dwight Spink was no follower of Darwin.

Valentino climbed carefully the short flight of spongey wooden steps to the stage where live acts had once been performed before the curtains parted behind them to expose the screen. His footsteps reverberated in the rafters, redolent with the smells of decaying wood, mildewed canvas, and old hemp drying and unraveling in the desert air. Suddenly, timbers groaned and a creature dropped with a thud to the stage, dusting its palms. It was Spink, shaped like a lightbulb, in his uniform of black polyester, streaked now with dust, wearing a construction helmet over his naked crown. He looked like Alice the Goon from *Popeye* and preambled his greeting with that ragged two-note cello stroke that never quite cleared his throat of its British bile.

"Mold," he said. "Black, and quite advanced. You'll have to delay construction until it can be removed."

Valentino peered up into the flies. "It looks like tar from here. Every time the place changed hands it found the next level of poverty. Someone smeared on fresh tar to stop a leak and save the cost of repairing the roof."

"It's mold. A severe respiratory hazard. It will void your insurance if you don't bring in a licensed professional to neutralize it."

"Did you take a sample for analysis?"

"No. I know mold when I see it."

"I think I'll take a sample and have it examined."

"That's your privilege. I've made my decision."

"I can appeal it."

"There is nothing to prevent you from submitting your case to the system, but the resolution will take months, and the authorities tend to find for the official who made the call in the first place. Meanwhile, construction is suspended."

"How much does mold removal cost?"

"I can't say. That isn't my area." The inspector cleared his throat. "I understand you've had the original pipe organ removed for restoration."

"I have. Does live music violate any of the zoning ordinances?"

"Not the music itself, only the volume. Naturally, the question of whether the neighborhood peace is disturbed can only be answered when the owner of a local residence or business files a complaint. A crew would then be dispatched with equipment to measure decibel levels. Acceptable amounts are lowered exponentially during evening hours, when I assume the theater will be drawing much of its audience. Should the noise level exceed the minimum, a court order may be issued demanding the offending instrument be made to conform or be silenced."

"I'm sure the musician can be persuaded to comply. But is that even a matter for a building inspector to consider?"

"Not directly. However, I'm concerned about cracks in the foundation. As things stand they can be repaired, but repeated vibration from the organ, compounded by the inevitability of shifting in the tectonic plates beneath the City of Los Angeles—You're aware of this phenomenon?"

"Earthquakes," Valentino said.

"Just so. The combination could over time compromise the integrity of the infrastructure, in which case condemnation would almost certainly follow. That decision would depend to a great degree upon the inspector's notes made during construction."

"I've put down a deposit on the organ project. If I thought it would be no more than a prop, I'd have left it inoperable. These are more than just serious financial considerations, Mr. Spink. We're discussing my ruination."

"Safety demands a high price, Mr. Valentino." The inspector took off his hard hat, dabbed with a handkerchief at his scalp, which looked as dry as papyrus, and replaced the helmet. "I should point out that these are worst-case scenarios, which can be prevented at a cost within your budget, if they're implemented early enough. A stitch in time."

The lunch hour was over. A power saw was whining in the lobby and someone was hammering on a sheet of tin, but the noise receded from Valentino's notice. "What are you suggesting?"

"A favorable report from my office at this point in the construction would repel any suspicions farther down the line. I'm a reasonable man, whatever else you may think of me."

"How reasonable?"

The cello scraped in Spink's throat once, twice. He glanced around, leaned close, went up on the balls of his feet, and whispered hoarsely in Valentino's ear.

Valentino felt himself pale. "That's a substantial amount. What guarantee can you give me our agreement will be honored?"

"Well, I'm sure you understand the inconvenience of giving you a receipt. Upon delivery—of your assurances that the concerns I've mentioned will be addressed to my satisfaction—I will issue you a certificate of completion of inspection, approving all the work conducted on this site." He held up a dusty finger. "There is one caveat: that you show it to no one until the building is ready for public occupancy. I will in the meantime make periodic visits, but they will be for appearances only, to be recorded in the log I submit to my superiors in the department. You'll be in possession of the document you require in order to open your doors."

"When do you wish these assurances?"

Spink consulted his Timex, as if it contained all the details of his schedule. "Nine o'clock Monday morning. The official purpose of my visit will be to ascertain that the mold issue has been resolved. You understand I have to file a report on today's discovery, to justify the return visit on Monday."

"I'm meeting with the university administration then, to discuss the department budget. I can't miss it. Can we reschedule?"

"I'm inspecting an industrial park that's going up in the Valley all this week, and most of next week an entertainment arcade in Pasadena; it has serious problems. The Oracle's on the way, that's why I could squeeze it in. We're looking at a week from Friday otherwise, at the earliest."

"With construction stopped all that time."

"Yes."

Valentino exhaled. "I'll make other arrangements for the meeting. Nine o'clock Monday morning."

The inspector smiled, exposing his rickrack bottom teeth. "I knew you for a rational man the moment I set eyes upon you." He held out his hand.

Valentino clenched his throat and took it.

The next day, Smith Oldfield in the UCLA legal department called him at his office. A former corporate attorney now semi-retired to a consultancy, the sexagenarian was avuncular and sly, in voice and appearance as deceptively harmless as an exploding cigar.

"I've been on the phone all morning with representatives of Kirk Kerkorian," he said. "I'm sure you know who he is."

"General Motors, Daimler-Chrysler, and Metro-Goldwyn-Mayer. Something tells me you didn't discuss cars."

"MGM's subsidiary branch is interested in issuing a two-disc DVD of a pair of Greta Garbo films previously unreleased in that format, with a short feature called *How Not to Dress* included among the extras. I understand we own that property, thanks to you."

"*How Not to Dress*, yes. What are the others?"

Paper rattled on Oldfield's end. "*Love* and *Two-Faced Woman*. You're familiar with them?"

Valentino felt his nose wrinkling. "*Anna Karenina* with a happy ending, and a dumb comedy that ended her career.

They're scraping bottom. How did they find out we have *How Not to Dress* so quickly? The ink's still wet on the catalogue entry."

"Kerkorian seems to have taken a special interest, and he *is* Kirk Kerkorian. Apparently Garbo continues to cast her spell from beyond the grave, with additional support from recent developments. In any case his people have made a generous offer for reproduction and distribution rights."

"They already own title to the others. How much will go to the Film Preservation Department?"

"A portion, you can be certain." The lawyer hastened on. "The reason I called you instead of the head of your department is they're asking you to audition to record the commentary for *How Not to Dress*."

He laughed. "For God's sake why? I'm not famous and I'm not a professional announcer."

"As to the second point, that's why they want to audition you. As to the first, your face appeared on every local TV station and newspaper front page throughout the shooting affair, plus three seconds on CNN, which is more than the president got that day. In the absence of in-focus footage of Matthew Rankin prior to his arraignment, you were the celebrity of the hour, inextricably attached to the story."

"Hour is right. The parking attendant here on campus still doesn't recognize me."

"These are entertainment people. Face time is face time. Are you interested? The honorarium is rather substantial for an amateur."

"Substantial as in how many zeroes?"

Oldfield told him the amount. It wouldn't begin to pay for improvements and delays inflicted by Dwight Spink, let alone the inspector's bribe; but Valentino was in no position to decline remuneration of any kind. "Tell them I'm interested, if I can get in a plug for the department."

"I was confident you would be, although I was a bit concerned you might have developed a phobia involving microphones."

Valentino wasn't surprised the story had spread throughout the campus. L.A. was a small town for all its sprawl, and the university was smaller still. The attorney spoke again before he could offer this piece of stale wisdom.

"I'll apprise Henry Anklemire of this situation. I'm sure he'll want to exploit it."

"Tell him there's no hurry." He hadn't considered the fact that any outside attention brought the eager little Information Services flack charging from cover. Although he had more patience with Anklemire than anyone else on staff—particularly Kyle Broadhead, who crossed against traffic whenever he saw him approaching—Valentino had never been able to spend even five minutes with him without feeling as if he'd gone ten rounds with a boxing kangaroo. On steroids.

There was little more work to be done that day, but he managed to stretch it into evening, when it was still too early to go back to the drab little room he'd booked at a residential hotel on Ventura. Harriet was working, and now that Broadhead had become determined to contribute to society, he was either away from his office immersed in mysterious research or not much company at all when he was available. Selfishly, Valentino missed the crusty but amiable dilettante devoted solely to the task of taking up tenured space until someone in Human Resources discovered how far he was past the age of mandatory retirement. The archivist found himself resenting Fanta for awakening his friend to his crepuscular potential.

He excavated that day's *Variety* from the wreckage that littered his desk and opened it to a filler piece informing him that a female impersonator working a popular club on Sunset had jettisoned all his other celebrity impressions in order to center his act around Greta Garbo. *Garbo Speaks* had sped to the top of the bill, and jaded Angelinos were amused to observe long lines of sophisticates, punks, and androgynous patrons in evening gowns, picture hats, and blue-smudged chins strung around the block waiting to get in. A postage stamp–size publicity mug of the ersatz G.G. showed a flattish face and heavily mascaraed eyes set as wide as a Pekingese dog's, more Susan Sarandon than Swedish Sphinx.

He flung aside the newspaper. Okay, so *Law & Order* wasn't rock bottom; surely this was. But deep down he knew that while the sky was the limit, the earth was not, and that there were depths yet to be sounded, that only God's poor clay could reach. Mae West, that anti-Garbo, would have loved it, even worked it into her Vegas act, in which she'd slunk, in her sixties, sequined from her celebrated bust to the platform soles that put the lie to her petite sixty inches of relentless pulchritude, on the arms of half a dozen Mr. Universe wannabes in loincloths and body oil.

"I want to be *let* alone," Garbo had said offscreen; not, as her character in *Grand Hotel* had said, "I want to be alone." The difference was tangible. She had been no hermit in her later days, but rather a low-profile jet-setter who'd divided her time between her luxury flat in Manhattan, her favorite Paris haunts, and her beloved Sweden, socializing with her small circle of loyal friends, shopping for unique objets d'art in high-end antiques stores and open-air flea markets, wrapped in capes and floppy hats that cast her famous features in shadow, and sitting on the floor in her living room with great sheets of butcher paper designing rugs for the use of her friends and herself. She had not been Gloria Swanson's Norma Desmond, festering away in her musty mansion, planning a comeback that would never come and autographing ancient publicity photos for nonexistent fans; fabulous offers had streamed in incessantly throughout middle and old age, and she had ignored them. It had been the unexpected, guilty pleasure of handfuls of New Yorkers and tourists to have experienced headwaiters point her out on the street. A young man, finding himself in an elevator with the legend, had made so bold as to ask her the time of day. He'd dined out for years on her reply: "You look to me like a young man who could afford a watch. I suggest you buy one." *Garbo actually spoke to me!*

She had spent her declining years in comfort: Her early real-estate investments in Beverly Hills, when acres were available for pennies on the dollar, had put her in possession of most of Rodeo Drive, where she had been Gucci's landlady. But all the money on earth could not separate her from her past. She had died just in time, on the edge of an era that would witness marauding paparazzi hounding Princess Di literally to her death, subject the royal to indignity beyond her grave with tattletale memoirs and profitable interviews granted by her trusted butler and even her own brother, who would charge tourists for admission to her final resting place. Legions of stalkers—would-be rapists and murderers—would make living hells of the lives of John Lennon, George Harrison, even actors in forgettable TV sitcoms. Their own popularity had made prisoners of Elvis, the troubled and haunted Michael Jackson, and Hollywood's A-list, cooped up in their bulletproof palaces with security goons and savage dogs patrolling the walled perimeters with the insatiable media clawing at the gates, helicopters turning their private airspace into a scene from *Apocalypse Now*. Garbo had died in the fullness of her years and fame, and not a moment too soon.

Desperate for distraction, Valentino took a remote control from a drawer—shoving aside the brochure for Midnite Magic Theater Systems' new spy toy, the latest assault on personal privacy—and switched on the thirteen-inch TV/VCR combo he now used almost exclusively to see what was on the air.

It was a mistake. He caught *Entertainment Tonight* in the middle of its opening fanfare, with its collage of overexposed faces, breathless hyperbole, and Not Ready for Family Hour subject matter, followed by Mary Hart's red-carpet headline splash:

"*ET* exposes the GARBO HOAX!" (Cue graphics.) "We bring you the exclusive details behind the STUNNING police announcement that the infamous GARBO LETTER is a FAKE!"

At last, Valentino thought; but too late. Just late enough to inject insulin into a story that should never have been told to begin with.

16

LOCKING UP, HE remembered the budget meeting he had to bug out on in order to link up with Spink. Ruth was shutting down her computer, preparatory to going home or fluttering up to her belfry or wherever she went when she wasn't drawing her salary. "Ruth, when Professor Broadhead comes in tomorrow, please tell him I'd like to talk to him."

"What's wrong with right now? He's in his office."

He glanced at the old-fashioned electric clock high on the wall behind her desk, thinking his watch was wrong. "He never stays this late."

"If you say so, but there's a pretty good holographic image of him sitting at his desk."

"Go away."

Valentino knocked again. "Kyle, it's Val."

"Go away, *Val*."

"It's important."

"Do you smell gas or see smoke?"

"No."

"Then it's not important. Go away."

He knocked a third time. "Open up, Kyle. I don't have time to start a fire."

Broadhead said something he must have picked up in prison in Yugoslavia. "Open it yourself. I misplaced the key ten years ago."

He found his friend glaring at the monitor of his venerable Wang computer. The only light in the room came from the screen, illuminating his face in acid green with *Bride of Frankenstein* shadows in the hollows. His desk, normally as bare as an airport runway, was stacked with volumes bound in cloth and paper and fusty numbers of cinema journals stitched, stapled, and held together with brads. "Did you know Leonardo DaVinci conducted early experiments in photographic reproduction?"

"Was that before or after he covered up for Jesus?"

Broadhead popped his lips in disgust and cut the power. The ventilating fan inside the computer whirred to a stop. He sat back, rubbing his eyes with the heels of his hands. "For a little while there I entertained the conceit I could produce the closest thing to a complete history of cinema that's ever been written, but the backer I go the backer *it* goes. I'm beginning to suspect Aristotle beat Griffith to the invention of the close-up by twelve hundred years. If this keeps up the project will run ten volumes before I get to *The Great Train Robbery*. Gibbon took only six to polish off Rome, and he was thirty-five when he started. They'll have to trace my lifeless carcass through the piles of notes by the stink of putrefaction."

"Maybe you should narrow your focus."

"You think? I've a hunch somebody already wrote *The Idiot's Guide to World Cinema*."

"You'll come up with something. I need to ask you a favor."

"The key's in the planter by the front door. There's a dead plant in it. I'll be here a while longer, committing suicide by the death of a thousand paper cuts."

"I'm not asking to move back in with you. I need you to sit in for me at the department budget meeting Monday morning. I've got a conflict."

"You do for a fact. I haven't attended a meeting at this institution since the three-cent stamp. The complaint was we weren't getting enough money from Washington. Is the program different now?"

"Sometimes there are cookies. Look, I wouldn't be asking you if it weren't important. The jocks in the sports department swing a big bat with the fiduciary committee, and we're pared to the bone as it is. Someone has to defend us from any more cuts. I'll give you all the facts and figures you need."

"Get somebody else. That little creep Anklemire likes you, and he can con the tattoos off a carny."

"The problem is no one likes Anklemire. You've got cachet. You're an ornament of this university."

"You know where ornaments go the day after Christmas."

Valentino said nothing. Broadhead looked around, lifted books off the stack and replaced them, found the stem of his pipe stuck between leaves as a bookmark, pulled it out without bothering to keep his place, and bit down on the end. "What's so important you can't sit in for yourself?"

"While you're listening to complaints about Washington, I'll be bribing a public official of the County of Los Angeles."

"Spink showed you his belly? How much?"

Valentino told him.

"Can you swing it?"

"I don't have any choice. It's the American Dream to fall into debt for life, but going broke is a nightmare. I can't afford to have him go on nickel-and-diming me into bankruptcy after I've invested so much."

"I seem to recall warning you of this eventuality when you took the plunge."

"I was pretty sure you were the type not to say I told you so."

"That privilege is one of the joys of breathing. You made the right decision. Most disastrous failures take place in the name of principle."

"Harriet thinks I should nail the little pisher."

"Women will sometimes surprise you with an understanding of the concept of honor. You know where I stand on straying outside one's specialty. The last time you set out to bring a felon to justice you almost wound up being arrested for committing felony."

"You were an accomplice, as I recall."

"I blame Fanta. Youthful enthusiasm is contagious. Fortunately, the experience innoculated me against a relapse in the future." Broadhead removed the pipe and made a face at it. "Misdemeanors, however, are as hard to resist as the common cold. Right now I'm considering violating state law and university regulations and putting this instrument to use as it was intended."

"I really need your help, Kyle. Will you sit in for me?"

"I suppose I will. I may even call in some markers from our illustrious administration and shake down a couple of plums from the money tree. My connections with the motion-picture industry are nearly as vast as the inestimable Ruth's, and there are still a few venerated academics I haven't managed to alienate entirely. Our president is starstruck when it comes to commencement speakers. What would you say to a jazzy new digital projector for the screening room?"

"A bauble," Valentino said. "It'd be obsolete before you got it out of the packing material. Meanwhile something timeless is lost to ignorance and the ravages of weather and pollution. I was thinking more along the lines of wiggle room in the travel budget, and broader discretion in the area of acquisitions."

Broadhead shook his rumpled head. "The treasury is a Chinese box. The bean counters think they'll be struck by lightning if they take money from one account to invest in something that the money in another account is designated for, as if it didn't all come from the same source. They understand tangible things: supplies and equipment. Pencils, yes; rescuing the lost *Metropolis* footage from the subbasement of the Polytechnic Institute in Berlin, no."

"*Metropolis* is in the subbasement of the Polytechnic Institute in Berlin?"

"Lay off geekhood for one minute. I'm being hypothetical. *Metropolis* is fine as is, and Loch Ness is pretty enough without a monster to mess up the surface. You must resign yourself to the plum lying on the ground as opposed to the riper specimen that may or may not reside on a branch near the top of the tree. Chances are it'll taste like my Aunt Ernestine's pudding, which sent half my family to the emergency room on Christmas Eve nineteen-forty-nine."

"How old *are* you?"

"Old enough for Social Security, but too young to ask my pharmacist for Viagra without blushing. And how is *your* prostate?"

Valentino ignored it as a rhetorical question. "The fruit analogy confuses me. If what you're saying is a new digital projector is the best we can hope for, that's light-years better than a reduction. I can put you on to the most persistent salesman I've ever met, by the name of Red Ollinger."

"Sounds like the name of a pirate."

"Oh, he's on record as opposed to piracy." Valentino gave him a brief summary of his two encounters with the representative of Midnite Magic Theater Systems.

Broadhead's pipe had proven too bitter even for him. He laid it in an ashtray fashioned from a lower human jaw he'd smuggled from the Roman catacombs. "I've been reading too much ancient history. Society has always celebrated the Henry Anklemires of the world while submitting the Galileos to censure. But at his most brilliant, the sage of the Renaissance never managed to get the goods on Shylock. Have you considered the awesome power of the weapon this cretin Ollinger has offered to place at your disposal?"

Valentino, who was by no means the scholar his friend pretended to consider him, took several moments translating his language into practical terms.

"That's diabolical," he said at last.

"You're at a serious cultural disadvantage," Broadhead said. "You lack the benefit of a lifetime in the City of Angels."

17

THE ATMOSPHERE IS *one of forced gaiety, enshrouded in a time of global bereavement. Rudolph Valentino, the Italian meteor, has finished his supernal ascent in death at age thirty-one; the phosphorescent glow was still visible above the train bearing his body from the pandemonium of its lying-in-state in New York City to its final resting place in Hollywood, with grief-stricken women all along the route threatening to throw themselves beneath the wheels. On this day after the national event of the funeral, John Gilbert and Greta Garbo are to wed.*

The affair has been planned along the lines of a sneak preview, with few aware that the ceremony uniting director King Vidor and actress Eleanor Boardman will be a double event; Garbo's relentless pursuit of privacy has drawn Gilbert into a conspiracy of silence.

Gilbert, excitable by nature, is strung tighter than usual. He arrives at Marion Davies' lavish Beverly Hills mansion just before 6:30 P.M., still in Bohemian costume from the set of La Boheme *and Lillian Gish's arms, and borrows one of Miss Davies' ninety rooms to change into evening dress. When he emerges, Garbo has not yet arrived. She is, as usual, tardy.*

The stars of the advertised attraction are gracious. Vidor and Miss Boardman stall for time by calling for another session of photographs and another round of champagne for the quests. The Great Lover's classic features display little of the spirit of the occasion in the pictures in which he appears. The guests grow restless. Some are inebriated, Gilbert included. He snatches stemware off passing trays and deposits the empties on the next.

The minister clears his throat and whispers to Vidor; he has another appointment. A glance passes between the two prospective bridegrooms. Gilbert jerks a nod.

Immediately after the ceremony, Gilbert withdraws to a guest bathroom, where Louis B. Mayer, the mercurial chief of Metro-Goldwyn-Mayer, is drying his hands on a monogrammed towel. Mayer smiles and claps a hand on the actor's shoulder. "Cheer up, Jack. Why marry her at all? Sleep with her and forget it."

Gilbert snatches Mayer by the lapels and shoves. Mayer falls backward, striking his head on the tiles, his wire-rimmed spectacles flying.

Drawn by the noise, guests help the studio chief to his feet. They restrain him from charging the actor, and the actor from finishing the job on Mayer.

"You're finished, Gilbert!" Mayer's voice is shrill.

Eddie Mannix, manager of MGM, turns Gilbert aside as Mayer storms out, a sycophant hurrying after him with his spectacles. "Go home, Jack," Mannix says. "I'll smooth things over with L.B."

Gilbert, calming, flashes his famous grin. "Don't grovel on my behalf. I just signed a contract for a million dollars. What can he do to me?"

"You've gone beyond obsession into psychosis," Harriet said. "You aren't even the star of your own dreams anymore."

Valentino said, "It isn't even history, it's Hollywood hokum. We only have Eleanor Boardman's word the scuffle even took place, or that Garbo and Gilbert were to be married that day. There's no wedding license on file."

They were in line at Starbucks, a drive-by date arranged in deference to their crowded schedules; he had a pile of facts and figures to prepare for Broadhead's appearance at the budget meeting, and crime in Los Angeles wasn't taking any holidays while she caught up with her caseload.

She said, "I always heard Mayer doctored Gilbert's voice on his first talkie to make him sound ridiculous, and that's what ended his career."

"They disliked each other from the start, but Mayer was too frugal to throw away a million bucks for spite. There was nothing wrong with Gilbert's voice, in person or otherwise. The problem was he was still acting for the silent camera. He came off like a ham. He was fine opposite Garbo in *Queen Christina* three years later, and he should've won on Oscar for *The Captain Hates the Sea*. He drank himself to death at thirty-six."

"So why dream about him now?"

"Search me." He was sorry he'd told her. He'd awakened in the middle of the night, the images still so vivid it had taken a minute to convince himself he hadn't been one of the wedding guests. He'd thought the dream amusing enough to share, but he'd forgotten that Harriet analyzed things for a living. "There's no work at the office and I'm useless at the theater. Maybe I'm fixated on failure."

"I'm glad you admit it. I think you should stay away from the Oracle for a few weeks and let Kalishnikov look after the details."

"I'll consider the advice." He hadn't told her about his assignation with Dwight Spink; her opinion of submitting to extortion was on record. "How come it took so long to release the truth about the fake Garbo letter to the press?"

"Why are you changing the subject?"

"You were right. I need to stop thinking about the Oracle."

"I don't believe you, but I'm tired of hearing about it. We wanted to be sure the letter was fake before we gave Beverly Hills the green light. After we established the similarity in penmanship, we borrowed a consultant from the USC English Department to do a computer analysis of the writing style. Everyone has his own, whether he's conscious of it or not: habitual turns of phrase, idiosyncratic punctuation, vocabulary. By programming in a broad sampling of the author's correspondence, an expert can match points of individuality the same way we match fingerprints. That's how they exposed the hack journalist who wrote that dumb political novel several years ago."

"I remember. It's also how Elizabethan scholars hope to prove who wrote Shakespeare. Why Southern Cal? UCLA has an English Department."

"My suggestion." She asked the barista for a jumbo latte. "My team captain thinks we've got one too many connections to UCLA as it is, and I like this job."

"Oh."

She paid for her order. "Anyway, after comparing it to the samples from Stockholm, the consultant's one hundred percent sure Garbo didn't write the letter. There were language mistakes no Swede would make, and as to the rest there was too little Garbo and too much of someone who was trying too hard to sound like Garbo. Case closed."

"But if—oh, sorry." He realized the young man behind the

counter was waiting and asked for the special. "If Akers' Swedish was so bad, I'm surprised Rankin didn't suspect the letter. He said he'd picked up quite a bit from listening to his wife and her mother."

"I didn't spot it myself, but I'm second-generation American. My father would have. The mistakes were only obvious to someone who was fluent; the consultant confirmed them with a colleague from the Foreign Languages Department. Whoever wrote the letter knew enough to get by, although it might have sounded pidgin to a Swede. It was as good as it needed to be for its intended target."

"As long as that target wasn't the LAPD."

On the sidewalk, Harriet tore a notch out of her lid and drank. "I'm working this weekend, but I've got Monday off. Why don't you play hooky and we'll spend the day together, not talking about Greta Garbo and Matthew Rankin and the theater that ate Valentino?"

He hesitated. "I can't."

"Why not? You said things are slow at the office."

"I've got a budget meeting Monday."

"Damn. Between the rising crime rate and your gypsy life, we never see each other."

She pecked him on the lips and took off through the crowd, in the opposite direction of where he was going. Watching her, he took too big a sip of coffee and burned his tongue. *Serves me right,* he thought, brushing at the stain on his shirt.

He spent the morning gathering papers and nursing the blister on his tongue. His filing system was similar to his eye for decor, and he found billing statements, ticket stubs, and other evidence that his department needed cash jammed into the backs of drawers, stuffed under the telephone standard, and anchoring cobwebs woven behind the credenza. When he was reasonably assured he'd assembled everything in intelligible order, he slid it into a ten-by-thirteen manila envelope, wrote *Kyle Broadhead* on the outside, shoveled the paper fallout into his wastebasket, and went out to give the material to Broadhead. Passing Ruth's desk he remembered to stop and ask if he was in his office.

"He's in the projection room, watching movies on university time."

"That's part of his job."

"That's not a job. Mopping floors is a job. Which reminds me: Leave your key. The cleaning crew's coming in today."

He put it on her desk. "Make sure they sweep behind the credenza. The spiders have built an entire condominium back there."

"Nice to know someone's working on this floor."

He didn't feel he had the moral authority to press the issue. Lying to Harriet had left him with a knot in his stomach. Hoping to loosen it with food, he gave Ruth the envelope to give to Broadhead and went to lunch at his and Broadhead's favorite restaurant, a blatant tourist trap plastered with stills and posters and everything on the menu named after a dead star or director; but the prices were moderate and the food was good, even if the Hitchcock Loaf had been discontinued for lack of interest because the chef insisted patrons remain in suspense about what it contained. But the knot was Gordian, and not being able to stop thinking about his appointment with Spink did nothing for his appetite. He pushed away his plate and made a decision.

Back at the office, he found the cleaning crew had taken its standard lick and a swipe and moved on. He opened the top drawer of his desk, groped inside, pushed it shut, and opened all the others in turn. He looked in his wastebasket, but in that instance the crew had been thorough; it was empty. With a sinking feeling he got out the Yellow Pages and then the metropolitan directory and looked through the business section. The listing he needed wasn't there.

He went back out to the reception desk. "Ruth, I think I accidentally threw away something important. Are the cleaners still here?"

"They just left."

He cursed beneath his breath.

"I heard that."

"Do they start here and work their way down to the ground floor, or is this their last stop?"

"How should I know? We don't trade professional secrets."

He went to the elevator, got out at every floor, quizzed receptionists, knocked at doors where the desks were unoccupied, and finished at ground level, where too late he realized he should have come straight there. He stepped outside just as a maintenance van rolled away. Standing in the middle of the paved drive he waved his arms, but the driver either didn't look in his mirror or ignored him.

When he turned back toward the building, he saw a white-haired man in coveralls raking leaves on the little patch of grass. The half-grown maple tree planted there seemed hardly worth the effort. Valentino asked him if he knew where the trash was taken. The man stopped what he was doing, considered, then inclined the handle of his rake toward a Dumpster standing next to the building.

By the time he found what he was looking for, Valentino had a pretty clear idea of the dining habits of his fellow employees;

it remained only to connect the faces he saw every day with the Chinese take-out cartons, chip bags, granola wrappers, salad containers, and barbecued spareribs gnawed to the bone. Other tastes were more difficult to pin down. *High Times*, *Forbes*, *Cosmopolitan*, and *Superstars of Wrestling* were all bunched together as if they'd come from the same floor, and apparently two people had decided simultaneously to rid themselves of a VOTE REPUBLICAN button and a Dixie Chicks CD. He thought he really ought to socialize more often with his neighbors.

At length he scraped a glop of macaroni and cheese off a glossy advertising brochure and was relieved to unfold it and find a business card tucked inside.

When he stepped off the elevator on his floor, Ruth did a double take. "You look like you've been out on the town with Mickey Rourke."

He told her he had an important call to make and not to interrupt him.

"Okay, boss."

Locking his door behind him, he decided she wasn't being ironic. Wading up to his armpits in garbage seemed to have given his tone an edge of authority.

"Red Ollinger, Midnite Magic Theater Systems."

Valentino introduced himself and told him what he wanted.

There was a brief pause on the other end. "Normally, we arrange demonstrations at our own facility. Grauman's was a big order, so we made an exception there, but—"

"How big a deposit would you need?"

"I'll have to get back to you on that."

"Never mind, I'll pay it. I need it set up this weekend."

"That soon? I'm not sure we can—"

"Mr. Ollinger?"

"Red."

"Red, you work on commission, don't you?"

"Yes, *sir*!"

"Good. Here's my shopping list." Valentino opened the brochure.

18

WHEN THE WORKERS were absent, the full weight of The Oracle's desolation came down like a leaden curtain. Only the echoes of Valentino's footfalls greeted him from distant corners; the abandoned ladders, drop cloths, and buckets of paint drew a stark picture of progress halted, for days, months, possibly years.

Not so long ago, throngs of women struggling in ordinary circumstances had swooned before the desert dash and smoldering sexuality of Rudolph Valentino, and men and women had recoiled from the naked face of Lon Chaney in *The Phantom of the Opera* and believed Al Jolson when he told them aloud that they hadn't seen nothing yet. Hundreds of blonde chorines had formed Busby Berkeley's intricate test patterns while time-stepping to the tunes of Harry Warren and Al Dubin, Errol Flynn and Johnny Weissmuller had swung from vines, Cary Grant had swept Irene Dunne off her feet, James Cagney had dragged Joan Blondell across the floor. Humphrey Bogart had gone straight, Rock Hudson had pretended to,

Marilyn Monroe had set the screen aflame in Technicolor, and scores of cowboys, Indians, and U.S. cavalrymen had galloped and shot and tumbled from their saddles through the talents of about three stuntmen. Charlie Chaplin, Jerry Lewis, and Dustin Hoffman had rocked the auditorium with laughter; Garbo and Barbara Stanwyck and Debra Winger had drenched it in tears. For the price of a ticket, America had come there asking Hollywood to cast a spell upon it every night and on Saturday afternoon, chapter by chapter, with cliffhangers to keep it coming back. And Hollywood and The Oracle had complied.

Stripped of its program, with streaks of acid rain weeping from the ducts of cast gargoyles, Greek masks, and cherubim, the building was only a barn where the remains of forgotten civilizations were stored. A sparrow fluttered from the Chinese Imperial Gardens in faded oils to the mouth of a gilded lion where it was building a nest, throwing its shadow on the new screen Valentino had just had installed. The pure white of the synthetic material brought out the dust and tarnish and tatters by contrast.

"Bit early for finishing touches, isn't it? I ought to cite you for that. No work is to be done until the most recent violation has been corrected and approved."

Dwight Spink's accent, an unpleasant mix of low cockney and West End affectation, turned Valentino away from the screen. The inspector was making his way up the center aisle, a hunched figure who led with his shoulder. He seemed to walk sideways, like a crab.

Valentino put his hands in his pockets. "I wanted to try it on for size. I'd hoped you might overlook one little whim in honor of our understanding."

"I overlook nothing." Spink stopped and swiveled his football-shaped head right and left, his eyes shifting like ball bearings, searching corners and the spaces between the rows of rotting seats. At length he seemed to have satisfied himself that the two were alone. He closed the distance between them. "I still think this place ought to be razed. Even wicked Rome offered bread with its circuses. You'll charge people five dollars for a small bag of stale popcorn."

"The real money's in the concessions; everyone in the industry knows that. I'm surprised you disapprove. If I didn't think the place would show a profit, I wouldn't have agreed to this meeting."

"I'm glad to see you've given up that pose of preserving the arts. The usher who caught me sneaking into *Irma La Douce* in Manchester didn't bore me with speeches. He boxed my ears and threw me in a filthy alley. I was ten years old."

"You should've bought a ticket."

"I'd have got worse from my parents if I had and they found out. We hadn't money to throw away on trifles. As it was I got a caning for coming home with a rip in my trousers. They thought I'd been fighting."

"Don't make me feel sorry for you, Spink."

"That wasn't my intention, but hear me out. No doubt you think I'm a low character."

Valentino said nothing.

Spink went on as if he'd agreed. "I wore patches on my clothes all through school; badges of dishonor that made my childhood a living hell on the playground. I thought things would be different when I emigrated here, to the land of equal opportunity. Your movies sold me that load of cobblers." His eyes brightened. "Oh, yes, when I began clerking in a government office I managed to scrape together a few shillings to attend a matinee from time to time.

"Equality is a despicable myth, Mr. Valentino; aided, abetted, and packaged for profit by the industry whose lies you intend to preach from this pulpit. I wear the best suit I can afford on a civil servant's salary. It might as well be covered with patches when I knock on a door in Beverly Hills. That tune changes when I click my little pen. And how will you greet the first little boy who sneaks past the ticket booth to gobble up your propoganda?"

"Well, I won't offer him a bribe to stay away. Unless he grows up to be like you."

The little man's face grew feral. The corners of his lips lifted to show his eyeteeth. "But isn't that the American way?"

"Can we get this over with? I have a salary to earn, and I'm not much better off than you. Worse, probably. I've gone into a hole on this place as it is and I haven't seen the bottom yet."

"Not so bad as that, surely, or you wouldn't be in a position to meet my terms."

Valentino drew a thick envelope from his inside breast pocket. "This is every penny I have left. I've already had to take on commission work to keep this project going. My employers are understanding, but their patience won't last if it starts affecting the work they pay me to do." He pulled it back when Spink stuck a hand out. "Aren't you forgetting something?"

The inspector reached inside his own coat and brought out a long fold of stiff paper. He held it close to his breast. "The envelope, please." He wiggled the fingers of his other hand.

"I want to be sure what I'm buying. In return for this money, you're giving me a certificate signed by you, stating that all the construction performed on these premises has met the requirements of the Los Angeles County Building Code, and that no further approval is necessary from your office to complete the project and open the building to private and public occupancy. Is that correct?"

Spink nodded.

"Say it, please."

"Why?"

"I want to be absolutely clear on what I'm getting for my money. Forgive me for being frank, but you don't impress me as the kind of man I can do business with on a handshake."

Spink was as suspicious as any burrowing creature. Once again he looked all around, and bent his knees to obtain a viewing angle of the maze of catwalks and crosspieces above the stage. In that position he resembled nothing so much as a tarantula. Finally he straightened, nodded, and repeated what Valentino had said, changing only the pronouns.

"You have a good memory. Something tells me you've done this before."

"That's none of your business, Mr. Valentino." He looked at his Timex. "Now, if you don't mind."

"Yes, the industrial park in the Valley. I imagine this is chicken feed compared to that." The archivist thumbed open the flap of the envelope and fanned out the corners of the bills inside.

The inspector's lips moved; he appeared to be counting the denominations. At length he nodded and let the fold of paper fall open so Valentino could read the legend and see the county seal in the corner next to his angular signature.

Cautiously each man took a step forward and extended his prize. The exchange took place in a simultaneous snatch and a crackle of paper.

Spink counted the bills again, whispering to himself. He tamped them all back in, tucked in the flap, and slid the envelope into his pocket. He pointed with his chin. "You'll want to replace the control panel backstage. The switches are corroded and something's been chewing at the wiring. I was considering red-tagging it on my next visit."

"Well, now that's none of *your* business, is it?" Valentino folded his paper.

"Just so." Spink started to turn. Then his narrow chest collapsed and filled, in and out, releasing a scratchy, broken wheeze through his throat, like an out-of-tune cello warming up. Valentino stared. He seemed to be having some kind of seizure. Then the wheeze broke into a high-pitched cackle. He was laughing.

"Do those bills tickle, Spink?"

"Forgive me." The noise stopped, although his sharp little eyes held their glitter. "It amuses me whenever someone who's had so many more advantages than I trades his last shekel for a dead pig in a poke."

"Excuse me?"

"This isn't the first theater I've inspected. That honor belongs to that miserable little enterprise in Manchester I was privileged to condemn after all those years. Gild and gussy it up all you please, this tower of Babel will fall back into disrepair when no one patronizes it and it closes its doors once again. Why should anyone bother to put on a shirt, fight traffic, and circle the block for ten minutes looking for a place to park just to pay ten dollars to see a feature he can download for two and watch at home? The snacks are cheaper and you don't have to put up with the loudmouth in the balcony."

"Your opinion, Spink."

"History's, Mr. Valentino. It's a fossil. All fossils crumble in time, and in this town they crumble faster than most. It may even happen soon enough for me to be the one who recommends demolition; but that's wishful thinking."

He patted his pocket. "With this and what I've gotten from your predecessors and one or two more, I plan to retire early.

My life's experience has made me a frugal man, but I'll be able to afford to take in a matinee before the place closes, for old times' sake and to refresh a pleasant memory. One of your American westerns, perhaps, where the humble are exalted and vice versa—through the intervention of a man of justice." He offered Valentino a mocking salute from his high bald brow and turned toward the exit.

Valentino raised his voice a notch. "Phil."

The auditorium flooded with light. A hidden speaker crackled.

"With this and what I've gotten from your predecessors and one or two more, I plan to retire early."

Spink turned back. The new screen was illuminated. His long face filled it from side to side and from just above his eyebrows to just below his pendulous bottom lip, an extreme close-up, Sergio Leone style. The high-definition digital reproduction showed his ivory-colored eyeteeth in stunning detail; Valentino was impressed by so much performance from a webcam no larger than the human eye. He was less pleased with the sound quality, which echoed tinnily and buzzed from a speaker installed too close to a wall, but the technicians had been in a hurry, and in any case the voice was readily identifiable. The tiny gun microphone had captured every word.

"Go back a little, Phil."

The image reversed action at quadruple speed. A confusing array of shots and angles flashed by.

"Stop. Play."

Spink again on-screen. "In return for this money, I'm giving you a certificate signed by me, stating—"

"Forward a bit. There!"

The angle was different, a two-shot courtesy of a camera set farther back: Valentino and Spink trading an envelope for a piece of paper.

"How close can you come in?"

The camera appeared to pounce. A face much more benevolent than Spink's filled the screen: Ben Franklin's steel-point image on a hundred-dollar bill.

"Down a little and to the right. Tight in."

Franklin vanished, replaced instantly by the gold county seal and the inspector's signature in royal blue ink.

"Amazing," Valentino said. "You just can't get detail like that on celluloid. Thanks, Phil. We'll save the rest."

The screen went dark. The shaft of light crawling with dust motes disappeared from the aperture belonging to the projection booth upstairs. Spink turned his head that way.

"I took down the plywood and put it back up after Phil climbed the noncompliant stairs," the archivist said. "I suppose I'm in trouble with whoever takes your place as building inspector."

Spink was still staring at the booth. A somewhat bullet-shaped silhouette showed against a light inside. One hand came up in a wave.

Valentino said, "I borrowed Phil from Matthew Rankin. He's a pro; he mastered the new technology in just one weekend. I could have operated it myself by remote control, but I didn't want to run afoul of the projectionists' union on top of that other violation. My life's experience has made me a law-abiding man."

Dwight Spink said nothing. When his face turned back it was gray and his mouth had fallen open to expose the tilted headstones in his bottom jaw.

19

"YOU FORCED HIM to resign?" Broadhead said.

Valentino nodded. "After he gave me back the money. That was the price of not turning my evidence over to the county for prosecution."

"Isn't that obstruction of justice?"

"Only the legal kind. He was bound to talk in return for a lesser charge. Why get a lot of desperate people in trouble just for agreeing to his terms? I was almost one of them. Anyway, I needed the money back. Midnite Magic demanded a stiff deposit to install all that equipment on a temporary basis."

"You returned it?"

"They're dismantling the sound equipment and spycams. I'm holding on to the digital projector; they've given me two weeks to try it out, and a payment plan if I'm hooked. The quality's perfect. I can use it to screen silent films until I get a more conventional audio receiver and speakers."

"Well, I guess you can move back in anytime. You've got Spink's certificate."

"I tore it up."

Broadhead smacked his venerable Remington typewriter with a palm and fell back in his chair. They were in the home office the professor maintained in a corner of his bedroom, with a freshly opened ream of paper on the writing table but no reference books in sight. "You're honest to a fault," he said. "A fault. The homespun pioneer principles that work so well in Fox Fart, Indiana, don't apply to Southern California."

"Fox Forage," Valentino corrected. "The paper was no good, Kyle. It was signed by Spink, and the record will show that he resigned his position months before construction was completed."

"Years. Decades. So what are you going to do when another Spink shows his face?"

"Call me idealistic, but I'm playing the percentages. They can't all be crooks or this city wouldn't be in a constant state of tearing down and building back up."

"The percentages would all be in your favor if you'd left him where he was and put that certificate in a safe deposit box."

"That would have made me no better than Roger Akers."

Broadhead charged his pipe. "I'd almost forgotten all about that."

"I haven't. If I refused Matthew Rankin's request to furnish blackmail evidence to stop Akers from blackmailing Rankin, I sure wasn't going to blackmail Spink to renovate the Oracle. I'd never be able to set foot in the place without remembering what I had to do to make it possible."

"That sounds like something Harriet would say. What did she say about your little undercover sting?"

"I haven't told her yet. She said I should nail him somehow, but I have my doubts she'd approve how I went about it. She works for the police department, after all." He changed the subject. "You haven't told me what happened at the budget meeting."

"Yes, about that." Broadhead put a match to the tobacco and popped his lips on the stem for thirty seconds before he was satisfied with the ignition. He blew a cloud and held the dead match until it cooled. "I tried to get the department a twenty-percent raise in its operating fund. I couldn't swing it."

"It was reckless to try. The best I hoped for was that the administration wouldn't make any cuts. Tell me you were able to talk them out of it."

"The subject didn't come up."

"They didn't table it! The last time that happened we were paralyzed for a year. I couldn't travel or make acquisitions without begging for every dime. By the time it finished crawling through the system, the opportunity was gone."

"They counteroffered with a fifteen-percent raise."

Valentino blinked. "I thought we were in an economic crunch."

"Have you ever known the administration to say we're flush? I reminded them of some of the properties the department's brought into the archives this past year, including *Greed* and Greta Garbo's film debut and the publicity there attendant. Your figures showing an increase in private donations after the *Greed* story broke didn't exactly queer the deal. Your being asked to provide commentary for *How Not to Dress* on DVD cinched it. I told you our president is starstruck."

"How'd you find out about that?"

"I've always known it. He almost soiled himself when I tagged Scorsese for a lecture series on European influences in American film."

"I mean how'd you find out I was invited to comment on *How Not to Dress*?"

"Ruth. Her intelligence network among the secretaries and switchboard operators on this campus makes Homeland Security look like two tin cans and a string."

"But why would she tell you? If she had her way, the university would turn our offices back into a power plant."

Broadhead puffed. "And what would she do then? No other department in this institution would have her. If she joined a retirement cruise, the crew and passengers would vote to maroon her on an island. Anyway, I asked her for help. That pile of papers you gave me wouldn't have done squat. So what about this Rankin thing? If you spring him, will he be properly grateful to the department?"

"Kyle, sometimes your cynicism isn't amusing. Justice should be its own reward."

"I got out of the habit of expecting justice a long time ago. That's why I don't dress like Napoleon to this day."

Valentino only half heard him. He was thinking about the budget. "This means I can go to Italy. A retired A.D. I've been pumping for information for years has been taunting me with some Fellini outtakes he claims to have in his basement. I can tell him face to face to put up or shut up."

"Where does he live?"

"Florence."

"Save your frequent flyer miles," Broadhead said. "The Tuscan government ordered all basements sealed after the Arno overflowed its banks forty years ago. He's probably trying to hit you up for a loan."

Valentino was disappointed. "Well, there's always Siberia. They say Stalin stocked a defunct salt mine with his favorite films in case he had to go underground to avoid a nuclear attack. He was particularly fond of Eisenstein."

"I bet a kid on Sunset sold you a map."

"The point is I can start dreaming again. Thanks, Kyle. Fanta's mistaken. You do contribute."

"Oh, her. She's going to have to come around on her own. I'm not pinning my legacy on a bureaucratic victory." He patted the typewriter.

"What's that?"

"A mechanical writing machine, a marvel of the age. It processes, paginates, and prints, and it's immune to electrical storms, power failures, hackers, and viruses. It will revolutionize the computer industry as we know it."

"I don't mean that. I mean that." Valentino pointed at the sheet rolled onto the platen.

"An Egyptian invention, originally fashioned from the pulp of the papyrus—"

"What's *on* the paper?"

"Oh. You didn't have to shout. It's the first chapter of my book."

"It says 'The.' "

"It's more than I've written in years. I have the rest in order." He tapped his temple with the stem of his pipe.

"You finally decided on a theme. Congratulations."

"Don't pop the cork until I'm finished. I've wasted a week in the library, the projection room, and that Mycenean monstrosity appropriately labeled the World Wide Web, only to confirm what I suspected at the start, that every stone has been turned and all the oceans plumbed to their depths. I have a new respect for the challenges confronting a modern musical composer, faced with the realization that every conceivable combination of notes on the scale has been exploited three times over. Am I the only one who noticed that 'Autumn in New York' and 'Moonlight in Vermont' are the same song, or that the refrain from Shania Twain's 'I Feel Like a Woman' is actually the rallying call at Dodgers Stadium?"

"I wasn't aware you knew she existed."

"Her opus sets the mood for a dozen Web sites. Someone should appoint a road commission to study the pointless detours and dead ends on the Information Superhighway."

"You're wandering off topic."

"So does the Net, but I at least can claim the privilege of senile dementia. There isn't a single aspect of the history, philosophy, and psychology of film that hasn't been poked, prodded, dissected with a scalpel, or bludgeoned beyond recognition with a blackjack. Film by decade, by year, by subject, by director, by actor, by character, by phile and phobia, by genre, by context, by politics, by cinematographer, by caterer, *subdivided* by individual food issues. Did you know Marlon Brando was allergic to peanuts? It explains his performance in *The Island of Dr. Moreau*, but no fewer than six pundits are at loggerheads over just what John Frankenheimer was eating when he puked out that one."

"You made your point. So what—"

"When I'm finished, I said. As we speak, an enterprising young philistine at Princeton is preparing a chronology on product placement in the movies, beginning with a tin of crackers in Georges Méliès' *Cinderella*, as his doctoral thesis. Doubtless some publisher will snap it up, and four hundred pages of slick advertising bound in cloth with an arresting dust jacket will occupy place of honor on Larry Kasdan's coffee table."

Valentino waited, reluctant to be scolded once again for interrupting. When Broadhead blew smoke rings, indicating intermission, he said, "Is that your theme? Nothing new under the sun?"

"I'd be worse than senile if I spent my remaining years repeating what the rest of the world has repeated to make the case for repetition. This senseless slaughter of trees must end somewhere. *I* am the theme. I'm writing from my own experience."

"I suggested a week ago you write your memoirs. Your response was ironic."

"It was not. I was sincere. I'm no theologian, but I'd deserve an extra week in Purgatory if I foisted upon an unsuspecting public the clinical details of the bloody nose I earned from Stinky Burnicki when I was six. I propose to focus on the one episode that may merit a respectable first printing."

It burst upon him. "The prison in Yugoslavia."

"Depressing; but Dumas mined similar material for Edmond Dantes without disgracing himself. Although it would be colorful to paint a portrait of myself scribbling *The Persistence of Vision* on bits of coarse toilet paper in the gray light seeping in through a single barred window, the truth is I bartered my rations for pencils and writing paper, and the electric bulb in the corridor was adequate until the guards turned it off at eight. I'm going to concentrate on the events that led me to that cell."

"You were falsely accused of espionage. Readers will lap it up."

Broadhead knocked out his pipe on the heel of his shoe. Plugs and ashes littered the floor the way dribbles of paint announced an artist at work. "How much have I told you about that period in my life?"

"Next to nothing. I don't think it's come up more than three or four times in all the years we've known each other, and you always change the subject when I start asking questions. I assumed you didn't want to dredge up a painful memory."

"It was certainly painful. When they threw me on the stone

floor, I scraped my knee, the scrape became infected, and by the time a physician was called I had to exhaust my small knowledge of Croatian to persuade him not to amputate. I nearly died of enteric fever, and when the U.S. State Department made up its mind after three years to acknowledge my existence, I walked out on crutches. Also, the entire country regarded central heating as a capitalistic myth. Is any of this new?"

"Almost all of it. You told me how long you were there, and what you were charged with, but you didn't give details."

"I thought not. I was pretty sure I never said I was falsely accused."

The meaning of this reply reached Valentino at glacial pace. He opened his mouth to say something.

Broadhead pointed his pipe stem at the ceiling, silencing him with this exclamation mark. "No questions. Nothing kills a book faster than talking about it. Close the door on your way out. I can't work in fresh air."

20

HARRIET WAS UNUSUALLY quiet. That made the break room, normally an oasis of peace in the middle of a busy police department, tomblike in its silence. A smock-clad criminalist Valentino had met once or twice came in, greeted them both, interpreted her monosyllabic reply as something less than cordial, and left quickly after snatching a juice box from the refrigerator. Harriet's fork rattled explosively against the plastic tray containing her pasta salad in the pall.

Valentino made a try at conversation. "Kyle's writing his book. Actually writing, not just talking about it."

"I know. Fanta told me." She didn't look up.

"I didn't know you two hung out."

"Girlfriends' network. That's how I know where you were yesterday morning."

"Whoops." It was the best he could come up with after three seconds.

"Well put."

"I told Kyle that in confidence."

"He told you about his book in confidence."

"I should have told you. I'm sorry. I thought if I did you'd try to talk me out of it."

"You're a grown man. If you thought it was that good an idea, you shouldn't have been worried I'd make you change your mind."

"You're right. I am sorry."

"Were you ever going to tell me?"

"I honestly don't know."

"The secrets just keep piling up." She pushed away the tray and looked at him. "I know you, mister. You only lie when you're ashamed of what you're doing. I'm the one who suggested you nail Spink, remember?"

"I was ashamed. I still am, even if he did have it coming. I never thought of myself as an extortionist, but that's what it amounted to. I tried to convince myself I did the right thing by forcing him to quit instead of putting him in my pocket, but you're right; if there was anything honorable about it I wouldn't have kept it from you." He sat back, twisting and untwisting the cap on his bottle of water. "I haven't been thinking right since this Spink business began. It wasn't just him; the hotel is the third time I've moved since I bought the theater, and then there was that mess with Rankin and the only serious fight I ever had with Kyle. I'm thinking of getting out from under, putting the Oracle up for sale and moving into an apartment with a nice long lease so I won't be tempted to tear up roots once again. Maybe the legend's right: The place is haunted."

"Demonic possession is no excuse for freezing me out of your life."

"Right again. But you have to admit it's original."

"Don't smile! Don't you dare. My last relationship ended

when he tried one too many times to charm himself back into my good graces."

He said nothing. He'd run out of options.

"How much do you think you can get for the place?"

His chest felt tight. He'd half expected her to try to talk him out of selling. "I don't know. I'd be surprised if I got back what I've put into it. When I bought it, Kyle said the smart thing to do would be to tear it down. Vacant lots are worth more than rickety old buildings in this town."

"Sergeant Clifford's husband is in construction. She might be able to get you a good deal on demolition. You bought some good will when you helped her clear up that old murder at the theater."

"I'll talk to her," he said after a moment.

They locked eyes. A nerve in her cheek twitched. Suddenly she broke up. The room seemed to go from gloomy black-and-white to Technicolor.

"I tried," she said, wiping her eyes with her napkin. "I couldn't sustain it. I wish I had a picture of your expression. You looked like a puppy with a bellyache. Val, you couldn't bring yourself to knock down that old barn if you struck oil in the basement. You can't sell it either. If you did and whoever bought it tore it down and put up a Seven-Eleven, you'd drive clear around the L.A. basin to avoid looking at it."

"I'd do it for you."

"If you did I'd drive the same route for the same reason. You *are* possessed, with a dream, and I'm not going to let you cast me as the Wicked Witch of the West by slapping you awake." She sat back, stirring the crushed ice in her fountain cup with the straw. "Anyway, that's where we met. What kind of girlfriend would I be if I demolished a romantic landmark?"

He ventured a smile. "Does that mean I'm forgiven?"

"No, Val, you're not."

He studied her face closely. Her cheek didn't twitch. She looked up. "We need a break," she said. "You can't cuddle up to that rat trap and me at the same time, and my work takes patience I can't afford to spread around." She held up a hand when he started to speak. "I'm not blaming you entirely. If I'd been thinking like a professional instead of mooning over my beau, I'd never have spilled information on an open police case by telling you what we'd found out from that phony Garbo letter. We both need a vacation, and not from work."

"How long?" he said at last.

"I don't know. It's not like making a reservation at a resort. We'll play it by ear."

He opened his mouth, closed it. He didn't want to say it. "I feel like we're breaking up."

"Maybe we are. I hope not. You're a pretty good guy, Mr. Valentino."

"You're not so bad yourself, Ms. Johansen."

She broke eye contact to lift a shopping bag from the floor beside her chair and put it on the table. It bore the Lord & Taylor logo; he'd assumed she'd spent her day off shopping and had wanted to show him what she'd bought, but she'd behaved as if she'd forgotten it. He asked her what it contained.

"A bunch of old letters. The originals are still in Stockholm and Beverly Hills has copies on file. They're just taking up space here. I thought you might like to add them to your collection."

He tilted the bag and looked inside. He recognized the script on the top sheet, as elegant as the hand that had written it, but so much more simple than the personality behind the words. The letter was in somewhat mangled English, an early experiment addressed to Greta Garbo's close friend Vera Schmiterlöw in Sweden from Hollywood, and characteristically unsigned.

Harriet interrupted before he could thank her. "This, too. They're issuing a press release, so don't think I'm falling back into my bad habits." She took a square fold of paper from a pocket of her smock and snapped it open under his nose.

The fax machine needed a new ink cartridge. The letters were faded, but legible. The message was signed by an inspector with the Swedish Ministry of Police.

Ray Padilla's office was tidier than he was, but then it had been stripped of everything personal and whatever paperwork it had contained had been transferred to someone else with the Beverly Hills Police. The lieutenant slid a bowling trophy into the cardboard carton on the desk and replaced the shredded Kool between his teeth with a fresh one from the pack. His rusty blazer had a fresh hole burned in the left sleeve—apparently he did more than just chew them when he wasn't under official scrutiny—and he'd gotten rid of the bolo tie.

"What's so important I had to delay my unpaid vacation?" he demanded.

Valentino held out the fax.

"I've seen it. When's the last time you changed your cartridge?"

"It isn't mine, it's LAPD's."

"That was my next quesiton. You've got a cheap pipeline. All you have to do is buy it flowers and feed it from time to time."

"I don't think that's a road you want to go down, considering the reason you're cleaning out your desk."

"I thought tipping the press to what was in the letter might send Rankin over the edge, force him to make a mistake that would reopen the investigation. Maybe I need some time off at that." Padilla upended a coffee mug full of pencils into the box, started to put down the mug, then shrugged and put it in too.

"It's possible I owe you an apology. I thought you had it in for everyone who was better off than you, and would frame evidence just to bring him down. Now I'm beginning to think you're the only cop in Beverly Hills who hasn't forgotten what justice is all about. Do you know what the fax means?"

"It's in English, and I can read. The cops in Stockholm arrested the guy that stole Garbo's letters from the military archives, a replacement janitor. Congrats to them. What's it got to do with a cold case in California?"

"It's warming up. All the material reported missing was recovered from the janitor's flat. It never left Stockholm. What does that do to the theory that Roger Akers stole it and used it to falsify the letter he blackmailed Matthew Rankin with?"

"Maybe he and the janitor were in cahoots. Maybe he borrowed them long enough to make copies and gave them back. The janitor's end would come out of whatever he got from selling them."

"You ran the background on Rankin and Akers. How long were they in Stockholm on that visit?"

"They came home after four days." Padilla chewed on his cigarette. "Not much time to set up a heist. Akers might've planned it long distance before they made the trip."

"How was his Swedish?"

"I didn't ask him. He's dead."

"He'd need more than you can get from a tourist's phrase book to communicate something as sophisticated as a conspiracy to commit grand theft. If he'd studied the language formally, there'd be a transcript; if he got it from Berlitz, he'd have tapes or CDs at his place or in his car. Even if he got rid of them, there'd have to be a paper trail of some kind."

"Maybe the janitor speaks English. I'm always hearing how European schools are better than ours when it comes to teaching languages."

"Something nudged me when I found out that whoever faked the blackmail letter needed at least a working knowledge of Swedish," Valentino said. "I wasn't in a frame of mind to know what it was at the time. Whether or not the actual thief speaks English, Akers had to be bilingual in order to fool Rankin, who knew enough to get by. I doubt the schools over there are so good that a janitor could pull it off."

"Nothing in Akers' file says he spoke or wrote any other language well enough to order in a Mexican restaurant. Rankin did all the talking when they were abroad. I've still got some credit with Records and Information; I can check those other things. But maybe Akers had help over there besides the janitor."

"He wasn't extorting enough from Rankin to pay that many accomplices. We'll know more when the police over there finish interrogating their suspect. Meanwhile we need to let go of the Garbo angle if we're going to clear this up."

"We," Padilla said. "A disgraced cop and a stamp collector. The dream team."

"Any reinforcements you can suggest are welcome."

The lieutenant made a face and dropped the cigarette into his wastebasket in two halves. He plucked a shred of tobacco from his lower lip and flicked it away. "There's a little crack in your theory. If Akers wasn't squeezing Rankin, there's no motive for shooting Akers. We can't blow apart Rankin's story that Akers attacked him when he refused to go on paying him without discarding the only other reason Rankin had for killing him. It's like one of those damn number puzzles where you can't slide one tile where it belongs without pushing another one out of its slot."

"Those puzzles are designed to be solved," Valentino said. "And Roger Akers didn't shoot himself."

"We know who shot Akers. Rankin admitted it."

"Let's ask him why."

He wanted to put his plan into operation immediately, but he remembered he had a meeting scheduled with Henry Anklemire in Information Services. Backing out wasn't an option; Smith Oldfield was enthusiastic about the deal with MGM, and the way Valentino's life had been going lately he needed a friend in the legal department.

The little publicist's office was the only one on campus less commodious than Valentino's. His abrasive personality had banished him to a monastic cell right next door to the boiler room in the basement of the UCLA administration building. During winter cold snaps—when skateboarders in Malibu wore scarves with their Speedos—the pipes rattled like maracas and the very walls seemed to sweat. Curling photographs in cheap frames showed Anklemire shaking hands with celebrities from both sides of the earthly pale. Some of the poses were putative; the ones with Richard Simmons and Gary Coleman looked genuine, but Bill Clinton and Henry Kissinger screamed Photoshop, and most of the autographs appeared to have been written by the same hand.

Anklemire popped up from behind his painted-plywood desk to wring his visitor's hand, mauling bone and grinning exactly as in his pictures with teeth courtesy of the university's dental school. He was a youngish man, but wore secondhand hairpieces he obtained from contacts in studio wardrobe departments, and his shiny-slick suit fit his tubby frame like the skin on a bratwurst.

"Garbo!" He spoke in sentence fragments and exclamation points, like the blurbs on an old-time movie poster.

"No, Valentino."

"You think I forgot your name? I'm still spending the bonus I got on the mileage from that *Greed* deal. Murder! Skeletons! A haunted moompitcher house! Boo! My onliest regret is we couldn't sit on it till Halloween! Sit down! Not there, that one's busted. I keep it around in case the director of the department comes to visit. Fat chance!"

Valentino sat in an orange plastic scoop chair that looked as if it had come from a high school, working his hand until circulation returned. The little man couldn't climb a flight of stairs without wheezing, but a lifetime of glad-handing had put him in shape to arm wrestle Mr. T.

"Cigar?" Back behind his desk, Anklemire shoved a box of White Owls the other's way. Valentino had visited many offices, but no one had ever offered him a cigar before. The man lived in a time warp.

"No, thanks. Will this take long? I've got an important call to make."

"I never chaired a meeting longer than five minutes. Words are for the rubes. Garbo!" It was the most singular case of Tourette's Syndrome the archivist had encountered. "I vant to be alone! Ha-ha!"

"Actually, she didn't say—"

"You're an ornament of this institution."

The statement, and the sudden grave expression that accompanied it, set him aback. He shifted uncomfortably. "Well, you know what happens to ornaments the day after Christmas."

"I'm on the level. Football, phooey! Endowments from old

geezers that can't fit into their old varsity jerseys, horse puckey! This town was built on moompitchers. Where'd Hugh Hefner be without boobs, I ask you?"

"I really can't answer that."

"In the crapper, that's where! You got to go with your long suit. I was in London last year, can you pipe that? I had frequent flyer miles burning a hole in my pocket, and Israel was at war with somebody or other. I seen some punked-up teenagers bopping through Picadilly, they had on T-shirts with movie stars on 'em. You think it was Larry Oliver and that tribe? Hell, no! Marilyn, Bogie, Jimmy Dean, *American* what-you-call icons! Detroit can't compete with the Nips, and those geeks in Silicone Valley can't get it up with even the South Koreans, but our junk culture—I'm swiping the phrase from those fossils in the English Lit Department—our junk culture has muscled its way clear into Baghdad. Those ragheads can keep their weapons of mass construction. We got Garbo!"

"Look, I've only been invited to an audition. I'm not much of a public speaker. It's highly possible they'll pass me over for someone who's a bigger draw. When I agreed to this meeting I thought you wanted to write up my bio, something to throw to the reporters who write for the entertainment page."

"Hell, I could cobble up something dynamite without taking up your time. As to the rest, I can get you a dialogue coach from Tri-Star. This guy taught Gwyneth Paltrow how to speak English. I asked you here to give me some ideas on how I can turn this canned ham into a honey-baked West Virginia."

Valentino rubbed his temples with his thumbs. He never came away from a meeting with Anklemire without a thumping headache, and the racket from the pipes next door wasn't helping. "I may need that dialogue coach. Right now I'm not sure we're speaking the same language."

"Look, Garbo's dead what, fifteen, sixteen years? That's forever in PR if you can't come up with a hook to make it whatyou-call relevant today. *Greed* was good, it was great; we had that murder. I got up my adrenaline when that shooting went down in Beverly Hills, and when that dyke thing broke I thought we was golden; but it's been weeks, and I need a sure-enough Dr. Frankensteen to keep it alive till *How to Dress* hits Best Buy."

"*How* Not *to Dress*."

"Schlemiel, Schlemozzle." He waggled a hand. "Give me input. How can we pump blood into this carcass, make it stand up and shout, 'Mazoola?'"

"I've no idea. I'm an archivist, not a publicist."

Anklemire studied his face, then sat back, squirming in his blown-out Naugahyde chair; the pernicious hemorrhoids that had driven him from Madison Avenue to this backwater were evident. "Well, I'll fire up some kind of rocket. I ain't dead yet."

"I wouldn't give up hope."

Valentino had intended the encouragement to be rhetorical, but it was a mistake to underestimate Henry Anklemire's powers of interpretation. He hounded Valentino with questions all the way to the exit. The man was as bad as the jackals from the press.

21

HE CALLED MATTHEW Rankin's house, but was told by the housekeeper that her employer was meeting with his board of directors in San Francisco and wouldn't be back until tomorrow. Ray Padilla took in the information over his cell phone and told Valentino to call him when he had an appointment.

"I wish we were wrapping this up tonight," Valentino said. "This waiting is murder."

"Murder is murder. Having second thoughts?"

"I had those an hour ago. Right now I'm halfway between my third and my fourth."

"I'd never trust you with this if I were in solid with the department; there's nothing like having a fat detective sergeant by your side and a prowl car purring at the curb for leverage. Rankin trusts you. If I try to get my foot in the door he'll call his lawyer and I won't be able to come within five hundred feet of him without a trunkload of probable cause."

"I'm not backing out on you, Lieutenant. I just needed a

pep talk. I'm still hoping this whole thing turns out to be a monstrous misunderstanding."

"I don't. But then I've got a pension going down for the third time." The connection broke. He had the telephone etiquette of an alligator gar.

Valentino's cell rang while he was driving to his residential hotel. It was Leo Kalishnikov.

"Spink resigned, did you hear?" he said by way of greeting.

"Through the grapevine. Any more good news?"

"Indeed, my friend. The zoning board has conferred and voted to extend you a temporary variance for the remainder of this term, to be reviewed next spring, when if there are no outstanding violations the members will consider making it permanent. Until then you are free to take up residence in the Oracle once again."

"What about the stairs to the projection booth?"

"Spink withdrew the objection when he submitted his resignation. Evidently he misinterpreted the ordinance." The Russian made a decorous noise in his throat. "Perhaps you have some insight that can shed light on this surprising turn of events. I myself have none."

"I didn't really know the man. Maybe he had an epiphany of some kind."

"With a bus, maybe, crossing Santa Monica against the light."

Valentino drove half a block in silence. When Kalishnikov spoke again, his Old World manner was back in place. "I look forward to making your better acquaintance throughout this project. You have facets that do not reveal themselves in the course of casual conversation."

"I'm not exactly a Fabergé egg." He thanked the designer sincerely for his efforts with the zoning board and said good-bye, relieved to have broken contact. Beneath all his preposterous pretensions, so carefully tailored to California culture, the Russian was dangerously perceptive.

He checked out of the hotel that same day. A crew was at work in the theater; he greeted them cheerfully, raising his voice above the noise from the power tools, and borrowed a framing hammer from a carpenter to tear down the barricade from the stairs to his apartment in the projection booth. He unpacked immediately and was dialing Harriet to invite her to a housewarming party for two when he remembered they were on a break. That took the shine off the evening.

The electric generator he'd rented to power Midnite Magic's equipment had gone back, and the one the construction workers used would leave with them at the end of the shift. He lit the Coleman lantern he used most nights and stretched out on his sofa with the shopping bag Harriet had given him on the floor beside it, sorting out Garbo's letters in English, saving the rest for translation when he was back in Harriet's good graces, and reading the accounts of thoughts and events going back eighty years. He didn't bother to arrange them in order—few were dated, just as she preferred not to sign them—and so he found himself moving back and forth in time, sharing intimacies intended for friends that reflected naive youth, wordly age, temporary elation, deep despair, and a surprisingly long list of prosaic details of a life spent moment to moment, and so far outside glamour as to shout out in protest against it.

He pictured her, pale to the point of transluscence, chain-smoking cigarettes in her apartment in Hollywood, her condominium in New York City, her hotel in Stockholm, scribbling, scribbling; pouring out her experiences unedited, and managing to break down her life hour by hour without a single salacious confession and no insight deeper than her decision to buy a hat. John Gilbert, the love affair of her life, the tragicomedy of the nascent movie colony and the crack at the point of pressure that brought down the Great Lover in pieces smaller than Humpty-Dumpty's, was mentioned once in passing and never again. The only comments on her films involved a complaint about an unbecoming dress in *A Woman of Affairs* and her personal review of her performance in *Anna Christie*, the landmark that had made Garbo's voice as famous as her face: "Terrible." Valentino found himself chafing at her stubborn lack of appreciation. Garbo was wasted on Greta Garbo.

It was far from a complete record. The letters were addressed to Vera Schmiterlöw and a handful of other Swedish friends of many years' standing, not the fixtures in the industry that had turned a chubby peasant girl destined to marry some goatherd into a goddess for the ages, mysterious and unobtainable, and gaps in the continuity suggested letters lost or withheld for reasons of privacy. Possibly she'd saved her innermost thoughts for expression in Swedish. But that left dozens of pages that read like the diary of a not very interesting woman who'd led a life so ordinary as to suggest a blind fear of anything that might be described as unique or adventurous. She was passionate about her rug designs, the antiques she collected, the curios she bought to rest her eyes upon when she locked herself away from the world. She had spent the rest on-screen, and left it there when she'd turned away from the Kliegs into the pale reflected sunlight of early retirement. It should have been a sad story, as drenched in pathos as Camille's, Anna Karenina's, and Grusinskaya's, signature roles that continued to burn with a silver flame in revival houses and home theaters in both hemispheres; but it was not. Camille and Karenina had died early, of wasting disease and suicide, and Grusinskaya was consigned to the living death of grief for love lost. Garbo had gone on living.

Whoever had framed a false letter purporting to drive Garbo from the closet obviously had not known her, or taken the time to learn more from her correspondence than the slope of her *l*'s. She was not the type to write a love letter of any kind, or to confide to anyone—at least not in writing—the details of her amours or even her impure thoughts. She had armored herself against not only the pryers and busybodies of her time, but of all time. Of all the heroes and legends of past and present, she alone had kept her feet of clay from public view. Garbo was gold: The only substance in the universe that would not deteriorate or even surrender its glow.

Valentino laid the last letter on his chest, closed his eyes, and slept without dreaming.

If Greta Garbo was gold, Matthew Rankin was stainless steel. It was the housekeeper's day off. For an octogenarian left to his own devices after a round-trip flight up the coast and a business meeting that must have been high-powered because it had required his presence, he looked as fresh and burnished as if he'd spent the time at a spa. His face was a healthy shade of bronze, his white hair was brushed and gleaming, and he was one of the very few modern men who could wear a smoking jacket and a silk scarf without looking affected or effete.

"You're looking well," Valentino said, understating it.

"You're kind, but if I'm not exactly falling apart I have Andrea to thank. She had a Swede's own idea of the price of health and put me on a regimen that has repaid the investment many times over. If you look as if you have the time to eat right and exercise and spend an hour or two on the beach, your shareholders tend to think their stock is in capable hands. You, on the other hand, look like a young man whose life has been leading him."

Valentino was touched by what appeared to be sincere concern. "It's been a rough patch, but not as rough as yours. It seems to be turning around. I want to thank you again for lending me Phil's services as a projectionist. They had an indirect influence on the result."

Over drinks in the study, he provided a brief summary of recent events. He left out his romantic troubles as too personal, and the scheme that had rid him of Spink; he'd asked Phil for his discretion, and had compensated him, but he didn't know how much Rankin might guess.

"I wish you'd confided in me earlier," his host said. "I have some contacts in government."

"Earlier you had problems of your own."

They were sitting in a leather-upholstered conversation area away from the desk. The bust of Garbo and its pedestal were not present. Their removal had lifted much of the oppression from a room where a man had died violently.

To Valentino's relief, Rankin didn't pursue the point. Perhaps he felt, as did his guest, that it was too early in the evening, and too close to home, to bring up the subject of extortion, no matter how well motivated it might have been in Valentino's case.

"So you're back home. I can't imagine what it's like to live in a movie house. If I'd set up domestic arrangements in one of my department stores, I'd have been accused of marrying my work."

"I have been, but it's work I love. I'm sure you can identify with that."

"Not really. My father-in-law was fanatically devoted to the business, but I'm still a chemist at heart. If I'd never met Andrea, I'd have been contented with a job in the research lab of some low-profile pharmaceutical company, developing serums that would save millions of lives in the Third World."

"I doubt that would give you much opportunity for innovation."

"You're probably right. In those days, a man who spent all his time bent over a Bunsen burner wouldn't have been caught dead socializing with a computer programmer or vice versa. Now, of course, the two professions are inseparable. Fortune put me in a position to apply my interest in the developing technology to save a dying business. I succeeded, but a healthy bottom line isn't a cure for the plague."

"You don't seem bitter."

"The young chemist would have been. But I have to say wealth and personal credit have their compensations. Given the value I place on privacy, had I remained where I was I'd be some penniless old hermit by now. *Recluse* is so much more genteel a term, but it requires a substantial income to support it." He smiled. "But you didn't ask to see me just to discuss the paths our lives might have taken."

Valentino set his drink on a marble coaster. "I'm sure you've heard by now about the arrest in Stockholm."

"All the monitors in the airport were tuned to CNN. I suppose I should feel sorry for the fellow, succumbing to temptation to escape a life of manual labor, and temporary employment at that; even in so progressive a country as Sweden, the next step from scrubbing toilets seldom leads upward. I hope they throw the book at him. G.G. didn't write those letters to entertain any troglodyte with an HP, or for any wretch to turn a buck putting them there."

"Whether or not the janitor intended to sell them, he never got around to it. He was found in possession of all the evidence. Every scrap was accounted for."

He frowned. "I hadn't heard that."

"The authorities haven't released all the details publicly yet. The police here have them."

"Ah. The hauntingly lovely and disconcertingly intelligent Ms. Johansen. How is she?"

"Busy. Even in so progressive a country as the U.S., the crime rate keeps going up. The police theory was that because Roger Akers was in Stockholm between the time the letters were last seen and when they were discovered missing, he had the opportunity to steal them and use them as models for the counterfeit he used to blackmail you. Without that connection, they're back to square one on their investigation."

"They have the photocopy."

"That's the problem. Your entire defense is based on your statement that Akers attacked you when you refused to go on paying him to keep the letter secret. I've told you about Ray Padilla, a lieutenant with the Beverly Hills Police. He has an unreasoning hatred for the rich, especially you, and it's about to cost him his job. There's no telling what he'll do to get himself reinstated, or bring you down with him if he fails. He's been badgering me for any morsel of evidence he can use against you. He thinks you forged the letter to put Akers in a bad light and make you look like a victim by comparison."

"That's ludicrous! How could I forge the letter without material to base it on? Andrea burned all of Greta's."

"He says we've only got your word on that."

"Did it occur to him *Roger* might have found some letters she'd overlooked and used them?"

"You had better access, he says. He's a rogue cop, the department has no control over him. It may even reopen the investigation just to put out any fires he might start. Being innocent, you've got nothing to worry about from them, but once the media get wind of it, they'll come swarming around all over again."

The ice jingled in Rankin's glass when he picked it up. He drank half its contents in a gulp; something the health-conscious Andrea would not have approved of. "The vultures. The bloodsuckers. They'd hound me into jail before they took their claws out."

"Akers liked money too much to have destroyed the legitimate letters after they'd served their purpose," Valentino said. "He could have sold them for plenty to collectors who wouldn't ask embarrassing questions. If they only turned up, the police could plug that hole, and they and the press would be off your back. But they made a complete search of Akers' apartment and came up empty."

"Complete, my foot. Who was in charge of the search?"

Valentino hesitated. "Ray Padilla."

"Once a rogue, always a rogue. If he found them, he kept it to himself. Destroying them wouldn't be above a creature like that."

"I wouldn't go that far. His job wasn't in trouble then."

"Over here, a policeman doesn't rate much higher than a janitor in Sweden." Rankin finished his drink. "Thank you, Val. You had nothing to gain by coming here, and that makes you the only person who's stood by me from the start without looking after Number One. By the time I'm finished contributing, the Film Preservation will have a new wing named after you." He stood, holding out his hand. "I hate to run you out, but I'm going to get Clifford Adams out of his La-Z-Boy and put him and his briefcase to work."

Coasting down the long sloping drive from the Rankin mansion, Valentino felt lower than he had so far in this, the lowest period in his life; and utterly alone.

IV

THE BRIDE OF RANKIN'S TIME

22

"'**NATURE IS FINE** *in luff—'"*

"Love."

"Love. I said this."

"You said luff. Pay attention to your labials."

Deep breath. "'Nature is fine in love, and where 'tis fine, it sends some precious instance of itself after the tang—'"

"Thing."

"T'ing."

"Th-ing! Thing!"

"'Th-ing it luffs. They bore him—'"

"Loves. 'Thing it loves.'"

"Gott! *This wretched language. Why could not Shakespeare be born a Swede?"*

"But he wasn't, dear. Try again from the beginning of the soliloquy, and remember, Ophelia is mad."

"Mad! She is spitting tacks!"

On the edge of the soundstage, outside the circle of light where the pince-nez-wearing female voice coach and her pretty project sit on tall stools before the microphone on its stand, Louis B. Mayer's spectacles make smaller circles of reflected light, like headlamps in a tunnel. His cigar smoke crawls toward the ventilating fan mounted in the soundproof wall of the booth where the cameraman is imprisoned so that the whirring of his equipment will not be heard on the soundtrack; for the time being, at least, the talkie revolution has banished sweep, and for that matter simple movement, from the moving picture.

Sotto voce, speaking out of the side of his mouth like the Chicago gangsters who fascinate him, Mayer addresses Irving Thalberg, who is completely enveloped in shadow at his shoulder. "What's the name of that dame we tested last month, the French girl without no accent? Colbert?"

"Colbert. Claudette Colbert. The t*'s silent in the last name. She signed with Paramount when I told her it would take seven years to make her a star."*

"Broads today got no patience. Who else we got don't sound like von Stroheim in drag?"

"Let's not give up on Garbo just yet. We've got a lot invested in her. We can't afford another Gilbert."

"It was worth every penny we lost on that S.O.B. to throw his ass off the lot. She's your baby, Irving. You can go down with the ship. I'm getting off at this station." A born showman, Mayer exits on this triumph of mangled metaphors, trailing smoke. The boom of the fire door shutting behind him turns the heads of the actress, her coach, and the sound man fiddling with his levels.

Thalberg raises his voice. "It's all right. Carry on."

"'Nature is fine in love . . .'"

This time, when Valentino sat up in bed, morning light fell fully on the screen visible through the square opening in the projection booth, and for a moment he wasn't sure if he'd been dreaming or watching a movie. But Midnite Magic's sound system had been dismantled and removed, and the dialogue was still ringing in his ears.

In any case, movies made more sense than dreams. By all accounts, Garbo's sound test had impressed everyone at MGM. She'd delivered Margaret's monologue from *Faust* in German, sung Solviet's solo from *Peer Gynt* in Swedish, and nailed Ophelia's insanity scene from *Hamlet* in flawless English, albeit with the heavy accent that would remain her trademark from *Anna Christie* through the end of her professional career. Her struggles with language had all taken place during her earliest days, when she had spurned the extensive studio system for grooming its contract players for public appearances in favor of private coaching, and unlike Mauritz Stiller, her mentor and probably her lover, she had proven a quick study. Stiller, meanwhile, had endured the confusion of actors and technicians who could not understand his directions in broken patois, bridled against the restrictions placed upon him by meddlers in the front office, and died a failure at forty-five, with his protégée's star firmly in the ascendant.

The female voice coach in the pinch-nose glasses had borne a suspicious resemblance to the identical character who'd despaired of teaching Jean Hagen's silent diva how to speak properly in *Singin' in the Rain*, a telling satire of the infant sound era in Hollywood. Valentino's subconscious mind seemed to have reached the point where staging remakes of actual cinema history was taking the place of reliable scholarship.

Ninety minutes later, seated in a glass-walled recording booth at a downtown studio leased by MGM/UA, Inc., he understood the emotions that had led to his dream. A producer ten years his junior had greeted him on the fly, bum's-rushed him down a corridor, sat him in a padded chair in front of a microphone, also padded, clamped earphones onto his head, and slapped a printed sheet marked up with unfamiliar symbols in red onto a table that pressed into his sternum when he leaned into the microphone; then the man had vanished, shutting the door on him.

The text, it turned out, was a personal introduction of the speaker and his professional credentials, the wording of which he recognized from his portion of a page on the UCLA Web site. Some studio supernumerary had downloaded it for use during his audition.

"Mr. Ballantyne?"

He turned, but he was alone in the room. Shadows moved about on the other side of the glass, but the booth was lit more brightly than that area and he couldn't make out figures or features. He realized then the address had come in over his earphones.

"Valentino," he corrected. "Like the actor."

"Who?"

He realized he was talking to the young producer. "Like the fashion designer?"

"Oh, Valentino. Sorry. We work at warp speed here. These facilities were originally intended for celebrity readings of movie tie-in books on tape, but then DVDs came along with all that room for extras. Jerry Lewis was sitting in that chair ten minutes ago, doing the commentary on *Cinderfella;* that'll be a three-disc set."

"You're doing three discs on Jerry Lewis and only two on Garbo?"

"I just produce them, Mr. Ballantyne. They don't ask me what I think."

"Valentino."

"Sorry. Can you read a few words from the sheet, so we can get a voice level?"

"'Hello. My name is Valentino. I'm—'"

"We didn't get that. Can you move closer to the mike?"

"I'm practically swallowing it now." But he leaned in until his lips nearly brushed the padding, the edge of the table cutting him in half.

Finally the wizard at the electronic board had his level, and he began reading for the demonstration tape. He got in two lines before the producer stopped him, getting his name right for the first time without prompting.

"You smacked your lips a couple of times."

"I did?"

"Everyone does, talking, and no one listening notices, or if they do they disregard it automatically. Our equipment is less forgiving; it's a bit of a tyrant, in fact. It takes in every little flaw and plays it back at a uniform level with everything else. During playback it sounds like you're chewing your cud. Try it again from the top."

Valentino had been pleased to note that the humdrum piece he was expected to read ran only about seventy-five words, which was as much as would fit on one page in oversize type cluttered with mystic symbols apparently understood by professionals on a level that was almost subconscious; but after four or five assaults, aborted when he took in breath audibly, or didn't take in enough and finished a sentence on a strangling note, or—greatly to his embarrassment—belched, even so short a speech loomed before him like the steps to the top of the Great Pyramid. There was a short break during which the producer, with a show of well-bred patience, called for someone to bring him a glass and a pitcher of water that looked like an old-fashioned milk bottle to lubricate his parched throat, but that strategy backfired when Valentino took too big a gulp on top of a heavy intake of breath and it backed into his nose, burning and making him cough explosively. Nothing like it had happened to him since grade school, when someone had made a crude joke in the cafeteria and he'd laughed so hard that milk came out his nose. The young man who had brought the water was dispatched quickly to slap him on the back until the spasm subsided. When his lungs reinflated he apologized, his cheeks burning. The producer's solicitous response only contributed to his humiliation. He felt like the victim of a sophomoric fraternity prank. If he didn't know that Kyle Broadhead was too immersed in his book, he'd have suspected him of setting up the whole situation; Broadhead had the lifelong academic's appreciation for low humor at a friend's expense.

Noon was approaching, and because Valentino had been too nervous that morning to hold down even a light breakfast, his stomach had begun to rumble (was the tyrannical equipment sensitive enough to pick up on the shameful behavior of his bowels?) when he managed at last to get through the text without interruption. He sat back, utterly depleted and damp under the arms. He had a new appreciation for the people who did voice-overs for a living; previously he'd thought them the fortunate recipients of a pleasing tone, with no more skills attendant than a strong man's in a circus.

His review came in the long pause that followed rather than in the polite words of the producer through his earphones: "Nice work. You should've heard Tom Hanks the first day he tackled *The Da Vinci Code*."

Outside the booth, the young man shook Valentino's hand with a torque that turned him toward the exit.

Not even an invitation to lunch, which in L.A. came as automatically as "Gesundheit" following a sneeze. Two minutes later he found himself in the sun-hammered parking lot, with no one expecting him anywhere at any time. So he grabbed lunch at a stand whose hot-dog shape had put it on the National Register of Historic Places and took his heartburn to the office.

He finished editing the footage of a Los Angeles that only still existed on film, sealed it in a can, and like any yeoman interrupted during the last stage of a project cursed when his intercom buzzed as he was hand-lettering the strip of masking tape that served as the label.

"What is it, Ruth?"

The short blip of silence on the other end of the apparatus dripped with glacial ice. But her voice sounded no less annoyed than usual. "A young lady to see you. Her name's Faygo."

Years of experience with the least receptive receptionist in Southern California had blessed him with the gift of instant interpretation. "I think you mean Fanta."

Silence again, during which she conferred with her source.

"Fanta, then. Are you in?"

"She's standing right there, isn't she?"

"I'll send her in."

He came out from behind the desk to extend his hand. The willowy brunette ignored it and wound her long arms around him. She smelled of fresh wheat; not a scent in a bottle, but her own natural fragrance. Today she wore a simple boatnecked top that exposed the perfection of her collarbone, a granny skirt, platform sandals, and one of those mod caps with a mushroom crown and a stiff visor that had somehow wound its way from 1964 to the first decade of the new millennium. When they broke, she said, "Free for drinks?"

"Are you legal?"

She touched a neat unpolished nail to a perfect set of teeth. "How long's the statute of limitations in this state?"

"You're the lawyer."

"Not yet. But I think we're in the clear."

She chose a popular undergraduate hangout a block off campus, staffed by Goths with black nails whose natural musk lingered behind their physical presence; but the booths had high backs that suggested private rooms, and Valentino considered that cocktails with more alcohol than mix destroyed the more harmful bacteria. Mausolea—the tiny name tag on her braless bosom brooked no argument—asked Fanta for ID. She glanced at her driver's license and handed it back. "Happy birthday."

When she left, Valentino said, "More of the same. Shouldn't you be celebrating your coming-of-age with Kyle?"

"That's why I asked you for drinks. But that can wait." She patted his hand. "How's the Oracle coming along? I have a proprietary interest in that place, you know."

"I certainly do know. Without your help it would still be a crime scene, and a seminal part of the history of the cinema would be moldering away in an evidence room of the West Hollywood police precinct. It's hit its share of snags, but I've begun to hope it will be open before you're on Medicare."

"That isn't saying much. The way things are going, the Baby Boomers will lick it down to bare metal before I get my first cataract; but that's not my area of law. Kyle told me about your nemesis in Building Inspection."

Valentino hesitated. "Are you speaking as a friend or as an officer of the court?"

She withdrew her hand. The gesture mortified him.

"I'm sorry. It's been a rotten few weeks."

"So I gathered." But she sounded sympathetic.

He told her what he'd done. Her eyes widened beyond the possibilities of his own generation. Finally she flashed her teeth in a short laugh that was not entirely approving.

"Rotten," she said. "Good choice of words."

"I'm not proud of what I did. If I'd known what it would cost me in terms of self-respect, I'd have gone another direction." He laughed then, in a way that was entirely disapproving. "There was another direction. Plenty of others have gone broke and started over again. There's no shortcut to self-respect."

"Poor Val." She patted his hand again. "You're too good for this world."

"So now I'm a joke." This time he withdrew his.

Their drinks came. She was silent until they were alone again. "The legal system's full of holes," she said. "Maggots like Spink wriggle their way in. If you wait for the system to do anything about them, they'll sprout wings and lay eggs, and before you know it you've got more maggots than holes. I'd've shot the son of a bitch."

"Are you sure you want to be a lawyer?"

She leaned in close and lowered her voice. "If you tell anyone, I'll deny it, but I'm a mole in the system. I'm going to undermine it until it falls under its own weight. Forget Spink," she said, sitting back. "By this time next year, he'll be a high-paid lobbyist in Washington. Meanwhile you'll be turning customers away at the box office."

"You may know the law inside out, but you don't have the slightest idea of how things work in the world of commerce. Next year at this time I'll still be fighting with contractors, and when the Oracle finally opens, I'll be in competition with home rentals, Internet downloads, and iPods from here to Catalina. I don't even want to be an entrepreneur. All I ever wanted was a place to sleep and a screening room I didn't have to stand in line to reserve for my own use."

"Feel better?" She lifted her glass to her mouth.

"You know, I do." He lifted his. "What shall we drink to?"

"Me and Kyle." Her voice was grave. "If there's any future in it. He dumped me, you know."

23

MAUSOLEA DRIFTED OVER, paused, then drifted on without asking them if they needed anything. She seemed uncommonly sensitive to the atmosphere at her station.

Valentino said, "As I understood it, you dumped Kyle; or at least turned down his proposal of marriage because he had no ambition."

"That's what Harriet said. If he wanted people to think that's what happened, I didn't see any reason to set them straight. I guess it's some kind of generational thing. He played the loser so I wouldn't have to. I don't care what he does with his time, as long as he's happy. He did plenty before I was out of diapers."

"Maybe he isn't happy. Maybe your coming into his life made him take a hard look at himself and he didn't approve of what he saw. It wouldn't be the first time a man cleaned up his act to make himself look better in a woman's eyes."

"But he kicked me *out* of his life!" Heads turned at nearby tables. She sat back stirring her swizzle stick until the red spots faded from her cheeks. "I'm sorry. You don't need this on top of what's been happening lately. I was going to keep my mouth shut, I was. But I miss Kyle. He makes me look at things, I mean really look at them. All my friends tell me how much wiser I am than they are. It's all Kyle."

"I know what you mean. Most of what I know about the world he told me, and I went out and found out he was right. He makes a strong case for reincarnation. One lifetime doesn't seem enough for the amount of information he's processed. Of course, he's also a world-class gasbag."

"Nobel quality." She laughed. "He doesn't believe half the things he says. He's a boy, shocking people just to see what he can get away with. I give him plenty of slack, but I think I've shocked him myself by calling him on a couple of points. He isn't used to that. You're partly to blame, you know," she said. "He says something outrageous and you think, 'That's just Old Man Broadhead being himself,' and you don't say anything. It encourages him to fall for his own line of crap."

"You *are* wise. You didn't get all of it from him."

"That's just dorm philosophy: Drink some Jack-and-Coke, do a little weed, and let the hot air out of everyone who gets too full of himself. You know I'm right."

"No argument. I'm probably as responsible for Old Man Broadhead being himself as anyone. But if I took a potshot at him every time he jumped the fence, I wouldn't have time to do anything else."

"That's my job. Or it was."

The ice had melted in their glasses. He got Mausolea's attention and ordered another round. They were silent until she brought the drinks and glided away.

"I'd like to help," he said then. "He needs you more than you need him, and seeing you together has blown up any prejudices I had about the age difference. But I wouldn't know where to begin. I can't even manage my own love life."

"Harriet told me that, too. We women can be cryptic, but this is one time when she means what she says. Give her a little space, and when you're back together, don't do anything you feel you need to keep secret from her."

"That sounds too simple."

"Complicated things usually are. That's Kyle talking, without the gas. If you weren't ashamed of something, you wouldn't hesitate to talk about it with the one person whose opinion you trusted."

"That's not Kyle talking. It's you." He reached across the table and gave her wrist a quick squeeze. "You said he makes you see things; that's what you just did for me. When two people you care about tell you the same thing, that's wisdom."

She smiled, and tossed her hair, throwing off blue haloes under the fluorescent lights. "You *can* help. When you're with Kyle, don't act like I'm dead and keep me out of the conversation. Talk about me."

"Even if he tells me to shut up?"

"Especially if he tells you to shut up. That's how you'll know it's working."

"Will you do the same for me with Harriet?"

"Nope. Different situation. The point is not to mention you at all. Let her bring up the subject."

"And if she doesn't?"

"Then you've lost her." She lifted her glass. "But isn't recovering lost things your specialty?"

"Yes, Ruth."

"Line One. Brian Ross."

"I don't know a Brian Ross."

"Says he's a producer with MGM. Maybe you've been discovered."

He couldn't remember if the young man had given his name in the rush to seat him in the recording booth. "Okay."

"Mr. Valentino, I called to say we won't be needing you for the commentary after all."

"That's a polite way of putting it, but I'm not surprised."

"Oh, there was nothing wrong with your demo. Everyone who heard it was quite impressed with your natural quality. However, the front office has decided to go a different way."

"What way is that?"

"Actually, it was a bit of luck. A man we thought was unavailable expressed his interest in the project. You might know the name. Craig Hunter?"

He knew the name. "I know him personally, as a matter of fact. We were involved in a couple of business deals years ago." He was reminded that Hunter had never paid back those loans.

"Then you know he was a popular action star before he announced his semiretirement. Apparently he's had his fill of golf and fishing. We were delighted to get him. The audience for this particular market has always reacted more positively to recognizable talent. Your many, uh, successes are well known in academic circles, but—"

Valentino was too soft-hearted to let him flounder. "Yes. Mother Teresa and Princess Di died the same week, but we all know who got the most coverage."

"I'm glad you understand." Ross was audibly relieved. It was always the pump jockey who took the brunt of high gasoline prices. "I want you to know we won't forget you. We'll keep your demo on file for future reference."

"Thank you for the opportunity. Please give Craig my regards."

Ruth came back on the intercom thirty seconds later. "Mother Teresa?"

"I thought you stopped eavesdropping on my conversations because they were boring."

"They're picking up."

"Man, you must've sucked."

Kyle Broadhead, hunkered in front of his pre-Columbian computer, had seemed too preoccupied with what was on the screen to have heard what Valentino had said; but he'd made his own share of bum investments in Craig Hunter for old times' sake.

"Big time," said Valentino. "He got a better chance at a comeback than Lazarus and still managed to drink himself out of a sweetheart contract with CBS. The last I heard he was just getting by recording books for the blind with the Library of Congress. They had to schedule all his sessions before noon, because he started drinking on the stroke of twelve and they had to pour him into a cab."

"*How Not to Dress* is a big deal to you and me, but it's not exactly the kind of thing that would bring Tom Cruise to cut short his honeymoon. How's your ego holding up?"

"Bloody, but unbowed. I told Smith Oldfield I had no experience. But—"

"Craig Hunter."

"Yes."

"Did you seriously compare yourself to Mother Teresa, or were you just trying to put a light touch on a tragic situation for your Uncle Kyle?"

"Hardly tragic. Ruth already gave me my lumps over that one. I was still in shock over their choice."

"Well, if it's any consulation, they'll have to give him a B-twelve shot so he can pronounce 'Greta Garbo' without stumbling." Broadhead sat back. "You're a connoisseur of faces. What would the physiognomists make of this one?"

The faded screen was fixed on a head-and-trunk shot of a severe Slavic face in a high-peaked military cap and a tight uniform with medals and epaulets. The caption was written in a language Valentino couldn't identify.

"Conrad Veidt?"

"Vladimir Bulganin, the Strong Man of Kosovo; the dispatches never use the name without the unofficial title, like 'Batman, the Caped Crusader.' He's the current favorite to head up the Ministry of Police in Bosnia. We called him Vlad the Impaler in the exercise yard. Among other things."

"You knew him in prison?"

"He was the warden. I hesitate to say 'commandant'; those Serbo-Croats can hold a grudge till the cows come home, and World War Two was yesterday. I'm thinking of dedicating my book to him."

"Was he kind to you?"

"He made Stalin look like Tickle Me Elmo. One could see he was destined for great things even then."

"Then why—"

"Hitler was *Time*'s Man of the Year in nineteen thirty-nine. Humanitarians rarely set the course of great events in motion, although I hesitate to refer to my humble incarceration as a great event. The book would not be possible without Bulganin. I wonder if he'd be open to writing an introduction?"

"I'm beginning to think this book is a bad idea. Are you sure you want to dredge up those old memories?"

"My dear young friend, a memory that requires dredging up is hardly worthy of the name. This particular memory remains as fresh as a malarial relapse." He punched a key: The bony, sun-blanched face of the Strong Man of Kosovo shuddered and vanished from the screen, to be replaced by Fatty Arbuckle's uncreased innocent on the wallpaper.

Valentino felt the need to change the subject. "I had drinks with Fanta today."

"Drinks? Oh, yes, the big birthday. Don't let me forget to send her a virtual card. Whatever possessed you two to go clubbing?"

"Two drinks isn't clubbing. She invited me. She needed a friend. Why didn't you tell me you were the one who decided you should stop seeing each other?"

"Chivalry is a tubercular old wheeze, but it pleases my sense of self to give it a shot of oxygen now and again. In her set, rejection is regarded as evidence of damaged goods, whereas in mine it's a periodic inevitability. How is she?"

"She misses you."

"She'll recover. Twenty-one is a resilient age; as it must be, for what's expected of it. What a nuisance she was, insisting upon seeing something in me that wasn't there to begin with."

"There's more to it than that."

"Think back to when you were that young—last week, wasn't it? Did your dreams and aspirations include trimming the hair sprouting from an old man's ears? The prospect is just as distasteful for the recipient. Can the wonderful world of incontinence be far behind?"

"That's just vanity. What you're describing is a committed relationship."

"Commitment indeed. It must have been a confirmed bachelor who coined the term. Last week I caught myself lingering in the Health and Beauty aisle in Safeway. The instructions on the Just For Men box were enlightening. I remembered how I struggled to mix the contents of those two little tubes of epoxy evenly enough to create a bond that would hold together the parts of a wooden model airplane. I'm older than plastic, you know.

"That led me to reflect upon just how many decades had passed since it mattered to me whether those parts stayed together, and how neatly Fanta's entire life span fit right into the middle with room for another on each side. I never cared for math, or for that matter any discipline that won't bend to reason. I sat down with her the next day and announced my decision."

"You're a fool, Kyle."

"A distinction we share. You let the fair Harriet fly away."

"That was her decision, and I'm going to put in the time and effort necessary to reverse it. I'd be as brass-bound an idiot as you if I'd sent her off."

"But you did. She gave you an ultimatum and you ignored it. I at least didn't shift the burden to her."

"I've never been in love before. Two women have loved you, against all odds. One died and you sent the other packing. Just today Fanta and I were talking about how wise you are. You're right. We've got a lot to learn."

Broadhead looked up from the pipe he was charging. Then he nodded, and went on nodding for a moment as if he'd forgotten to stop. He looked like a bobble-head doll. *Pathetic*, thought Valentino; and with the thought felt the physical ache of another illusion torn from him.

"I'm no longer your mentor, it appears. Thank God. I've been all these years terrified of falling on my prat in your estimation. Anticipation is far more painful than the reality." He struck a match. It shook a little, but he got the tobacco burning and blew a plume of smoke at the fire marshal's warning tacked to the wall. "What of your friend Matthew Rankin? Perhaps he can be groomed to take my place."

"It's been a bad week for role models," Valentino said. "I may have helped stick him with a murder."

24

THE WORKERS HAD left for the day, but their traces remained in the buckets of spackle, litter of Gatorade bottles, waffle-patterned footprints in the sawdust on the floor. Rorschach patterns of damp plaster stained the walls and there was withal a musk of perspiration and sour breath to advertise the fact that The Oracle was no sanctuary from the world and would not be for many months to come. Valentino stood in the unfinished grotto of the grand foyer, keys dangling from the ring on his finger, and considered that he'd moved out of the residential hotel with three more days paid for; the square brass key was still on his ring. The room wasn't much bigger than a cell, but it offered electric light, a mattress less eccentric than his sofa in the projection booth, and basic cable for escape. He was turning toward the exit when his telephone rang.

"Padilla," said the lieutenant. "My chief of detectives has invited Rankin and his lawyer to a conference in his office tomorrow at nine A.M. I thought you might want to sit in."

"What's the occasion?"

"After the story broke on the arrest in Stockholm, the chief ordered another search of Roger Akers' apartment. The officers found a bundle of letters under a loose floorboard in the bedroom. They were all addressed to Andrea Rankin in Greta Garbo's handwriting."

Valentino said nothing.

"You might want to put on a necktie," the other went on. "I am. Rankins' counsel demanded the press be present to record a formal apology from the City of Beverly Hills and my resignation."

He slept in the theater after all; it was closer to Beverly Hills and his best suit hung in the closet where a succession of projectionists had stored the cans and cans of feature films, cartoons, newsreels, and travelogues they had shown over and over again every evening and during Saturday matinees. When he gave his name to a uniformed officer outside the chief of detective's office, the anteroom was already filled with people, many of them reporters and technicians reading their notes and doing systems checks on their equipment. The man who'd blacked Valentino's eye with his microphone looked straight at him and passed his gaze onward without sign of recognition. He was deader than old news; so far as the juggernaut of celebrity and notoriety was concerned, it was as if he'd never been news at all.

These were the unanointed: journeymen news gatherers who never sat down on camera or never appeared there, condemned to sweep up morsels of commentary from principals in flight from the actual press conference, after colleagues with more cachet had finished recording the breaking story firsthand, whose jumbled images and three-second sound bites were edited to orbit and enhance the footage that would lead the broadcast. They dressed—if they were to appear at all—from the waist up, in blazers and pins displaying their stations' call-letters, and from there on down in denim and dirty sneakers. Those who would not appear looked like the homeless waiting for the doors of the shelter to open. Valentino had set himself apart from them merely by putting on a matching suit of clothes and tying a scrap of cloth around his neck.

At long length the officer returned and beckoned him to follow. The crowd parted, eyes now following the man who'd been granted access, and the officer opened a paneled door and held it, neatly inserting himself into the only possible avenue of assault from aggressive media not yet resigned to their place. Valentino swept through the breech and the door shut behind him.

The office was larger than Valentino's and Broadhead's combined, with three times the floor space of his apartment in The Oracle, and corner windows looking out on the wealthiest four square miles in California; but it was standing room only. Cameras, cables, lights, and sound equipment created an obstacle course for the invited people crowding in for a better look at Chief Conroy seated behind a big desk with a bare polished top, Ray Padilla standing behind him, and Matthew Rankin and Clifford Adams sitting next to each other in comfortable-looking chairs arranged at a right angle to the desk. Rankin looked tense and pale inside that tight circle of eager bodies, his attorney as calm as if he were resting in a first-class lounge at the airport. Today he wore a burgundy suit and a yellow tie that complemented his sleek black close-shaven skin, with a pale blue shirt that would photograph crisp white on television. A briefcase, burgundy also, lay in his lap; a prop he had not thought necessary during his visit to Valentino's office. His long legs were crossed comfortably and cordovans glistened on his feet.

Conroy adjusted his gold-rimmed glasses and cleared his throat, silencing the buzz of voices. "Ladies and gentlemen. As you know, you've been invited here at the request of Mr. Rankin and his attorney to set the record straight regarding the tragedy that took place in Matthew Rankin's home some weeks ago. I'm going to ask you to hold your questions until we open the forum. Lieutenant Padilla has a statement to make."

Lenses changed and microphones shifted angles as Padilla stepped forward. He looked almost respectable in a dark blue J.C. Penney suit and a black necktie knotted too evenly to be anything but a clip-on, but his face was as gray as Rankin's; he would never be a public animal like his burnished chief of detectives. His hands shook slightly as he unfolded a sheet of paper from an inside pocket and began reading in a monotone. Asked to speak up by a man holding an aluminum rod with a microphone dangling from it, he swallowed and started over.

"Yesterday at approximately six P.M., a forensics crew working with the Beverly Hills Police Department was dispatched to Roger Akers' apartment in Century City to search for further evidence in the investigation into Mr. Akers' fatal shooting. During that search, the crew discovered this item." He reached into another pocket and placed a stack of yellowed and dog-eared envelopes bound with a rubber band on the desk. Some of the envelopes bore red chevrons on their edges, indicating that they'd been sent by overseas air mail. The crowd on Valentino's side of the desk leaned forward in a body. Cameras tilted to secure close-ups of the bundle. "The item represents a collection of eight personal letters written and mailed over a period of approximately twenty years by Greta Garbo, the late retired motion-picture actress, to Andrea Rankin, the late wife of Matthew Rankin. Some were written in Swedish, and these have been translated. All have been read by department personnel and copies of them made.

"Mr. Rankin and his attorney, Clifford Adams, have asked me to state that the communications were of a friendly nature, attesting to a long-term relationship that was close, but nonsexual. They are not love letters."

Valentino was aware of a general deflation of atmosphere. Outside of a funeral service, there was nothing so bleak as a room full of reporters who have witnessed the destruction of a scandal.

A blonde female reporter in a red blazer spoke up. "Why weren't the letters found during the first search?"

"I asked that you hold all questions until invited to ask them," Conroy snapped. "You will all have ample opportunity—"

"I'll answer it," Padilla said.

The chief glared at him through tinted lenses, but said nothing. Valentino knew the two would discuss this departure in private.

"During the second search," the lieutenant said, "a crowbar was used to sound the floor, and a hollow was discovered beneath an eight-inch section of floorboard beneath a wall-to-wall carpet in the bedroom. When the carpet was lifted, the board was removed and the letters found in the hollow space. The department is investigating the circumstances behind the failure to find them the first time the room was searched."

This satisfied no one. A rumble coursed through the spectators, interrupted by a crackle of paper as Padilla turned the sheet over and read from the other side. "Early in the investigation, Matthew Rankin stated that the deceased had extorted money from him by threatening to make public a letter purporting to show that Ms. Garbo and Mrs. Rankin were involved in a lengthy same-sex affair whose exposure would invade Mr. Rankin's privacy and cast a shadow on the reputation of his late wife, and that when Mr. Rankin refused to continue paying Akers, Akers advanced upon him holding a heavy marble bust in an aggressive manner, which Mr. Rankin believed to be an attempt upon his life. He stated that he shot Akers dead in an act of self-defense.

"When the letter Akers was alleged to be using for blackmail was determined to have been forged, and a number of Ms. Garbo's authentic letters were reported missing from the Swedish Military Archives, this department speculated that Akers had had access to the stolen material and used it to create the forgery, using a computer. At that point the charges against Mr. Rankin were dismissed. However, subsequent events demonstrated that in fact that access did not exist. When the stolen material was recovered by the authorities in Stockholm, no chain of possession could be established to link them to Akers. The two events, Roger Akers' shooting and the theft of the actual Garbo letters, were unrelated."

The press broke its leash. Padilla stood stone-faced, eyes fixed on his prepared statement, while the questions washed over him, an incoherent babble. Chief Conroy showed remarkable restraint, allowing the first wave to recede before rapping his knuckles sharply on his desk like a judge with a gavel.

"I've explained the conditions twice," he said. "One more display and this conference is over. You can all wait for the press release. Go on, Lieutenant."

"Yes, sir. It was at Matthew Rankin's request, submitted through his attorney, that the second search was made of Roger Akers' apartment. The Beverly Hills Police Department speculates that the letters were found in the Rankin house, overlooked when Mrs. Rankin burned the others as Ms. Garbo requested.

We have determined beyond reasonable doubt that they provided the material necessary to forge the spurious love letter." He refolded the sheet and returned it to his pocket. A sheen of perspiration glistened on his forehead.

"Mr. Adams?" The chief's tone was level. Valentino could not tell if he was playing a winning hand or throwing in his cards.

"Thank you." The lawyer uncrossed his legs and crossed them the other way. He left his briefcase buckled and had nothing in his hands. "My client, Matthew Rankin, has asked me to say that this entire episode has been a nightmare for himself and an embarrassment to the City of Beverly Hills. In spite of my advice to the contrary, he wishes not to prolong it with the several legal actions it is his right to pursue. Said actions would expose a campaign driven by vindictiveness and personal ambition, based upon no evidence, to destroy his privacy, assassinate his character, and drag the memory of his beloved wife through the sewer. No judge in this country, once the facts were placed before him, would fail to find for my client and against the Beverly Hills Police Department, and recompense him in the amount of one hundred million dollars."

The sum started the room rumbling all over again. This time, Conroy let the noise die down on its own. Adams, whose quietly theatrical tones were as well suited to a theater as a courtroom, had his audience in his pocket. Rankin, pale as ever beneath his tan, stared at the floor.

"Patently, Mr. Rankin doesn't need another hundred million dollars, and it would do nothing to erase the memory of the ordeal through which he has passed. His is a simple demand, representing a fair and forgiving heart. He wishes only a formal apology from Chief Conroy for the conduct of his department and the immediate resignation of Lieutenant Ray Padilla, with forfeiture of benefits and pension. It is because of this man's blind, unreasoning hatred toward my client that this bitter affair did not end weeks ago."

The camera swung on Padilla, perspiring heavily now under the lights.

"Lieutenant, I believe you have another statement to make at this time," said Conroy.

"Yes, sir." He patted first one pocket, then another, and produced a printed card from a third. "Matthew Rankin, you're under arrest for the murder of Roger Akers. 'You have the right to an attorney. . . .' "

Valentino didn't hear the rest, and neither did anyone else including Rankin and Adams, gripping the arms of their chairs as they stared at Padilla. The room went up in a roar of questions.

25

CONROY WAS TRUE to his word. At a signal from him, a troupe of officers left their station at the back of the room and formed a cordon to drive the jabbering defenders of the First Amendment out the door. There were casualties: A bank of TV lights mounted on a pole slipped more or less accidentally, cutting a policeman's forehead with a sharp corner, and a lens was smashed when a shoulder-mounted camera struck the door frame on the way out. The chief raised his voice, promising a statement later; a reporter shouted a different sort of promise back, and then Valentino was alone with the Beverly Hills Police Department, Matthew Rankin, and Clifford Adams, who was on his feet now and glaring down at Conroy behind his desk.

"Consider the lawsuit reinstated," he said. "Consider the amount doubled. You just earned yourself a place in the unemployment line behind Padilla."

The chief was calm. "Please sit down. I'm doing your client the favor of not having him placed in restraint. His age and his standing in the community entitle him to that courtesy, but it doesn't extend to tampering with the evidence at a police crime scene."

Rankin spoke for the first time since Valentino had entered the room. His coloring remained sickly, but his voice was steady. "Come to the point, Chief. Not even your man Padilla found anything in my study to support his suspicions of me."

"I wasn't referring to the room where you shot Roger Akers. How long have you had a key to his apartment?"

"Don't answer that," Adams said.

Rankin ignored him. "I've never had one."

Conroy said, "My guess is he kept an extra set in his desk at your house, though I don't suppose we'll find it now. You'd have thrown it away after you planted the letters in his bedroom."

"You're burying yourself," Adams said.

"Sit down, Clifford. When a man sets out to commit career suicide, it's a mistake to stand in his way."

Adams took his client's advice. He opened his briefcase and took out a legal pad and a gold pencil. "You don't mind if I take notes. I wouldn't want to forget a grievance in the blizzard."

"Certainly not. Lieutenant?"

Padilla had stopped sweating. Valentino half expected him to risk Conroy's wrath and stick a cigarette between his teeth, but he stood without moving, his hands at his sides. "That space under the floorboard led to a heating duct before the apartment building was renovated. The register was removed and the board cut to fit. Akers may never have known about it. There was nothing but dust in the hole the first time we checked it out."

"Can you confirm that?" Adams asked.

"We took pictures. The camera dated them digitally. I sent a crew back a second time to record every possible place in the apartment where a bundle of letters could be hidden, just before I asked Valentino to tell Rankin we were reopening the investigation."

Rankin and Adams looked at Valentino for the first time. They hadn't seemed to notice he was in the room. He fidgeted.

"It was the only way I could think of to bring those letters out into the open," Padilla said. "No judge would issue a search warrant for your house to make a case everyone wanted to go away, and I couldn't be sure you hadn't hidden them somewhere else. I knew they existed; you'd needed them to fake the evidence to support your claim of self-defense, and I gambled on the fact you hadn't destroyed them because of their intrinsic value. No one makes billions by forming a habit of throwing away thousands, and you needed a surefire backup in case the Stockholm angle didn't pay out."

Adams said, "This is all storytelling. You haven't a shred of proof my client planted those letters."

"Sergeant Stimson?"

A woman in uniform stepped from her corner. "Yes, Lieutenant."

"The shoes."

"Yes, sir." She left the room, drawing the door shut behind her on the pandemonium outside; either the media had successfully thwarted attempts to ban them entirely from the premises or Chief Conroy had considered the effort not worth the expenditure of taxpayers' time.

Padilla said, "When those letters surfaced, I took them and the crime-scene photos to a judge and got that search warrant. That's why it took so long to get this show started. I had to make sure you were out of the house long enough to get what I needed and run tests."

"*What* tests?" Adams lifted his pencil from the pad. "What shoes?"

No one answered him. Moments later the sergeant returned, carrying a plastic bag stenciled PROPERTY B.H.P.D. She placed it on the desk. Padilla opened it and withdrew a pair of walking shoes, thick-soled and obviously handmade; meticulous stitching showed where the mass-produced product was usually glued.

"You have a lot of shoes, Mr. Rankin," Padilla said. "We left the dress pumps for last, on the theory that you'd choose stealth over style. Not that it narrowed things down as much as we'd like; a health nut like you has plenty tied up in athletic footwear."

Valentino sneaked a look at Rankin, leaning forward in his chair with his hands gripping the arms, staring at the shoes as if he'd never seen a pair to compare with them. Padilla placed them to one side, reached back into the bag, and took out a gooseneck lamp with a metal shade. Sergeant Stimson, still close to hand, uncoiled the cord and stooped to plug it into an outlet behind the desk.

"Lights?"

The officers at the back of the room stirred. One found the switch to the overhead fixture and manipulated it. Now the only illumination came filtered through smog by way of the windows.

"Not exactly state of the art," Padilla said as he switched on the lamp. "You're a high-tech guy, and I couldn't be sure you wouldn't spot a surveillance camera. So I fell back on an old wheeze: infrared powder, invisible except when exposed to black light." He picked up both shoes and turned them soles up under the dim ray from the lamp. They gave back a bluish glow.

"We scattered the powder on the floor in every room in Roger Akers' apartment," Padilla went on. "After we found the letters, we took pictures with an infrared camera. Footprints in the powder matched the soles of these shoes."

"Entrapment!" snapped Adams, when the overhead light was back on. "You took the shoes from my client's house and manufactured this evidence."

"No, sir, we did not." Conroy folded his hands on the desk. "I don't mean to tell you your business, but you'll have a hard time convincing a jury that any member of this department had access to those letters except by removing them from your client's house; which brings us right back to the incontrovertible fact that they have been in his possession this entire time. With malice aforethought, he set out to murder his assistant, and used the letters to create a computer-generated letter containing scandalous material to suggest that Akers was a blackmailer, and that when his blackmail scheme failed he attacked your client, providing just cause for your client to take Akers' life. Without the letter there is no blackmail, and without the blackmail, there is no motive for malice on the part of the victim. That leaves a clear-cut case of murder in the first degree."

Adams curled his lips back from his bright teeth; shark's teeth. "You've overlooked two important considerations. To prove Murder One, you need to establish motive."

"Deposits in Akers' bank account match withdrawals in Rankin's," Conroy said. "Some kind of blackmail was going on, and that's a strong enough motive for any jury."

"You just hit upon the second consideration, and the one that explodes your own theory. He *was* being blackmailed, and when he decided to put an end to it, Akers attacked him, giving him reason to take steps to defend his life."

Conroy gave no sign that they had reached an impasse; which was proof enough for Valentino that they had. He was an efficient administrator, and—one of the big surprises in a day packed with revelations—a staunch defender of even so unsavory a subordinate as Ray Padilla, he of the cheap haberdashery and undiplomatic demeanor—but he was not a good working detective. He was the reason why the Ray Padillas of the world remained in the trenches. He looked to the lieutenant for support.

Padilla was more than ready. He snatched off the clip-on tie, stuffed it into a pocket, and opened his collar to restore circulation to his brain. His tobacco-stained leer was a match for the lawyer's polished orthodontry. "What was he being blackmailed over, counselor? And what was so bad about it that dragging his marriage through the sewer was brighter by comparison?"

"That's your end, Lieutenant." Clifford Adams, the poster boy for dignity under fire, folded his hands on his legal pad. "The burden of proof is on the prosecution."

"Shut up, Clifford. Game over."

A curtain of silence fell upon the room, with lead weights at the bottom. A dozen pairs of eyes turned upon the bloodless face of Matthew Rankin.

"Roger was a good assistant at the start," he said. "If you've never had one, I can't make you understand what he represents: priest, mistress, wife. You find yourself confessing things to him you'd never tell your closest friend. The worst mistake I ever made was to tell him I murdered Andrea."

26

"I POISONED MY wife."

Matthew Rankin's aristocratic facade was peeling. Seated in his chair facing the tripod-mounted video camera that had been brought in to record his statement, he was an old man with a sagging face, his trademark tan as thin as cheap gold leaf. Clifford Adams sat beside him scribbling in his pad, coiled to raise objections for the record. The muscles stood out on the sides of the attorney's jaw; the confession was taking place over and above his protests.

"I was a good chemist," Rankin said. "I spent two years developing a drug to prevent cardiac arrest, and I was close to a breakthrough when the funding for the experiment was withdrawn. At that point I had a toxin that counterfeited the symptoms of a heart attack, causing death in laboratory animals. The company panicked over the implications; my samples were confiscated for disposal and I was ordered to destroy my notes. But no one could destroy what was in here." He touched a temple.

"When was this?" Ray Padilla had taken Conroy's place at

his desk. The chief of detectives, deferring to the lieutenant's interviewing skills, stood in a corner with his hands folded behind his back.

Rankin smiled thinly. "Before you were born. My Horatio Alger story begins many years later, when I met and married Andrea and went to work for her father in the department-store business." He turned in his chair to look at Valentino, standing among the officers at the back of the room. "I told you Andrea started out as a salesclerk in one of her father's stores, so she could learn the business from the bottom up; that was the bond that held her to Greta, the shared experience. When I came along the old man was ailing, and he hadn't time to bring me up through the ranks, so he put me in charge of the chain. He was impressed by my technical knowledge, and was convinced, as I was, that computerizing the operation would reverse the decline brought on by competition from shopping malls.

"Andrea never forgave him for that. She'd been told her whole life that the business would be hers someday, but when push came to shove he bowed to convention and gave it to one of his own sex."

He returned his attention to Padilla. "After the old man died, she transferred her resentment to me. Nothing takes place overnight: When the profit picture was slow to improve and the malls continued to drain customers from our downtown stores, she blamed me for poor management. I was incompetent, I was a spendthrift, pouring millions of company capital into a computer system that was profligate and unproved. As she saw it, in a few months I'd succeeded in driving a sixty-year-old institution to the brink of ruin.

"She couldn't break the will that named me chief executive officer, but she owned twice as many shares as I did, and if she could convince enough stockholders that I was a threat to the company, they would vote with her to remove me at the annual meeting. I was just a glorified employee, after all. All the time that campaign was going on, I remembered the frustration and humiliation I'd felt the last time someone in authority pulled the rug out from under me on the verge of triumph. It was a short leap from there to that toxin I'd developed. At the time, no autopsy could prove that whoever ingested it hadn't died of simple cardiac arrest.

"I put it in her tea," he said. "You see, we continued the charade of a contented married couple at home. I really think she believed it was possible to separate our public squabbles from our domestic life. If she'd lived a bit longer, she'd have learned that you can't exist in both worlds. I chose privacy."

"It seems you did all the choosing for both of you."

"I'm sorry she didn't live longer. She'd have seen the computer program I designed drag her father's company into the twentieth century and reverse its fortunes in spectacular fashion. Of course, that wasn't possible, because if she had lived, she'd have fired me, and my only satisfaction would have come from witnessing the inevitable collapse."

"Is that the same program you used to forge the Garbo letter?" Padilla asked.

"Hardly. That program was grammar school beside the business plan I invented. Any dunce can create a font from a model of someone's handwriting. The trick was to make it look good enough to have fooled me in a distracted state, but not so good it couldn't be exposed when the time was right."

"Where'd you get Garbo's letters? You said your wife burned them."

"I swiped a bundle when she wasn't looking. They were

worth something, and I'm too practical a businessman to stand by and watch sentiment get the better of profit. At the time I didn't know just how valuable they'd prove to be."

"Tell us about Stockholm. That theft was too timely to be a coincidence."

"I had nothing to do with that. A man approached me in the lobby of my hotel, offering to sell me some letters written by Garbo; he'd heard I was a fan. He showed them to me. I knew right away they were genuine, and that he couldn't have come by them honestly; for all I knew, it was a trap set by a competitor to arrest and embarrass me. I sent him on his way.

"Later, of course, I saw that the episode could be of use, as the theft was bound to be discovered sooner or later, and there was Roger Akers, in Stockholm with me at just the right time. It's not always easy to know the precise moment when a plan was conceived, but I can trace it to that encounter."

"How did you come to tell Akers you'd killed your wife?"

"I actually don't remember telling him. I was drinking pretty heavily at the time, and I must have been in a confiding mood. He made sure to remind me of the conversation when I was sober. I haven't had more than one drink in an evening since. I couldn't take the chance of betraying myself in front of someone else and adding another blackmailer to the list."

"When did it start?"

"Just before the Swedish trip. I spent most of my time there thinking about how many improvements had been made in criminal science and worrying what a modern toxicologist would find if the body were exhumed. That fellow in the lobby came as a godsend. I couldn't very well kill Roger and tell the police he was holding me up for murdering Andrea, but if I was protecting her memory from a scandal, it occurred to me I might squeeze by on self-defense, or if not, escape serious punishment because public sympathy would be with me and against a man who exploited a man's loyalty to his dead wife.

"I almost succeeded. I paid him without protest for months, building up evidence to support my story. I even tricked Roger into putting his fingerprints on the fake letter by pretending I'd mixed it up with some documents I wanted him to file. He gave it right back without guessing what it was. I knew he wouldn't, because I wrote it in Swedish, a language he didn't read; but the police would have a hard time proving that."

"How'd you get his prints on the bust he was supposed to have threatened you with?"

Rankin smiled wanly. "I told him his latest payment was in an envelope under the bust. He thought I was being churlish. When he picked it up, I shot him."

"What made you choose Valentino as your witness?"

"It could have been anyone. I'd made up my mind to plant the story with him only the night before, there in the study where I carried it out." He shuddered, and looked again at Valentino. "Lord, that girlfriend of yours gave me a turn when I saw her in that costume. I thought Garbo had come back from the grave to spoil my plan."

"For the record," Padilla said, "here in the presence of your attorney, Clifford Adams, Valentino, a civilian, and officers of the Beverly Hills Police Department, you, Matthew Rankin, confess to planning the murders of your wife, Andrea Rankin, and your assistant, Roger Akers, and carrying out those murders."

"Yes. If it will spare me from the executioner."

At a signal from Conroy, Sergeant Stimson came forward and switched off the video camera. The chief then nodded at

Padilla, who asked Rankin to rise and present his wrists. He was manacled in a moment.

"Lieutenant," said Conroy, when Padilla turned his prisoner toward the door behind which the press continued to prowl. The lieutenant looked from his superior's face to Rankin's, which was dead white now. Padilla stripped off his suit coat, folded it, and draped it over the tycoon's shackles.

At the door, Rankin stopped and turned toward Valentino. "Not very sporting, young man. I gave you *How Not to Dress* and lent you my projectionist."

"Those weren't the reasons I wanted to help you. I thought you were innocent."

"What changed your mind?"

"When the police were slow to announce the letter was a fraud, you were in no hurry to set the record straight. I knew then you weren't as devoted to Andrea's memory as you pretended. At that point, Padilla's suspicions started to make sense."

"How very righteous. That's the very same attitude that got me where I am."

"Are you ready?" Padilla asked.

At that moment, Valentino ceased to exist for the man in custody. He stared at the door, behind which the murmur of reporters discussing the case among themselves and over cell phones rumbled like low-grade thunder. He took a deep breath, lifted his chin, and nodded.

Padilla placed his hand on the knob, hesitated, and withdrew it. "Sergeant?"

Stimson presented herself. The lieutenant stepped away. After a pause, the sergeant placed a hand on Rankin's shoulder and turned the knob.

When the door shut against the jabber and bright lights, Valentino said, "You're missing your fifteen minutes."

"I guess whatever Garbo had was contagious." He held out his hand.

Valentino took it. "You know, you clean up pretty nice."

"Keep your voice down." He was whispering. "Conroy wants to put me in for captain. If he gets his way I'll have to wear a necktie all the time."

He didn't go from there to the office and he didn't go home. Instead he went to the campus projection room and watched *How Not to Dress* alone for the first time. He laughed sympathetically at young Greta Lovisa Gustafsson's first awkward flirtation with a camera that would fall in love with her soon enough, and probably too soon for a peasant girl of sixteen. She'd started out eager for attention, appreciation, and celebrity, even played the Hollywood game, granting interviews, making public appearances, and colluding to invent a past for herself commensurate with the glamorous roles she played; then, without warning, had stopped—the first in her profession to do so, and in so doing made herself more sought after than before. She'd done the same with poor John Gilbert, hurling herself into a romance with all the publicity potential of a Pickfair or, in a later day, a Brangelina, then, abruptly, turning and sprinting in the other direction. Too much had happened too soon, and she had better than sixty years to go. Meanwhile her legend fed upon itself and upon whatever fleeting scraps fell to the public—crossing a street in Midtown Manhattan, bundled in scarves and sweaters and the ubiquitous dark glasses, boarding a plane at JFK bound for Sweden, sunbathing nude on a private beach on the Riviera. No lurid romantic interests fueled the fire, no sordid scandal; not even so much as a scuffle with a reporter. She'd asked to be let alone, and that was one favor the world refused.

She looks out upon the East River, a moving picture shot by a stationary camera. Tugs, pleasure craft, stately cargo ships glide past, oblivious to the icon at the window. Today is like yesterday, tomorrow will be like today. Perhaps she will put on a disguise and visit the flea market on Broadway; but, no, she was out yesterday, and a young man in the elevator had recognized her and made bold enough to demand of her the time. She'd replied that he should buy a watch. That was foolish; how much better that she should ignore him, give him not so much as the time of day. Such stories were retold and reshaped, and only added to the compost. No, she will stay home and design a rug, sit cross-legged on her own floor with her colored pencils and butcher's wrap, drawing and smoking cigarettes, creating a screen They cannot penetrate.

"I am on the lam." She smiles as she says it aloud: American gangsterisms have always held a fascination. Her earliest attempts at English came from reading pulp magazines with missing-link thugs and naked women on the covers, and she is drawn to movies where the antihero spends the last reel evading platoons of police at the wheel of a powerful automobile; the kind of movies in which she never appeared, because she would have spent too little time on-screen. Invariably she leaves the theater before the end, when the lobby is deserted and the fugitive is still at large. "I am on the lam," she says again. "You will never take me alive."

When the film finished flapping through the gate, he stirred himself from a doze, removed the take-up reel from the projector, and sealed it in its can. The ancient librarian—shrunken, androgynous, and completely deaf—checked in the material without comment and returned it to its cabinet.

Valentino checked his cell for messages. He had none. Kyle Broadhead and Harriet were working, but always before they'd found time to maintain contact. He called Ruth, but she said the lines had been silent at the office. The rush hour hadn't started; he drove up to a take-out window without having to wait and took home his order through four lanes of scattered traffic. No one was at work in The Oracle. He went up to the booth, ate, read a chapter in a book, and got up to look down at the rows of seats slumbering under drop cloths in the dark. He wanted to call out, but he was afraid there would be no echo.

His cell rang. He answered without checking the number.

"I don't want to be alone," Harriet said. "Do you?"

His heart bumped. It felt as if it were starting again. "Where can we meet?"

"What's wrong with right here?" And he realized her voice was directly behind him.

CLOSING CREDITS

The following sources were instrumental in the writing of *Alone*:

BIBLIOGRAPHY

1. Greta Garbo

Bainbridge, John. *Garbo*. New York: Holt, Rinehart, and Winston, 1971.

This is probably the best biography published during its subject's lifetime, updated twice by the author.

Cahill, Marie. *Greta Garbo: A Hollywood Portrait*. New York: Smithmark, 1992.

Basically a picture book, formatted for the coffee table. Photos tell the truest story of Garbo's life on film, and the text, although brief, is informative and accurate.

Conway, Michael, McGregor, Dion, and Ricci, Mark. *The*

Complete Films of Greta Garbo. Secaucus, New Jersey: The Citadel Press, 1991.

The Citadel series is the Bible of professional information, actor by actor, and this volume is no exception. Parker Tyler's thumbnail biography and analysis of Garbo's screen persona is a valuable addition to this exhaustive filmography since its first appearance in 1968.

Gish, Lillian. *Dorothy and Lillian Gish.* New York: Charles Scribner's Sons, 1973.

Lillian Gish, who was present when the first flicker of light appeared on the silver screen, was an accomplished wordsmith (particularly for a silent-screen star!) and a keen observer of the motion-picture industry throughout its first eighty years. This book shed some light on John Gilbert's appearance in *La Bohème*, whose set he abandoned to attend his infamous wedding-that-never-was with Garbo.

Horan, Gray. "Greta Garbo: The Legendary Star's Secret Garden in New York." Los Angeles: *Architectural Digest*, April 1992.

Architectural Digest's "Hollywood at Home" issue, recently reinstated as a recurring feature, is a treasury of personal and professional information on contemporary and classic movie icons. Horan's article, the first exhaustive piece to appear following Garbo's death in 1991, provides details of her later years hitherto kept from the public by the small circle of loyal intimates with whom she shared it. The cover story coincided with Sotheby's auction of personal items from her fabulous estate.

Swenson, Karen. *Greta Garbo: A Life Apart.* New York: Charles Scribner's Sons, 1997.

This is the first major posthumous biography, and the best to date. Swenson takes an unblinking look at the Swedish Sphinx from life to death and beyond, closely examining rumors regarding her sexual preferences, exploding myths, and casting doubt on cherished portions of her legend, while avoiding the salaciousness and contempt for her subject that usually travel hand in hand with so frank a book.

Uncredited. "Garbo's Letters Missing." Press release, December 11, 2005.

Three inches of tantalizing newspaper coverage of the discovery that two letters and two postcards written by Garbo to her friend, Vera Schmiterlöw, had been removed from the Swedish Military Archives and not returned. Despite an alternative development written into this book, the correspondence remains missing and the circumstances of its disappearance are unknown.

2. General

Anderson, Brett. Photographed by Phillip Ennis. *Theo Kalomirakis' Private Theaters*. New York: Abrams, 1997.

A sumptuous picture book, with an extensive text, showcasing the world's premiere designer of high-end home theaters for the Matthew Rankins among us who can afford them. Exquisite reproductions of Golden Age picture palaces scaled down for the manse (one diminution includes a miniature shopping mall annex complete with a well-stocked jewelry store and a dealership displaying classic cars), these salivary treasures are lovingly presented in full color, closely detailed. (Yes, "Theo Kalomirakis" does look like "Leo Kalishnikov" when you squint.)

Castle, Steven. Photographed by Phillip Ennis. *Great Escapes: New Designs for Home Theaters by Theo Kalomirakis*. New York: Abrams, 2003.

The sequel. If The Oracle winds up looking half as good as the basement haven of best-selling horror novelist Dean Koontz (who furnishes the introduction), Valentino will be ecstatic—and in debt for the rest of his life.

Corey, Melinda, and Ochoa, George. *The Dictionary of Film Quotations*. New York: Three Rivers, 1995.

This is a quick, entertaining celebration of the terse wit and wisdom of movie dialogue, although at 413 pages of text it's necessarily less extensive than the Nowlands' 741-page (not counting the index) *"We'll Always Have Paris,"* about which more anon. The editors' personal screening of every film cited, as diverting and enjoyable a task as it must have been, spares the harried researcher thousands of hours of time and effort.

Doherty, Thomas. *Pre-Code Hollywood: Sex, Immorality, and Insurrection in American Cinema 1930–1934*. New York: Columbia, 1999.

There was a code of decency prior to 1934, but the enforcers were mostly looking the other way while the first generation of talking-picture artists forged a subversive response to the accepted mores of the Great Depression. This one is a real eye-opener to those who believe the cinema didn't lose its innocence until the 1960s.

Halliwell, Leslie. *The Filmgoer's Companion*. New York: Avon, 1977.

Halliwell was a terminal curmudgeon, but his annual film guides were invaluable (Leonard Maltin's are better known, but he leaves out the names of studios), and remain so under the direction of his successors. This encyclopedic study of movies belongs on the shelf of anyone who considers himself a cineaste. It first appeared in 1965, and by this edition had been updated five times.

LaSalle, Mick. *Complicated Women: Sex and Power in Pre-Code Hollywood.* New York: St. Martin's Press, 2000.

How those jazz babies did carry on. LaSalle makes the point that the 1934 crackdown froze the revolutionary development of film for more than thirty years, and that if it had not taken place, open political dissent, graphic sex, and full nudity would have reached the screen by the end of the 1930s.

LaSalle, Mick. *Dangerous Men: Pre-Code Hollywood and the Birth of the Modern Man*. New York: St. Martin's Press, 2002.

The inevitable sequel, but freestanding and just as progressive in its vision. Clark Gable's 1939 Rhett Butler was a wuss compared to the characters he played just as heroically years earlier. LaSalle states that mature males in our time are hesitant to call themselves men, with all that entails, and enforces his claim.

Nowlan, Robert A., and Nowlan, Gwendolyn W. *"We'll Always Have Paris": The Definitive Guide to Great Lines from the Movies*. New York: HarperPerennial, 1995.

Unlike more recent books that concentrate on lines from films made since the collapse of the studio system, this monster volume squeezes most of the twentieth century for the best and most memorable passages, and credits them to screenwriters rather than to the actors who spoke them, a revelation to moviegoers who think Bruce Willis is witty. *Casablanca* alone is cited forty-seven times, and each example is superior to Quentin Tarantino's entire output. ("Burger Royale," indeed!)

Wilhelm, Elliot. *Videohound's World Cinema*. Detroit: Visible Ink, 1999.

The *Videohound* franchise is fast overtaking Maltin and Halliwell. Most film guides display native prejudice for the USA and the U.K. Wilhelm provides a balanced view of every civilized (and some not so) country's contribution to the moving image.

(See "Closing Credits" in *Frames*, the first Valentino novel, for more recommendations of value to this series.)

FILMOGRAPHY

1. Greta Garbo

The following is an abridged list of Garbo's landmark films, all currently available on DVD:

Torrent. Directed by Monta Bell, starring Ricardo Cortez, Greta Garbo, Gertrude Olmstead, Edward Connelly, Lucien Littlefield, Martha Mattox, Lucy Beaumont, Tully Marshall, Mack Swain, Arthur Edmund Carew, Lillian Leighton, and Mario Carillo. MGM, 1926.

Meddling parents break up an unsuitable romance between the classes, with results that satisfy no one.

This was Garbo's first American film, hence her billing beneath Ricardo Cortez (né Jake Krantz). He was recruited in the 1920s in a failed attempt to fill the Latin-lover gap left by the death of Rudolph Valentino. If Cortez is remembered at all today, it's as the first Sam Spade in the 1931 version of Dashiell Hammett's *The Maltese Falcon*. He was more effective than Warren William in *Satan Met a Lady*, the 1936 remake, but the role will always belong to Humphrey Bogart in the third adaptation in 1941. Considering how thoroughly he was upstaged, charity demands we single Cortez out as Garbo's first Hollywood leading man, and one of the few not to sport a silly moustache.

William H. Daniels, whose career spanned *Foolish Wives* (1922) and *The Maltese Bippy* (1969), photographed Garbo here the first of many times, discovering the ineffable quality that projected her far beyond the footlights; none of the studio brass took much notice of her until the rushes. (Daniels also filmed Erich von Stroheim's notorious *Greed*; see *Frames*.)

The Temptress. Directed by Fred Niblo, starring Greta Garbo, Antonio Moreno, Marc MacDermott, Lionel Barrymore, Armand Kaliz, Roy D'Arcy, Alys Murrell, Steve Clemento, Roy Coulson, Robert Anderson, Francis MacDonald, Hector V. Sarno, Virginia Brown Faire, and Inez Gomez. MGM, 1926.

Garbo's vamps were hard on Latin types. Having fallen in love with her at a masquerade ball, and learning she's married, Moreno flees her charms all the way to Argentina. She follows him there and takes a swipe at Barrymore, who kills a friend in a duel over her. Years later, strolling Paris with Faire, his new fiancée, Moreno encounters Garbo, who's become a prostitute and cannot recall him from among the many men she's known.

The Swedish Sphinx was never more luminous, and most of the men who saw the film probably sympathized with Moreno's tragic attraction to her. Roy D'Arcy, as the villainous Manos Duras, was extremely effective, and one wonders whether she'd have been able to manipulate him as easily as she had most of the rest of the male cast. It's a stirring film, brilliantly photographed by Tony Gaudio. This was to be Garbo's first Hollywood collaboration with Mauritz Stiller, her mentor and presumably her lover, but his inability to work within the strictures of the studio system got him replaced by Niblo, who also directed the stunningly successful *Ben-Hur* in 1925.

Flesh and the Devil. Directed by Clarence Brown, starring John Gilbert, Greta Garbo, Lars Hanson, Barbara Kent, William Orlamond, George Fawcett, Eugenie Besserer, Marc MacDermott, Marcelle Corday. MGM, 1926.

Married again, Garbo has an affair (again), this time with Gilbert, who is forced to kill her titled husband in a duel. Once again the New World embraces a shattered lover, leaving Garbo to marry Hanson, Gilbert's best friend. Upon returning to Austria, Garbo sets her cap a second time for Gilbert, who is challenged by Hanson to yet another duel. Garbo sees the error of her ways and sets off across a frozen river to prevent bloodshed; she falls through the ice and drowns. Gilbert wounds Hanson, who recovers, and the friendship is reinstated.

Garbo's love scenes with Gilbert burned up the screen, as well they might have. They fell in love for real on the set, precipitating the first of many celebrated on-again, off-again affairs that have become as endemic to Hollywood as sports cars and divorce.

This was the last time Garbo received less than top billing. By the time the pair were reunited on screen in *Love* (1927), a bowdlerized adaptation of Leo Tolstoy's *Anna Karenina,* Gilbert's name had slipped to the second spot.

Anna Christie. Directed by Clarence Brown, starring Greta Garbo, Charles Bickford, George F. Marion, Marie Dressler, James T. Mack, and Lee Phelps. MGM, 1930.

Garbo, having fled the cruel family in whose care her seaman father left her, quits the life of a prostitute to live with her father. After saving Bickford, a young sailor, from drowning during a storm, she falls in love with him, only to be abandoned by him when he learns of her past. He returns, himself a man far from perfect, to beg for forgiveness and propose marriage. She accepts.

This adaptation of a play by Eugene O'Neill, who had run afoul of the censors in New York during the so-called Roaring Twenties, was a dangerous choice for Garbo's debut in a talking film. No one could be sure that audiences would accept her in such a sordid role, let alone embrace her deep voice and strong accent. Her entrance, dog-tired in dowdy clothes she might have slept in, is so unglamorous as to draw all the drab details from the seedy waterfront bar where most of the action—such as it is—takes place. No simple drink order was ever anticipated so breathlessly, or celebrated with so much relief; that throaty contralto would eventually pave the way to stardom for Tallulah Bankhead, Lauren Bacall, and Kathleen Turner—and assure the livelihoods of a host of falsetto-challenged female impersonators. Garbo herself preferred the German-language version of the film she starred in later that year, and thought Marie Dressler, cast as father Marion's slatternly former mistress, stole the one shot in English.

Susan Lenox: Her Fall and Rise. Directed by Robert Z. Leonard, starring Greta Garbo, Clark Gable, Jean Hersholt, John Miljan, Alan Hale, Hale Hamilton, Hilda Vaughn, Russell Simpson, Cecil Cunningham, Theodore von Eltz, Marjorie King, Helene Millard, and Ian Keith. MGM, 1931.

Fleeing an arranged marriage with thuggish Hale, Garbo stumbles into the arms of Gable, a hunky construction engineer.

He plans to marry her, but while he's away on business, Garbo hops a carnival train to escape her father's pursuit. Gable returns, only to leave again when he learns that she's become involved with the owner of the carnival. When they meet again, she's changed her name to the eponymous Susan Lenox, and has become the mistress of a rich politician. Again Gable leaves, but she tracks him to South America, where he's fallen on hard times working at a construction camp in the jungle. Eventually all misunderstandings are swept aside, and they are a couple at last.

It's a steamy film—even the scenes not set in that ubiquitous tropical exile—and the viewer who knows Gable mainly as the hail-fellow-well-met-con/he-man of *San Francisco*, *Boom Town*, and *It Happened One Night* gets an unadulterated dose of the "Dangerous Man" of Mick LaSalle's take on pre-Code Hollywood. With the possible exceptions of the world-weary John Barrymore and the urbane Melvyn Douglas, Gable seemed the only man in pictures capable of handling Garbo, and of upstaging her in her own scenes. Perhaps that's why they were never matched again.

Mata Hari. Directed by George Fitzmaurice, starring Greta Garbo, Ramón Novarro, Lionel Barrymore, Lewis Stone, C. Henry Gordon, Karen Morley, Alec B. Francis, Blanche Frederici, Edmund Breese, Helen Jerome Eddy, and Frank Reicher. MGM, 1931.

Garbo is the notorious Mata Hari, spying for the Kaiser under the cover of a cooch dancer in Paris. Novarro falls for her, enabling her to secure military secrets he's been entrusted with as a lieutenant with the Russian Army. Recalled to Russia, Novarro's plane is shot down and he's blinded. Garbo comes to visit him, declaring her love. He's still in bandages when he goes to speak with her in prison; she convinces him she's in a hospital, recovering from an illness. He doesn't know that she's pleaded guilty to espionage to keep him from being called in to testify and find out about her past. After he leaves, she is taken from her cell to face a firing squad.

This is arguably Garbo's campiest role, celebrated mostly for its turgid earnestness and That Costume, which is reduced nearly to its headdress during her salacious dance with a pagan idol. Novarro, whose homosexuality is often cited for his apparent discomfort in macho roles (there's no sign of such conflict in his Ben-Hur), seems out of his element as an ardent swain; but that may have more to do with his inexperience acting in talkies. His career high was six years in the past.

Grand Hotel. Directed by Edmund Goulding, starring Greta Garbo, John Barrymore, Joan Crawford, Wallace Beery, Lionel Barrymore, Lewis Stone, Jean Hersholt, Robert McWade, Purnell B. Pratt, Ferdinand Gottschalk, Rafaela Ottiano, Morgan Wallace, Tully Marshall, Frank Conroy, Murry Kinnell, and Edwin Maxwell. MGM, 1932.

Garbo, a great ballet star undergoing deep depression, is prevented from committing suicide by John Barrymore, a down-on-his-heels aristocrat engaged in burgling her room at the Grand Hotel in Berlin. They fall in love, but before they can run away together, Barrymore is slain by Beery after robbing Beery's room in an attempt to secure valuables to free himself from his past. Unaware of this event, Garbo checks out, blissfully looking forward to her future with Barrymore.

Grand Hotel is a precursor of those Universal extravaganzas that placed Dracula, the Wolf Man, and Frankenstein's monster in the same feature; it's MGM, seeking to reverse the Depression's drain on the box office by placing as many of its "more stars than there are in heaven" in one feature as it can get away with. It paid off, and industry watchers were astonished when Joan Crawford, in one of several separate stories loosely connected to the others, garnered notices equal with the great Garbo's. (Beery, cast against his usual lug type as a ruthless and desperate business tycoon, merits special mention as the only one of several supposedly German characters to speak with an accent.)

This is the film in which Garbo speaks the immortal line, "I want to be alone"—several times.

As You Desire Me. Directed by George Fitzmaurice, starring Greta Garbo, Melvyn Douglas, Erich von Stroheim, Owen Moore, Hedda Hopper, Rafåela Ottiano, Warburton Gamble, Albert Conti, William Ricciardi, and Roland Varno. MGM, 1932.

Amnesiac cabaret entertainer Garbo is identified as the wife of Douglas, who believed her to have been slain during the Austrian invasion of Italy during the First World War. Seeking to break her ties to the Svengali-like novelist von Stroheim, Garbo flees Budapest to rejoin Douglas. Despite an abortive attempt by von Stroheim to brand her as an imposter, she remains with Douglas, although she is still in doubt as to whether she is whom he thinks she is.

This film has more Hollywood history than most movie documentaries. Garbo, cinematographer Daniels, and von Stroheim are reunited, albeit this time von Stroheim is in front of the camera, not behind it, as when he directed *Greed*, and this is the first feature to pair Garbo with Douglas, who was one of the few to hold his own. Legendary gossip columnist Hopper makes one of her last acting appearances; and any picture that lets von Stroheim wear his monocle is worth a look.

Queen Christina. Directed by Rouben Mamoulian, starring Greta Garbo, John Gilbert, Ian Keith, Lewis Stone, Elizabeth Young, C. Aubrey Smith, Reginald Owen, Lawrence Grant, David Torrence, Gustav von Seyffertitz, Ferdinand Munier, and George Renevent. MGM, 1933.

Christina, Queen of Sweden, falls in love with Spanish ambassador Gilbert and abdicates her throne so she can marry him and avoid a diplomatic wedding with the King of Spain; but before the lovers can run away together, Gilbert is killed in a jealous rage by a former love interest of Garbo's. Alone, she sets sail toward an uncertain future.

The plot has a stronger historical base than *Mata Hari*, and until Edward VII gave up the English crown to marry a commoner, represented *the* great worldly sacrifice in the name of romance. The film also lays to rest the myth that Gilbert had a high, squeaky voice that cut short his career when the screen learned to talk. It was a pleasant light baritone, and he'd mastered subtlety since his unfortunate first attempt; but it was too late. He died three years later.

Mamoulian, it's said, coaxed that haunting, enigmatic last shot of Garbo at the prow of her ship by telling her to make her mind absolutely blank. It's an iconic moment, and makes up for an awkward early scene in which Gilbert manages to mistake Garbo for a boy because she's wearing trousers when they meet.

Anna Karenina. Directed by Clarence Brown, starring Greta Garbo, Fredric March, Freddie Bartholomew, Maureen O'Sullivan, May Robson, Basil Rathbone, Reginald Owen, Reginald Denny, Phoebe Foster, Gyles Isham, Buster Phelps, Ella Ethridge, Joan Marsh, Sidney Bracey, Cora Sue Collins, Olaf Hytten, Joe E. Tozer, Guy D'Ennery, Harry Allen, and Mary Forbes. MGM, 1935.

The Tolstoy chestnut about a respectable married woman who throws everything away for the love of a dashing military officer, then throws herself in front of a train.

She made it once before, as a 1927 silent that stripped the epic novel of most of its social elements and even its title: *Love*, moreover, was presented in modern dress, with no counts or czars. The second version is closer to its source but, like every other attempt to translate a sweeping novel of class war to the big and small screen, reduces it to a bourgeois love triangle.

(NOTE: For all his knowledge of cinematic history, Valentino is not infallible; in *Alone*, he scorns *Love* for its tacked-on happy ending. In fact, both adaptations end with her suicide, although in the first American release of *Karenina*, she survives. However, most existing prints preserve the tragic ending that appeared overseas.)

Ninotchka. Directed by Ernst Lubitsch, starring Greta Garbo, Melvyn Douglas, Ina Claire, Bela Lugosi, Sig Rumann, Felix Bressart, Alexander Granach, Gregory Gaye, Rolfe Sedan, Edwin Maxwell, and Richard Carle. MGM, 1939.

Garbo is sent by the Soviet government in Russia to expedite the sale of the imperial crown jewels in Paris. Discovering that the three plenipotentiaries who preceded her in the mission have been corrupted by the West, she at first repels the advances of Douglas, working on behalf of former Grand Duchess Claire, then embraces him as he in turn falls in love with her. Claire offers a bargain: Surrender Douglas, Claire's pet, go back to Russia, and she'll give up her claim to the jewels. Garbo agrees for the sake of her countrymen, but with the help of the three corrupted comrades, Douglas lures her back outside the Iron Curtain and into his arms.

This is the best romantic comedy of all time, and makes one wish Garbo had sampled the genre much sooner (although her next foray, *Two-Faced Woman*, was a disaster and may have influenced her decision to retire from the screen at thirty-six). "Garbo Laughs!" exclaimed the publicity, and the scene where she loses it is Hollywood gold.

Remade as *Silk Stockings,* a musical, in 1957, the story still worked, thanks to the pairing of Fred Astaire and Cyd Charisse, a fabulous Cole Porter score, and Rouben Mamoulian bringing his Garbo chops to the director's chair, but it won't make you forget the original. (If only *Dracula* star Lugosi could have been resurrected to repeat his rare comic cameo. . . .)

2. Related

Garbo Talks. Directed by Sidney Lumet, starring Anne Bancroft, Ron Silver, Carrie Fisher, Catherine Hicks, Steven Hill, Howard da Silva, Dorothy Louden, Harvey Fierstein, Hermione Gingold, and Mary McDonnell. MGM/UA, 1984.

Bancroft, returning to type as a feisty old broad, is terminally ill, and makes one last request of her son, with whom she has a difficult relationship: She wants to meet her idol, Greta Garbo. Son Silver, reprising his trademark schlep, stalks the elusive recluse throughout New York City, corners her at last (at a flea market), and persuades her to visit Bancroft on her deathbed. The actress playing Garbo (Leonard Maltin says it's Betty Comden, of the comedy-writing team of Comden and Green, but another source says it's a professional Garbo impersonator) doesn't speak onscreen until the final scene, when she encounters Silver on the street after his mother's passing: "Hello, Vincent."

It's a breezy little film, funny and sad by turns, with a dynamite performance by Bancroft, who was never less than memorable, and belongs on the same bill with other Hollywood cannibal fare like *Being John Malkovich* and *Abbott and Costello Meet the Killer, Boris Karloff*. (Garbo, it's said, was Not Amused, and peeved at her old studio for making her au courant—and fair game for the paparazzi—once again.)

MGM: When the Lion Roars. Directed by Frank Martin. Turner Pictures, 1992.

A retrospective documentary celebrating the rise and fall of Metro-Goldwyn-Mayer, copiously illustrated with archival footage interspersed with interviews with surviving contract players, directors, studio executives, and other eyewitnesses.

This three-part series, aired on the TCM network and issued on VHS (now out of print), is a matchless history of the studio that ushered motion pictures into the industrial age and ended its sixty-year reign with a chilling memo from Kirk Kerkorian, a robber baron out of the nineteenth-century school of Jay Gould and Jim Fisk, announcing to the world that MGM was now primarily in the hotel business. The remastered footage is glossy and gorgeous, and the interviews, many of them with people who are no longer with us, are fascinating and suggest total recall. It's emceed by an unusually buoyant Patrick Stewart on an eye-popping Art Deco set drenched in Metrocolor. Garbo, Gilbert, and all the rest of the giants live again here.

ABOUT THE AUTHOR

Loren D. Estleman has written more than sixty novels. He has already netted four Shamus Awards for detective fiction, five Spur Awards for Western fiction, and three Western Heritage Awards, among his many professional honors. He has written twenty Amos Walker mysteries, the most recent of which, *The Left-Handed Dollar,* will be published in April 2010. He lives with his wife, author Deborah Morgan, in Michigan.